STRANGE FUGITIVE

T0164427

STRANGE FUGITIVE

Morley Callaghan

Introduction by
James Dubro

EXILE editions

Library and Archives Canada Cataloguing in Publication

Callaghan, Morley, 1903-1990
    Strange fugitive / Morley Callaghan ; introduction by James Dubro.

Includes bibliographical references.
ISBN 978-1-55096-155-3

    I. Title.

PS8505.A43S8 2011   C813'.52   C2011-907131-2

Design and Composition by Hourglass Angels-mc
Typeset in Times New Roman and New Yorker at the Moons of Jupiter Studios
Printed by Imprimerie Gauvin

This novel is a work of fiction. Names, characters, places and incidents are the products of the author's imagination. Any resemblance to actual persons, living or dead, events, or locales is entirely coincidental.

Published by Exile Editions Ltd.
144483 Southgate Road 14 – GD
Holstein, Ontario, N0G 2A0
Canada   www.ExileEditions.com
Printed and Bound in Canada in 2011

 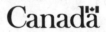 Conseil des Arts Canada Council
du Canada   for the Arts

Canada

 ONTARIO ARTS COUNCIL
CONSEIL DES ARTS DE L'ONTARIO

The publisher would like to acknowledge the financial support of the Canada Council for the Arts, the Government of Canada through the Canada Book Fund (CBF), and the Ontario Arts Council–an agency of the Government of Ontario, for our publishing activities.

Sales / Distribution:
Independent Publishers Group
814 North Franklin Street, Chicago, IL 60610 USA
www.ipgbook.com   toll free: 1 800 888 4741

Contents

INTRODUCTION

In the summer of 1923, as a brutal gang war for control of the lucrative bootleg trade raged in Southern Ontario, Morley Callaghan, then a twenty-year-old second-year student at the University of Toronto, landed a seasonal job as a cub reporter at the *Toronto Star*. His life was to change dramatically. Within a month he befriended one of the *Star*'s best reporters — Ernest Hemingway. The two shared many literary interests. Hemingway, after reading just one of Morley's stories, told him:"You are a real writer; you write big-time stuff." Two years later, having read several more of his stories, Heming-way wrote Morley from Paris: "If you want encouragement and backing let me tell you right now and you can cut this out and paste it in the front of your prayer book that you have the stuff and will be a hell of a fine writer and probably the first writer that's ever come out of Canada." This part of the Morley Callaghan story is well known.

But what isn't known or understood about Morley is that his first novel, *Strange Fugitive,* published by Scribner's in New York in 1928, grew directly out of his experiences as a reporter at the *Star*. Whether by direct involvement through interviews, research or writing, or just from the intense daily office scuttlebutt, Morley became familiar with the bootlegging scene, the speakeasies and the underworld characters in downtown Toronto in the immigrant "Ward" area.

A *Star* man Morley almost certainly met and worked with was Dave Rogers, a young crime reporter working exclusively on the deadly gang war (he also likely met Athel Gow and C. Roy Greenaway and other local *Star* crime reporters). Editor Harry Hindmarsh, along with publisher Joe Atkinson, had started a platoon system; the saturation treatment of sensational stories in which everyone from reporters to copy editors was thrown into coverage. Callaghan would have been involved, one way or another, in several major stories, especially this one:

On May 10, 1922, Mafia boss Domenic Scaroni had been killed after leaving a mob banquet in Guelph, clearing the way for well-known Hamilton Mafia boss Rocco Perri to become the undisputed head of the Calabrian Mafia in Ontario. Perri controlled a large part of the bootleg trade in and out of the province. For the Scaroni killing Rocco Perri used one of his Niagara Falls lieutenants, John Trotta (a.k.a. Trott) who, along with Mike and Tony Trotta (his two brothers), was a major bootlegger and booze exporter to the United States. John Trotta was the last man to see Scaroni alive and later also arranged for the murder of his brother Joe Scaroni in September 1922. The policeman investigating the two Scaroni hits was John Trueman of Thorold, and as he was closing in on Trotta, he was himself killed. Trotta was charged with the murder by the OPP. Rocco Perri then paid for his lawyer and sat directly behind Trotta every day of the trial which ended in a hung jury on November 14, 1925. (But in a second trial in February 1925, Trotta was convicted of killing Constable Trueman and got a life sentence.)

Within days, more bodies of victims were discovered in Hamilton and the *Star* editor decided to opt for platoon coverage of the war. On November 17, 1925, a breathlessly florid piece entitled "Mountain of Murder" began with "Hamilton Mountain has become a place of skulls, a mountain of human sacrifice. It is like one of the stone pyramids on which the bloodthirsty Aztec priests cut the throats of innumerable victims . . ." Another article that day, by Dave Rogers, gave the background for two of the killings and quoted sources as saying that the "king of the bootleggers" was directly involved.

Rogers followed this up in a few days with a remarkable exclusive interview with Rocco Perri and his Jewish common-law wife, Bessie, who proclaimed that Rocco was "the King of the Bootleggers" and discussed many of the inner workings of criminal mob activity including his theory about the killings, concepts of vengeance and honor. This was a major scoop and copies of the *Star* were sold out within minutes, with scalpers later that day selling the paper at astronomical prices. Rocco Perri became a household name.

In a few months, a mob-imported batch of poison brew killed forty-three people in Ontario and New York state and the public clamored for the arrests of the high-profiled Perri and his fellow bootleggers. Among those arrested were Perri, Ben Kerr, known as "the king of the smugglers," and three Toronto Jewish bootleggers (Max and Harry Wortzman and Harry Goldstein) but there was not enough evidence to convict these gangsters. Finally in 1926, there was enough public pressure to force the federal government to appoint a major Royal Commission on the bootleg trade. The hearings were another huge media event in 1927 with Harry Hatch of Gooderham and Worts, Rocco and Bessie Perri, and many bootleggers publicly taking the stand in 1927 even as Callaghan was writing *Strange Fugitive*. Rocco Perri received a six-month sentence for perjury, his only jail time in his long criminal career.

The story of *Strange Fugitive,* rooted in these actual events, is told through the eyes of Harry Trotter, an Ontario white Anglo-Saxon Protestant of self-described "pioneer stock," who establishes himself as a major bootlegger in the "foreign"-dominated multicultural underworld of 1920's Toronto. It seems certain that the name "Trotter" is an anglicization of Trotta, surname of three of the family who were Perri's Niagara Falls lieutenants.

There is little heroic about Harry Trotter. He is superficial, insufferably self-centered, domineering, sexist, promiscuous, bigoted, and psychopathic. Yet what makes the novel of this unimaginative thug fascinating is its vivid depiction of the underworld jungle he chooses to enter and of the boring, smug, middle-class Toronto everyday world from which he rebels. He is an early literary example of the modern alienated outsider made popular much later in the existential novels of Albert Camus and Jean-Paul Sartre, and discussed in the classic Colin Wilson study *The Outsider*, where criminals are depicted as "outsider" anti-heroes. In his Introduction to the last edition of *Strange Fugitive* in 1970, Robert Weaver remarked, "There is a prophetic strain in *Strange Fugitive*. Harry Trotter reminds me in many ways of the anti-hero of [Camus' 1942 novel] *The Stranger* . . ." At one point Trotter, as if he were a Merseault, tells his wife Vera that "he wants to be alone and not have to think about anyone. I want to drift wherever I feel like. I don't want to be tied to the thoughts of anyone." And Trotter throughout the novel, untied to his thoughts, loses his sense of identity many times. In the last part of the novel he sees his identity only through the items around him in his office at the book store, ". . . slowly becoming aware of every object in the room. He noticed the desk, its size, glass pen-container, four pens on it, big blotting paper, mahogany chairs, carpet, the pattern. He was alone in the room and each one of these objects had assumed an identity of being for him. He became so conscious of them he felt that he couldn't really be alone while they were in the room . . ." He often does not know who he is or why he is. He is not comfortable in the gangster world, or the mainstream world or, indeed, in his own skin. He is a misfit, a mistake, and we are spectators in his journey through the underworld where he loses his identity for real in a shootout in downtown Toronto.

The original title Morley had for the novel was *Big Boy* but Maxwell Perkins, Callaghan's New York editor, didn't like it, so Callaghan came up with *Strange Fugitive*. This is not an obvious title as Trotter is not a fugitive in any actual sense. Rather, he is a fugitive in a metaphorical and spiritual sense. He is a man on the run from himself. The classy art nouveau cover of the original Scribner's edition (reproduced here) plays up the "strange" and dark quality of Trotter whose image appears in a stark profile in black. The only text other than the title is "The Rise and Fall of One of Gangdom's 'Big Shots'." Uniquely for its time *Strange Fugitive* is a literary novel about a gangster told — for the first time — from the point of view of the criminal himself.

Strange Fugitive is, in fact, the first of the modern gangster novels, preceding by a year W.J. Burnett's *Little Caesar* about the career of the Chicago gangster "Rico" who, in many ways, is an American version of Trotter, and whose rise and fall is as inevitable and whose murder is as predictable and justifiable as Trotter's. It would be interesting to find out if Burnett had read and was influenced by Callaghan's earlier gangster novel. There is a direct line from *Strange Fugitive* and *Little Caesar* (and the later 1930's short stories of Damon Runyon) to novels like *The Godfather* and *Prizzi's Honor*. Hollywood producers considered *Strange Fugitive* as a film in 1930. Warner Brothers thought of having actor James Cagney play Trotter but opted for the Chicago setting of *Little Caesar*, using Edward G. Robinson as the star of the first of many gangster films. [If only *Strange Fugitive* had been made into a movie Canadian criminals would have been become known for their very pivotal role in the American bootlegging scene.]

On one level *Strange Fugitive* is a simple morality tale of a gangster and murderer receiving his appropriate punishment ("a just reward for my misdeeds my death doth plain declare," says the hero in *Cambyses*, an early Renaissance morality play). It is a novel of Harry Trotter's descent from respectable Toronto lumberyard foreman (Morley worked two weeks one summer in a lumberyard and witnessed a nasty fight similar to the one described in the novel) into the underworld (literal and figurative) of 20's Toronto — a world of speakeasies, promiscuous sex, violence — a place inhabited by whores, killers, "kikes," "wops," "chinks," "niggers," and "foreigners." William Carlos Williams eloquently stated that Callaghan "seems to prove by laying his tale among bootleggers and whores that the tragic principle holds as good with ignoble metal as with noble, as good here as with the mythological King of Attica . . ."

The novel is divided into four parts:

Part I: This is Trotter's life in the "straight" world of provincial Toronto. Trotter loses his job after a fight with an Italian employee. Trotter's soulful wife Vera is a major character in this part. Vera is a figure that is at the heart of the novel. While she is essentially out of the novel by a third of the way through, she is always in Trotter's mind and thoughts. She represents literally "truth" and she is Trotter's light, his rock, and what little there is of his spiritual life. William Carlos Williams told Callaghan that he felt that she was crucial to the novel and that Trotter even became an "appealing figure" because of his "bewildered circling around the flame of his love of Vera." At one point early in the novel, Vera tells Harry that she is thinking of becoming a Roman Catholic. But Trotter is not interested in religion at all. God is not on his radar screen and he tells Vera that "that is a queer notion." When directly asked if he believes in God and original sin, he tells his lover Julie casually, "It doesn't appeal to me." Trotter is too self-absorbed, amoral and nihilistic to bother with even the simplest of theological concepts.

Part II: Here Trotter dabbles in the Toronto underworld — drinking, whoring and visiting the dance halls and speakeasies in a multicultural world of "oily Jews, " "big wops" and even an elegant, rouged, "lipsyled" homosexual. (Trotter is only told that the man is "on the outside of things," but Trotter's gut reaction is, "He gets on my nerves . . . how I hate that guy.") It ends with Trotter and Nash stealing a truckload of a bootlegger's shipment and selling it to an Italian-owned speakeasy.

Part III: In this longest section of the novel, Trotter establishes himself as part of the underworld. He rises from small-time bootlegger to big-time gangster and wealthy booze exporter. It ends with his murder of his rival Al Cosantino (a lesser version of the real Rocco Perri), and his shameless appearance at the funeral as a mourner. He also shacks up with Anna, a promiscuous femme fatale.

Part IV: This is the decline and fall of Trotter, complete with a mob banquet and a major mob sit-down (probably the first mob summit in fiction), where Trotter only further alienates his mob colleagues by his virulent anti-semitism and lying about his role in Cosantino's murder. This section and the novel end with Trotter's inevitable murder on the streets of downtown Toronto. The last sentence is a lyrical firsthand account of his death from gunshots from his rivals' hit car: "He saw the wheels of the car go round and round, and the car got bigger. The wheels went round slowly and he was dead."

There are equivalents in the real world of most of the characters and names in *Strange Fugitive*. The big Irish bootlegger O'Reilly is a composite of the real-life Hamilton bootlegger, Ben Kerr, and Rocco Perri — and like Perri, O'Reilly makes most of his money in the export trade to the U.S. and gives a rather fulsome and unnecessary interview to a Toronto newspaper on the bootleg war. The name of Rocco Perri's well-known lawyer before the 1926-27 Royal Commission was Michael Reilly, and the chief accountant for the commission who, along with Reilly, was quoted in the paper daily, was A.E. Nash, (the name used for Trotter's young partner in crime is Jimmie Nash). The real Jewish gangsters who controlled a lot of the booze in Toronto were the Wortzman brothers and Harry Goldstein, who were all called before the Royal

Commission in 1927. Trotter himself has a bit of the background of Ben Kerr, the "king of the smugglers," and a pinch of the flare of the Perri hit-man and bootlegger, John Trotta, his real-life namesake. (The name of the main Toronto Jewish gangster in the novel, Asche, is similar to that of Morley's close friend Nathan Asch, son of the great Yiddish writer Sholom Asch.)

Strange Fugitive is remarkably innovative in its style, its dialogue, its "lean crisp prose" — to quote one reviewer — and its unique realism. Callaghan pushed the boundaries of taste by the use of local slang, colorful colloquialisms, and racist terms. (Princeton-educated and refined gentleman that he was, Scott Fitzgerald would never have a character in *The Great Gatsby* referred to as an "oily Jew" or "kike," as Trotter or his narrator do.) Callaghan himself wrote in the *London Times Literary Supplement* in 1964: "I had become aware that the language in which I wanted to write, a North American language which I lived by, had rhythms and nuances and twists and turns quite alien to English speech. I had decided that language of feeling and perception and even direct observation had to be the language of the people I wrote about." In *Strange Fugitive*, the main character is a bigoted Toronto gangster and so the dialogue and language is appropriate and realistic. And the use of racist epithets like "kike" had a charge in them since they were never used in the literary fiction of the time. (This is much like the innovative freshness that came in the 1950's with Henry Miller's use of "fuck" and other colorful sexual language).

In a review of *Strange Fugitive* in the *New York Times* in 1928 the critic said "so fresh and vivid is Mr. Callaghan's style, so sharp and convincing his characterization, so sparkling his dialogue, that one has a momentary urge to place the laurel crown on the brow without much ado . . . No one interested in what is really alive and vital in the writing of the younger generation of novelists can be ignorant of Mr.

Callaghan's work. . . . His style is a joy in an age which suffers from too much hack writing. . . ." Also trumpeting Morley was Nobel laureate Sinclair Lewis who opined in 1929 on the front page of the *NY Tribune* that "No one today — if one claims Toronto as part of the American scene — is more brilliantly finding the remarkable in the ordinary than Morley Callaghan. Here is magnificently the seeing eye. . . . His persons and places are of the most commonplace, his technique is so simple that it is apparently not a technique at all . . ."

Callaghan in *Strange Fugitive* is showing the Toronto bootleg world as he sees it and, as a result, Trotter is not a sophisticated or educated man. His literary antecedent might be Melville's 1856 Bartleby, a character who is inarticulate and whose inability to communicate rationally has similarly fatal consequence. Trotter is just such a primitive, instinctive man. It is a characteristic that Joseph Conrad — as if he were describing Trotter — noted in a 1916 letter about the Irish nationalist, Sir Roger Casement, when he described him as "a man, properly speaking, of no mind at all. I don't mean stupid. I mean he was all emotion . . . and sheer emotionalism has undone him, a creature of sheer temperament . . ." The implications of, and justification for this inarticulateness in Trotter and his immaturity, was commented on by Maxwell Perkins in a letter to Morley in 1931: "In almost all of your writing your characters were the common run of people who have not had the chance to develop much intellectually or emotionally. That has led many readers . . . to regard you as a hard-boiled writer. Some say a delicacy of perception was one of your marked and most distinguishing qualities, and that it was expressed with corresponding subtlety in your writing. They should have seen that even in your first novel about a bootlegger. But you were writing about a bootlegger and you naturally dealt in what I call realism. Many unpleasant details had a significance in that narrative and you put them in, and quite rightly."

Morley Callaghan's stark description of Trotter's killing of his rival in Part III of the novel reveals a lot about Callaghan's technique:

One of the men coming out the side door was Cosantino, short and dark. The two men with him were taller and wore caps. Cosantino's overcoat was open, a white scarf flapping loosely over the blue coat. They were on the sidewalk. They were crossing the road. The car passed, moving very slowly. Harry fired three times at Cosantino. Eddie [Trotter's hired gun] fired twice . . . Cosantino and one of his men fell on the road . . . At the first corner Eddie spun the wheel,the car swung around, coming back along the street. The woman who had come out of the store screamed and ran, the car passed within a few feet of Cosantino who was sprawled in the middle of the road, his face down, one knee hunched up. The white scarf had gotten tangled around his neck. His hat had fallen off. The car passed over the hat and close to Cosantino and Harry fired two more shots into the body, and the car leapt forward swinging around the corner . . . People running along the road were yelling. A cop on a bicycle came along and he blew his whistle. They turned north. "We got the wop," Harry said, "we got the wop." The blood seemed to be surging into his head. He heard the whistle again and laughed out loud . . .

The American poet William Carlos Williams, who read the book in proofs, told Callaghan in a long letter in early 1928 that he stayed up all night reading the novel and found that the book "frightened" him:

"There is a truth or a principle which governs the book . . . it is the tragic principle of classical drama . . . the book is a play of studied moves. It does not grow. It is made by terrifying rules from which the characters do not escape, but they do live. Thus the truth of the writing is outside the story. There is much of the starkness of the tragic drama in Callaghan's book. It may be Greek; it may be Racine; it may be Ibsen . . . My own interest is in asking what is this thing? It is the Vera of the story. Harry wavers around it like a moth. Its failure in Harry is his death, his inherent inability to realize it and to hold it under any circumstances is his tragedy."

Writing about crime in such realistic fashion as Morley does can provide remarkable insight into society. For example, in the bootlegging world of the 20's, it is clear that there are a lot of respectable people who were otherwise known as legitimate distillers and yet were hypocritically involved in the criminal export of booze. Also, there was rampant police corruption as a major part of the bootleg trade (as there is today in the drug trade), and at one point in the novel Trotter complains about how much of his profits he has to pay to corrupt cops to keep his illicit operation unmolested. He also notes how easy it was (and still is) to recruit cops for protection: "These policemen [the first four he put on the payroll] had been useful in getting others who were easier because not many wanted to miss anything."

Crime writing however has seldom been considered worthy literature — even today — by most critics, academics and intellectuals. Thus many belittle Morley for writing about crime as he saw it. For example, the *New York Times* critic in 1928 said that "when Trotter participates in a cold-blooded murder with sawed-off shotguns he goes about it as calmly and unemotionally as though he were kicking a dog which barred his path. In this last fact lies the weakness of the novel. It is interesting to read of a murderer only when the murder has a decided effect upon his character . . . Our interest in Trotter the murderer is sustained by the expertness with which the story is told, not the story itself . . ."

More recently, the critic George Woodcock, in the *Oxford Companion to Canadian Literature,* wrote that the novel is "gauche and tentative in manner and implausible and melodramatic in plot." And Edmund Wilson lamented the lack of a moral life in Harry Trotter. But I would say that very few successful gangsters — from the fictional Little Caesar and Tony Soprano to the many real gangsters I have known well over the years — have any moral life to speak of. Trotter is no different — he is an armed robber and killer — a psychopath with no conscience — and Callaghan would have been remiss in his portrayal of Trotter — a nasty brutish thug — to give him any moral life of substance. What inner life there is in Trotter is only hinted at (the book is only from Trotter's point of view) in his reflections over his treatment of Vera, his long-suffering wife, and his brooding over his mother and the loss of his Eden — his childhood home in the horse-and-buggy town of Maydale (Maydale may very well be Markham — with its long history of gang violence), an hour north of Toronto where Trotter visits after he kills Cosantino. (As a feeble act of atonement he puts up an enormous garish stone for his parents.) There is a hint of guilt over his treatment of Vera — a glimmer of a moral awareness which WIlliam Carlos Williams thought gave a "tragic" sense to the novel and Harry's fate. But in such a criminal a developed moral life or conscience would be highly unusual, to say nothing of it being counterproductive.

Strange Fugitive is unique in Morley Callaghan's opus — a gritty, innovative story dealing with something Callaghan knew about — the underside of a big city, Toronto. In this, his first novel, he became an important modern writer who broke significant new literary ground establishing the gangster novel in North America and the urban novel in Canadian literature.

James Dubro, Toronto, 2004

PART ONE

1

*H*arry Trotter, who had a good job as foreman in Pape's lumberyard, was determined everybody should understand he loved his wife. After they had been married three years he felt it necessary to show contrition every time he thoughtlessly spoke harshly to Vera, and when in the company of other people, she pouted, making it clear he had in some way offended her, he was eager to pet her, and talk baby talk to convince her he was awfully sorry. She was rather small and neat, and his big hands covered her cheeks when she cried, her head just reaching his shoulder. Afterward there was a temporary impetus to his passion.

He lay in bed one night, listening to Vera breathing and thinking he had loved her so much no other woman could ever give such satisfaction. He felt almost like crying, and wished he had encouraged her to have children. He was sure his increasing interest in other women had a direct relation to Vera, and that he would always be in love with her. It was a hot night and bedclothes were tight against his throat or he might have dealt more successfully with such a complicated problem. Then Vera moved beside him. She was awake. She began talking of an argument they had had before going to bed. She said sullenly that he thought more of his job than of anything else on earth. The thought startled him, and before falling asleep he decided she had been close to the truth. He was unhappy all next day, and in the evening he took a long walk by himself, and sitting on a park bench had many thoughts till he felt absolutely alone, and even thought of going away but couldn't seriously consider leaving such a good job. In the daytime, in the yard, he was ugly-tempered with the men and worked them savagely.

2

The nape of Trotter's neck caught the sun's stinging heat. He leaned back and looked up at the sun, then moved a step into the boxcar's shadow.

A plank swung out over the cross-bar on the car door into Trotter's hands. Glancing at it quickly, he called "Twenty-two common" to the tally-boy on the stool a few feet away, then swung it into the hands of one of the hunkies, waiting their turn in single file on the narrow shadow, who carried it on his hip, slowly out into the sun, piling it on the sawhorses.

He was unloading a boxcar on a siding in Pape's lumber-yard. From the milling plant came the sound of saw-teeth tearing through wood. The hot sun in a cloudless sky, shining for hours on the wooden platform, burned through heavy boot soles. When Trotter leaned forward he caught the stuffy smell of fresh pines from the boxcar door. A puff of hot air came along the platform. One of the men mopped his forehead with a big bandana handkerchief, and fanned himself with an old discoloured straw hat. The men went on slugging the lumber steadily. Trotter, checking the planks mechanically, let his eye wander beyond the limits of the yard to the jutting tower of a flour elevator. He was not thinking of anything in particular, watching big white letters on the red tower, and he called, "Twenty-three common; twenty-three good!" but kept his eye on the men. A big fellow in the line scratched his head, staring across the yard to the tracks where an engine was shunting a boxcar. "Hey, you big bum, snap out of it!" Harry yelled. "It's hot, but we got to get this done in a hurry . . . twenty-three common," he chanted, "twenty-three fair. Keep them stepping lively." He worked briskly. He liked knowing lumber so well. Only a few old-timers in the yard knew lumber better than he did.

In the gang were three Italians, an old, thick-set Scotch-man, a Swede, and a fellow working in the yard temporarily. A squat, long-armed, leather-faced Italian in a torn blue shirt, darkly blotched with sweat at the armpit, wiped his forehead with his hairy arm, and stepped out of the line to get a drink. Harry stopped marking planks for a few seconds, scowling at the broad back bending over the tap.

"Hey, big fellow, now you're over there, help Charlie put the chain around the pile," he said quietly.

Standing still, he watched Charlie drive the horse along the platform and throw the clanking chain around planks piled on sawhorses. The big fellow and Charlie buckled the chain tight, the Italian kicked away one of the sawhorses. Charlie backed the horse in and got on top of the pile. Harry, watching the horse move slowly along the platform, was thinking how the wop had stepped out of line, holding up the parade. If he didn't shake a leg he'd show him. But it was hard doing anything to old wops like that. They got into easy ways of doing things and you couldn't budge them. The men were working smoothly again. They didn't know how to feel important. You could get them under your thumb, and they wanted to hold the job.

He could inspect lumber, call to the tally-boy, and go on having his own thoughts. When his thoughts drifted into places beyond the lumberyard he worked slower, but afterward took it out of the men. He watched Jimmie Nash, the new man, too awkward to be effective at heavy work in the yard, carrying lumber patiently, piling planks clumsily. Harry noticed the tired droop of his shoulders, and the skin peeling from his sunburnt face. He liked Nash. At first he had wondered why a university man had ever taken a hunkie's job in a lumberyard, then had learned Jimmie was making some money, waiting for a job on a newspaper. They had had many interesting talks together, and had gone drinking in the evenings, and sometimes to see a friend of Jimmie's, Julie Roberts. Jimmie was quiet, but his mouth drooped a little from sneering, and he had a poor opinion of the yard superintendent, Hohnsburger, and the mayor of the city, the university, the police force, prohibition, ministers, thin women, so Harry felt flattered to discover Jimmie really liked him. Jimmie, carrying a plank, passed by, sweating a lot, but very indifferent.

"Don't fight the plank, Jimmie," Harry said.

"All right, I intended to ask you at noon time. Are you going up to Julie's tonight?"

"I don't know."

"Well, why look so sad about it?"

"I'm not sad, Jimmie.."

"I believe women bother you."

"Listen, Jimmie, you'll get sunstroke with that cap on."

"It's not so bad," he said, standing up straight, wiping sweat from his forehead with his sleeve. The hunkies in line stared across the yard, thankful for the delay, indifferent to Harry and Nash.

"There's a big straw hat hanging in a closet in the warehouse just as you go in," Harry said, gruffly agreeable.

As soon as Nash moved off down the platform Harry started making the men work very fast.

Factory whistles sounded five o'clock. The men working in the yard quit promptly. Harry went over to the warehouse to change his clothes.

In the three-by-four compartment he had erected for himself in the corner of the warehouse he started to clean up. He got the pail from a corner and went back to the tap for water. He took off his khaki shirt, his undershirt, and, bare-bodied, dipped the soap in water, making lather for his face and rubbing well down his shoulders and hairy chest. Scooping water in his palms he splashed his face, blowing out through his mouth and nose, and getting soap out of his eye with the thumb-joint. He stood up well-rubbed with the towel, peeled off his overalls, and kicked off his heavy boots. He remembered that tonight one of the ball teams practiced in the park near his place, and, standing in his underwear, putting on a clean shirt, wished he had time to make a place on one of the teams. The soft collar he circled with a sky-blue tie, snappy, conservative, the knot tied fastidiously. He looked squarely and seriously at his image in the jagged piece of looking-glass hanging on the wall, and wondered if Vera would want to do anything after supper that would prevent him from going over to the park. Slowly he brushed his thick hair, took a straw sailor from a nail and adjusted it at a sporty angle on his head. He handled carefully his shining, tan low shoes. He emerged from the warehouse, altogether aloof from the yard, no bum, not just a hunky boss, no cheapskate from a lumberyard. He walked confidently along the platform, the flash of thick blond hair under the hat brim well cut, his tanned, high-cheekboned face free from stubble, his stylish tweed suit with a high waist-line, well cut and form-fitting.

He nodded to Hohnsburger, the superintendent, whom he passed turning into the alley behind the office to punch the time clock. Hohnsburger nodded civilly but unsmilingly. They rarely spoke to each other after business hours. At first it had been all right working under Hohnsburger, but recently he had been looking at Harry as if unable to make up his mind about him. Nothing definite had ever happened. Harry simply had no use for the superintendent, and without trying to explain it to himself, he disliked uneasily Hohnsburger's solid, six-foot, double-chinned importance. Harry reached for his time-card in the rack. Neat men from the office were punching the clock. He was like them only better and stronger, neat as a pin, but could smash them if he wanted to. He carried no lunch-pail, and they knew it.

3

The Trotters lived in a duplex house on a street not far from the lake. A young lawyer and his wife lived on the ground floor. The Trotters lived upstairs. Vera Trotter had known Harry at high school, but had gone away to Chicago, and when she came back had met him at one of those Old Boy dances high schools have once a year. He had liked her sensuous ways, and the steady, wistful look in her dark eyes. She was two years older than he, and becoming aware that she should have her own life and not live in the way of her mother and father. Her mother, who did illustrating for magazines and a few book jackets, did not think much of Harry, who was working in the office of Pape's lumberyard.

In Chicago Vera had an affair with a man who had been expelled from college for his unnatural habits. He wrote soft, sticky poetry, but made love roughly and energetically. After an automobile ride one night he asked Vera to go to Paris with him. She thought him boyishly wayward, and hoped if they went away he would develop into a decent, respectable fellow. She thought she was in love, and wanted to go away with him. They talked of Paris, and the drop in the franc, but he was arrested on a criminal seduction charge, and sent down for a year.

Vera told Harry all about the man in Chicago, and showed him some of the poetry, and cried when she came to the last part of the story. Some of the feeling she had had for the young man who had been expelled from college came to her when talking to Harry, and she was eager to get married and have him become successful and amount to something. She imagined him growing strong and dominant while remaining close to her, and very faithful to her. There were mental qualities he lacked, and she was at first discontented, but liked his hard, lean legs and the deep wave in his fair hair, and the fierce eagerness inside him, and the strength of his arms, all of it becoming more important to her as she knew him better. And they got married.

Vera suggested that he leave the lumberyard and get into something requiring more character and more ability than a knowledge of lumber, but he got the foreman's job in the yard and a salary of fifty dollars a week, so she decided she could be happier if they remained practical. She got into the way of thinking it would be cruel to Harry to suggest for a single moment that he leave the yard, he was so strong in his own importance. Though making certain positive reservations she felt herself becoming a part of his world in which he was a boss, hard and firm, and confident. It pleased her at times to be sentimental and think of him as a man who in other days on barbaric islands would have been a tribal chief. The first time she thought of it, and had developed it, she told him the story and was glad he took it all so seriously.

She knew all about the yard, and the men in the gang, and Hohnsburger the superintendent.

Coming home from the yard at half-past five o'clock Harry smelled a stew cooking as he climbed the stair of the duplex house, a dish he liked, and Vera cooked it with small round new potatoes, oodles of onions, peppers, spices.

"Stew eh, Vera," he said, going into the kitchen. When she kissed him like that, closing her eyes, he felt that he had not known her very long and watched her move around the kitchen. He sat down on a kitchen chair. She bent over the sink and he mechanically shifted his gaze, aware, in a practical way, of looking closely at someone familiar to him, a waste of time over a curiosity that should have been satisfied long ago, but thinking suddenly of girls getting on a streetcar and his constant curiosity about the shape of legs, he was satisfied to go on watching Vera bending over the sink. She was trim, and deliberate.

"Did the paper come?" he said, getting up and taking off his coat.

"Yes, it did," she said. "Hang up your coat, Harry."

"My coat's all right. I'll be putting it on right after supper."

"Well, there's no harm in hanging it up."

"All right, I'll hang it up," he said, carefully avoiding argument, for there was no reason why he shouldn't hang it on the hall rack.

"Now for the stew, eh."

"It's a dandy stew tonight," she said, filling his plate.

"That's the stuff, Vera."

"How'd things go today? Have any trouble with Hohnsburger?"

"No, didn't bang into him. That guy's a real ham. Don't ask me why. He's just a ham."

He answered her irritably, determined not to go on talking about the yard, yet expecting her to persist, but she went on eating. The evening paper was on a corner of the table and he glanced at the headlines.

"Harry."

"What?"

"What would you think if I became a Catholic?"

"Holy smoke." He stopped eating, looking at her earnestly. She smiled, then was serious. He let his glance wander around the room. On a cupboard was a book. He could make out the name of the author, Philip Gibbs, the man who wrote the unknown-soldier story, and who must have been a good writer because the government had so many writers to choose from.

"That's a queer notion," he said.

"I've often thought about it." Her eyes got moist thinking about it. "I don't know why, but I know I'll feel happier if I'm a Catholic."

"Who do you know that's a Catholic?"

"I knew a couple of girls before they got married. Now they've sent their kids to a convent for schooling. If I ever had a girl I'd love to have her educated in a convent."

"Well, suit yourself," he said broad-mindedly, "only don't try and rope me in on it."

"Let's go down to the lake and sit on a bench by the water," she said suddenly.

"I hadn't thought of the lake, Vera."

"I was thinking this afternoon how we used to go down through the park and watch the lights on the lake when it got dark."

"I remember."

"Well, let's do it tonight."

"Tonight?"

"Yes tonight, go early, and watch the sun go down on the water."

"I hadn't thought of it, Vera. I wanted to go over to the ballpark and watch the practice."

"Aw, no."

"Gol darn it, I had looked forward to it."

She put up her elbow on the table, chin in her hand and said: "All right, go on over to the ballpark."

"Never mind," he said. "I'll go along with you."

"No, you won't."

"Don't be silly, don't you see I'm saying I'll go with you."

"Well, you certainly won't now."

"I will, I tell you, and please, I ask you, in heaven's name, don't be so contrary."

She got up, shrugging her shoulders, and shaped her lips for whistling, to show a lack of concern. He watched her going out of the room. She never could whistle. He got up to rush after her, angry words coming impulsively. He stood still, ashamed to think such an unimportant conversation should enrage him.

"I think I'll go over to the ballpark and watch the boys practice," he said.

"All right."

He found his finger-glove in the pantry and inspected it critically, slapping the palm a few times, then spitting on it, to soften the leather. "Vera won't really become a Catholic," he thought. "She gets worked up about things, but she'll get over it all right." He jumped over the back fence to take the short-cut across the vacant lot. Stan Farrel, the lawyer who lived on the ground floor, waved from the window while he was jumping the fence. Harry heard the crack of the bat against the ball, and a whoop and shout.

In the park he leaned against the rail watching the manager hit grounders to infielders. The stocky little manager in a red sweater-coat standing restively at the home-plate, nodded to the first baseman who waited on his toes. "On the hop," the manager yelled, swinging, the ball bounding down to the third baseman who, coming in quickly, scooped it up neatly, pegging hard across the diamond. "Atta boy, you're there kid," Harry yelled to the third baseman. Harry had played in this league before he had got married and was still fond of the game. Now he liked the way it took his mind off his work. Sometimes he went into the outfield and chased flies with the players. The practice was too serious tonight and he did not get into it at all.

The practice over, he went into the dressing room and talked with some of the players. He watched a fellow stretched out on his belly getting a rub down. He smelled the liniment, and thought maybe the fellow had a charley horse. Most players undressed slowly, singing and telling stories. They talked loudly and happily. Harry picked up a fellow's ball-shoes and whacked them on the floor, knocking the mud out of the spikes.

"Much obliged. You're a good guy," the fellow grinned.

"That's all right."

He left the dressing room with Sid Dodds and Curly Spencer and Charlie Duggan. They leaned against the fence, standing on the sidewalk, smoking. It was not quite dark but street lights were lit. Two girls sauntered down the street, slowing up under the street lights, and one grinned at Charlie Duggan.

Harry watched the fellows catch up to the girls and everything seemed to go nice and easy. He felt discontented, anxious for some interesting experience, and suddenly decided to go and see Julie Roberts.

4

He had met Julie at a time when too many evenings with Vera seemed dull, and he felt he ought to get interested in another woman. Julie astonished him, she suggested so much experience, a war widow who had been to France and lived for two years in Paris. Some of her best stories were about the voyage home. He met her in the book and novelty shop she had opened uptown, close to the good conservative district. He read a great many detective stories, and one night, with Jimmie Nash, he went into Julie's shop and looked over the mystery stories, while Jimmie talked to her about other books. Harry thought she had an excellent variety of mystery stories on the shelves, and, reading a synopsis, he happened to glance at her, and was embarrassed. She was smiling at him. She was about thirty-five years old, a serious woman with a round face and soft eyes. She stood up and he was disappointed, then astonished and interested in the size of her, the width of her shoulders and her strong legs. He stared rudely and she smiled at him and he felt that his thoughts were amusing her. Afterward Jimmie explained that she was a fine woman to know, if she liked you, and he made up his mind to get all his mystery stories from her library. He didn't expect her to be really interested in him because he was uncomfortable in the arty shop, and he told Jimmie that she was probably a damn sight too sophisticated for him. One evening she good-naturedly told him he was a husky brute, and talked for half an hour. He asked if he could call on her some night and at once felt very nervous when she agreed. She encouraged him to talk of the lumber business, but he insisted she was laughing at him. Several times, visiting her in the evenings, he talked of Vera, and after one of these con-versations, when he had decided he never could be as happy as he had been in the old days with Vera, on the way home he thought entirely of Julie. She was older and when he tried to make love she afterward smiled, as if capable of a great deal more than the surface emotion suggested. She understood that it was impracticable for him to take her out to shows, so they often took long walks up north at the city limits, and always he had the feeling of having made an astonishing discovery.

He refused to think he was definitely trying to replace a feeling he had had once for Vera, and when she irritated him, he avoided any direct comparison with Julie. Instead he talked of an old friend of Vera's, who had interested him, Grace Leon ard, who had gone away to Virginia. He told Vera that Grace was beautiful, though rather slender, and the most sympathetic woman he had ever met. But he never mentioned Julie to her because he didn't want the comparison, even for himself.

He went up to Julie's shop, after the ball practice, and didn't bother looking at the pattern of coloured glass bowls in the window, or the new flagstones in the path to the door. He opened the door and a bell tinkled. Julie was at the back of the shop, bending over the desk, getting ready to close for the evening. She was hardly surprised, and he was irritated. There was too much composure suggested in her heavy face and ample body. She was casually cheerful, taking it for granted, while she put on her coat, that he would walk home with her. "I wonder if she gets other people the way she gets me," he thought, aware that he was attracted by the suggestion of rich experience made the most of by her big body, a husband dead, two years in Europe, and all her stories about the voyage home, and the three or four languages she spoke fluently.

He held her plump arm while they walked four blocks to her cottage. She asked too politely for his wife, as though Vera's health was important to her. He didn't answer abruptly because she was deliberately teasing him. There was no light in the cottage so she went in ahead, telling him to go into the back room and stretch out on the couch, while she went upstairs, to change her dress. On the couch he closed his eyes. He didn't want to look at the funny pictures on the wall, the gold wallpaper, the grand piano. She came into the room wearing a blue dress with a wide skirt and long sleeves, her Russian peasant dress she called it, and began to light the four red candles on the desk by the couch. She took a pack of cards from a drawer and flipping them neatly across the desk, arranged them for solitaire. Usually, when she wanted to talk, she sat at the desk with the cards. He stretched himself on the couch.

"Why did you come along tonight?" She seemed mainly interested in the cards.

"Just to be with you a while, Julie."

"A quarrel with the wife, I dare say" She smiled at the cards.

He shrugged his shoulders and stared at her pale face and heavy red lips. "Come on over on the couch here," he said suddenly, but she paid no attention to him, smiling to herself. He was eager to put his arms around her, restless because he knew there would be a number of movements and motions before she consented. She swept the cards into a pile, starting over again, pausing to quote a few lines of poetry, and turning apologetically to say, "Milton, son." He crossed his legs on the couch, and thought vaguely that he loved her because he liked watching her. Sometimes he watched a pretty girl. Julie was not pretty, a big slow woman, but he loved the lines of her face, and had the feeling of a small boy conscious of the presence of a bold grown woman.

He got up quickly, put his hands on her shoulders, and jerked her over to the couch. She fell awkwardly over his hip and was quite heavy but he liked it. She lay there laughing. "What a big tough boy you are," she said. She made herself more comfortable and he put his hand on her forehead. "Let's be serious," she said.

"No, kiss me."

"Listen, do you believe in God?"

"Cut it out."

"No, I want to get a rather natural point of view. Tell me."

"I don't know."

"Think about it."

"I don't want to, it's too peaceful," he said, noticing a soft fold of flesh under her chin. "It isn't worth a kiss."

"I'm not suggesting that, but these nice discussions can be had only now and then." She told him she had had an operation for appendicitis, and just before the anaesthetic, had said to herself "There's no God." After coming out of it the same thought had astonished her. So they talked about God and a world where there was smallpox and crime and little girls who never had a chance. He held onto her plump arm, and she insisted all theological systems were absolutely impracticable. "God knows, for example, that a man born a cripple in this world will suffer terribly, why is it?"

"I don't know, Julie, for the love of Mike."

"But what do you think?"

"Because of original sin, I guess."

"It doesn't appeal to me."

"Me either."

So they kissed and he was happier. She looked at her wristwatch and said: "Augustus is coming here tonight, but if you want to stay I needn't let him in." Her guarded eagerness was uncomfortable. The lack of passion in the words was more embarrassing than if she had jumped up and taken hold of him tightly. She got up slowly and sat down again at the desk, fumbling with cards. He watched the flame at the tip of the red candle, and her plump fingers shuffling cards. Her leg moved under the dress and he looked up startled, but she was simply crossing her ankles.

"I think I'll go home all right," he said.

"You're really not too reckless."

"Let's not argue, Julie. Have a heart."

"All right, do you know I'm thinking of getting married?"

"Not to the little guy Augustus, the guy with the violin?"

"He's a dear boy. He'll be along any moment now. You should tell me when you intend to come here."

He was angry to think of her marrying the long-haired boy, chinless and pale-eyed, but was surprised to hear himself say: "Don't marry that little guy, Julie."

"I'm going to."

He was sorry for himself. He stood behind her, looking at the white part in her black hair. For a moment he thought of trying to explain there was something about her he couldn't afford to lose, but such words would suggest he took Augustus seriously. Instead he said: "I'll break that little guy's violin over his ear."

Someone rapped at the front door.

"That's Augustus," she said pleasantly, without getting up. "Well—"

"No, I got to go, Julie."

"Come up tomorrow night," she said nervously.

"No."

"Suit yourself, then, you big sweet-tempered boy."

He followed her to the door and passed Augustus coming in. Augustus bowed and said good evening very politely in a squeaky voice. He had two thick books under his arm. Harry grinned at him and Augustus stroked his cheek.

Augustus usually made him feel good-humoured. Walking along the street he laughed to himself. He always thought of Augustus by way of the picture Julie had shown him, taken in winter, a coon-skin hat pulled down over his ears and a kind of dog-skin coat. "God help Augustus," he thought, wondering what he was doing back in the room with Julie.

He walked through Queen's Park, walking very slowly. It was dark but there was a bright moon and the thick trunks of the tall trees were stark against the sky. Benches were in the shadows of the tree trunks, and in the dark he walked too close to one and heard a discreet cough. He turned on to the path again. A match was lit near a flower bed and low bushes along the main path, and he remembered he had sat on that bench with Grace Leonard the only time he had ever been alone with her. They were on the bench an hour and a half talking of trivial matters till nearly midnight. A policeman on a bicycle coming through the park had seen him light a cigarette and had come over to say that if they were respectable people they would go home at once, and leaning against his wheel, he had watched Grace suspiciously, as they moved away. He felt sad, thinking how Grace had gone away, and he half closed his eyes, walking in the shadow of a university building, to remember all the lines of her face that had become vague, but almost too beautiful, he was sure. He was walking on cement now by Gothic Hart House and, going down a short flight of steps, heard only the sound of his own footsteps, and had the uneasy, pleasant feeling of being alone. He began to think of good times he might have had with Grace. Her face, from one angle, was beautiful but at another, the features were a little too heavy. His feeling for her, now only a memory, had nothing whatever to do with Julie Roberts. He giggled to himself. Supposing he should grab Julie by the hips and simply lift her up, sending her sprawling on the couch, anything to disturb her confidence in herself, so he could measure her definitely. He followed the road south in the shadows, then watched the rays of white light from the searchlight in front of the parliament buildings, lighting up the white stone of the new wing. Out of the park, he got a streetcar going west. He got off at the corner near home. He was fairly happy, and even looked forward to seeing Vera and talking with her. He looked into the window of the Italian fruit-store near the corner, the light in the window shining on pyramids of oranges, plums and rosy apples. He went into the store and bought a bag of plums.

5

The Farrels came up next night at half-past eight. Vera respected Farrel because he was a professional man, a young lawyer with good prospects but making small money actually. Recently she had talked a good deal of a quarrel the Farrels were having over two dogs. It was rather a friendly quarrel, though sometimes it developed till they shouted loudly and were heard upstairs. Stan Farrel had an English bulldog, and his wife, a bad-tempered Pekinese. Stan paid a lot of money for his bitch. The two dogs quarrelled, so he tried to persuade his wife to get rid of the Pekinese, and when she refused, threatened to let his bitch tear up the little beast next time there was trouble. Stan was nasty to the Pekinese whenever possible, and once tried to coax Harry to take it away and drown it. Mrs. Farrel, hearing of it, insisted she would get even. The bitch was in heat and Stan kept it carefully in the backyard. One morning, after Stan had gone to work, Mrs. Farrel let the bitch out in the backyard. There was a litter of mongrel pups and Stan felt badly because he couldn't quite explain it. He talked of getting rid of the bulldog, but decided to keep it and offered the pick of the litter to Harry, who sympathized, though he didn't want a dog. Three nights ago the Trotters had been downstairs for some bridge, now the Farrels were coming up for a few talky easygoing hours. Mrs. Farrel and Vera, talking eagerly, went into the sunroom. Stan, slapping his hands, swaggered half the length of the room.

"How's the boy, Harry?"

"Fine. We haven't had an evening together for moons."

"No, not in a dog's age."

Farrel adjusted himself comfortably in an easy chair. Harry liked him for being so reassuring. Stan leaned forward in his chair, his paunch overflowing, fat around the waist all right, but his legs hard, and his shoulders wide and firm. A little boxing in the army had been useful, though he never could stand being hit on the nose. Anyway he was good-natured and his wife couldn't get sore at him. His cheeks were smooth and except for a few long hairs on a growth on his left cheek, he never had to shave. He had on his "gates-ajar" collar that he always wore, a mark of the professional man.

"How about going down to the office tonight?" he said.

"What's the idea? We couldn't stay long."

"Long enough. Let the girls strut their stuff by themselves, they'll never miss us."

"What's doing down at the office?"

"Bob Gibson'll be there, and if he hasn't got anything to drink we can slip over to Angelina's."

Mrs. Farrel and Vera came back arguing politely about an article in the evening paper, a division of opinion among the Baptists in the city over a proper interpretation of the Book of Jonah. Harry looked up. When Mrs. Farrel and Vera were together he felt slightly superior, though always aware that Stan was the professional man. Mrs. Farrel, a good talker when she got going, had a neat lean body, tall and rather good-looking. Her skirt hung loosely around her hips. Her feet were long and slender. At public school, kids had called her licorice legs, but her face was fresh and her hair thick. She was positive she was right and often said, "don't be silly," but when really puzzled she said, "I'll ask my husband."

"The teacup theologians," Stan grinned.

"I'm for the whale," Harry said.

"Maybe so, if you like being skeptical," Mrs. Farrel said.

"Did the whale swallow Jonah, or did Jonah swallow the whale?" Stan said brightly.

That spoilt the argument. Vera started a literary conversation with Farrel, unaware that he was treating her opinions good-humouredly. Farrel, talking, liked some of his own opinions so well he expanded and said, "I've always been fond of the company of bookish people and artists. Knew a lot of them in the army. We had a paper and I wrote some fair satirical verse in it, if I do say it myself."

"A poet, eh?"

"A bit of a poet, rather."

Harry got up. "Cut it short and let's do something. Stan and I were thinking of taking a little walk."

"I'm reading Philip Gibbs," Vera said, holding on to the conversation. "I think his descriptions wonderful."

"Philip Gibbs, eh, yeah, yeah, but I stick to the old stuff," Farrel said. "Hold your horses, Harry old boy. I mean I'm reading Montaigne's 'Essays.' There you have pungent humour in the classical vein and quite revolutionary too, mind you. Ever read it?"

"No. Come on. Stan, I'm laughing hearty."

"Harry doesn't like reading much," Vera apologized.

"Neither does my wife."

"I just don't like the books Stan likes," Mrs. Farrel explained.

"That's it, dear, you just don't like 'em."

"But Stan can tell you who wrote almost anything though. Go on, Stan."

Stan winked at Harry, smiling good-naturedly.

"Go on, try him, Mrs. Trotter," Mrs. Farrel said.

"Well."

"Go on, try and catch him."

"Tut tut, Mrs. Trotter, we'll just take it as read," Stan said, getting up. Going out the door, Harry said to Stan, "What do you think this is, your birthday, what the hell!"

They left the house and walked over to the corner to get a streetcar, and waited five minutes before the car came along. The hot August night was sticky, the air heavy and men passing were carrying coats and fanning themselves with sailor hats. Harry looked up overhead, no stars in the sky, then looked at Stan, the "gates-ajar" collar losing some of its stiffness around his thick neck. They hesitated, thinking it might be better to go over to the Greek's and have a cool sundae, but the car came. They got a seat together, and Harry on the inside jerked up the window, putting his elbows on the window ledge, a cool breeze coming as the car gained speed.

They walked slowly over to the office building, their coats under their arms. Stan, his handkerchief in his hand, mopped his forehead continually. In the office building the old fellow doing night duty on the elevator knew Stan and they held a weather conversation as they shot up to the eleventh floor.

They could see a light in the office at the end of the corridor. "Bob's there all right," Stan said, "but I'll try the door quietly, if it's locked we won't bother him."

"Who would he have in there?"

"The Lord knows. I don't."

The door was locked but the knob rattled. Someone yelled, "Come in."

"Now that's bright, all right," Stan said.

Then Bob Gibson opened the door, grinning, one hand in his pocket, a nice guy, slim, neatly dressed. Whispering softly he nodded to the back office, saying loudly, "Sure Stan, come on in. Come on in, Harry." He grinned foolishly at Harry.

The woman in the back office said merrily, "How's the old straw hat, Stan?"

"Do you know Harry Trotter, Anna?"

"No, but why not."

"Anna is our best lady friend."

"Your best client you mean."

"That's right," Stan said, "our best cash customer, she pays and pays."

"One more wise-crack, and you go out," Bob said, hunting for extra glasses in the drawer of his desk. He pulled out five or six napkins from Bowles Lunch. "I use them for handkerchiefs in the morning when I don't go home at night," he explained, carefully replacing them in the drawer.

Anna tilted back in the swivel chair, her long legs stretched out, her neck balanced on the back of the chair. She grinned generously at Harry and tried to look alertly genial.

Two more glasses were placed on the table. One bottle was in the waste-paper basket, another on the windowledge. Heavy green curtains were drawn over the windows.

"How's it going, Anna?" Stan asked, rubbing his hands, boisterously genial. "I had an idea you'd be here."

"I'm getting a divorce," she said enthusiastically.

"Even so, don't stand there like sentries, you two," Bob said. "Draw up some chairs and let's be a family."

"No more family stuff, thanks. Hey, Harry, are you married?" she smiled.

"I sure am."

"Like it?"

"Got nothing against it."

"That means you're a swell husband. Only I don't think I'd want one anyway."

"If you ever do?"

"Name's in the phone book, I getcha."

She got up and leaned against the windowsill, looking serious quite prettily. Harry was anxious to be friendly. She was lazy-looking and easy-going. There was a swing to her big body. She took off slowly her mauve silk hat and swung it on the tip of her finger. "Made it myself," she grinned. "How do you like it, Harry? Bob likes it. Stan likes it. Everybody likes it."

Harry sat down, smiling at Anna. He took the drink Bob gave him, then he laughed at her. He laughed outright as a relief from grinning, rather uncertain of himself. She was easy-going, and he was sure she demanded no effort, but knowing it, he couldn't find the right words to interest her.

"Tell Harry the crossword puzzle story, Anna," Bob said. "Stan's the crossword puzzle hero," he explained.

Stan beckoned to Bob, who got up and followed him to the next office. "Business, always business," he said pleasantly.

Harry got up and leaned against the edge of the desk, watching Anna out of the corner of his eye. She smiled openly, tilting back in the chair, half closing her eyes, her toe just touching his ankle gently, accidentally, but it startled him, and he stared intently at the neat ankle, following the curve of it till he nervously looked at her eyes, only half closed. Very slowly, he brushed against her silk stocking leg, closing his eyes, tilting back his head a little to enjoy fully the faint sound of a trouser-leg brushing against smooth silk, holding it there till his hands began to tingle. At the moment he didn't want it to go any further, and wished it had been dark, for it was enough to feel her rounded ankle pressed against his trousered leg. Mechanically he moved closer, touching her shoulder with his hand. He touched her coat with the tip of his finger very gently, then stared at her directly. She was breathing heavily, as though asleep, but he knew she was watching him. She didn't want to spoil it by opening her eyes. He rubbed his hands down her coat, slowly and lightly. He heard Bob and Stan coming, and stepped back, leaning against the edge of the desk. She reached out to squeeze his hand quickly, then yawned lazily.

Stan picked up his glass and emptied it. "Very good, Bob, now, I think we'd better leave you two to the pursuit of happiness, eh?"

"I like the boyfriend," Anna said suddenly, showing her teeth, and nodding at Harry. They were firm teeth, white and even.

"O Lord, that means you'll have to adopt her too," Bob said sadly.

"I'm a knockout at that." Harry went around the table to lean against the window ledge with her. She settled snugly against the ledge with him.

"Whose adoption is she now?"

"Bobbie's," Stan said mournfully.

"Yours last week, Stan. Tell about the crossword puzzle, Anna."

"No, I'm just her legal adviser."

"I'm her husband's," Bob said, still mournful.

"Forget the little runt," she said sharply. "Thank the Lord that's over."

Bill and Stan were exchanging wisecracks and Harry tried to whisper, his lips brushing against the hair over her ears. She couldn't hear him and pretended he was tickling. He was asking for her phone number, deliberately muffling his words, not sure he wanted her to hear him. They both enjoyed it. "It tickles," she said.

"You two are getting damn chummy mighty silently," Bob said soberly.

For half an hour more they talked, anxious to keep the conversation lively. Bob brightened up immensely.

Outside, the street, back from the main thoroughfare, was very quiet. A slight breeze made the air cooler.

"She's really nice, Stan, and she don't seem tough. Was she tight?"

"She's a fine-looking girl, I've always said it, I mean she's nice-looking, neat for a big girl."

"You bet your boots, she's got a hot way with her."

"Oh, I don't know."

"Don't know what?"

"I mean I'd lay off her if I were you. Would have been all right a few weeks ago, but there's too many fooling around her now. See?"

"Yeah."

"Yeah, it's so. Listen to that damn night-hawk screeching."

"You wouldn't think it would fly around these buildings."

At the corner they could see the twinkling yellow and pink lights of the new electric sign over the Hippodrome. A cop, on the corner, looked at them doubtfully. Harry thought of Bob and Anna back in the office, mainly of Anna. Then he thought of the night before with Julie Roberts. Two women entirely different. Julie puzzled him, exciting him inwardly, so he could never be effective with her, but he could reach out his hand and confidently touch Anna. She was young and carelessly eager. "Things'll go easy with that baby," he thought, looking forward to her with relief, since his thoughts of Julie, or Vera, and even the memory of Grace Leonard had often bothered him till he was confused and unhappy.

"Where'd you pick her up?" he said to Stan.

"Walked into the office one day."

"What with?"

"Her husband."

"What for?"

"A separation and an allowance."

"Does she like you?"

"I think she likes me because I'm fat. I think most women love a fat man. At least I find it that way. But Bobbie wants to watch out or his wife'll be landing down there."

"I didn't know Bob was married."

"Neither did any one else but me."

"Who's he married to?"

"You've seen him with her. Calls herself Miss Ross. Her name is Rosenberg. She's a Jewess. The poor bastard, I feel sorry for him. She made him think he had to marry her. Her people won't have anything to do with him and he can't take her around places with him because most of his friends know she's a Jewess but they don't know they're married. See? It would be better if he'd come right out with it. As it is, he's drinking himself cuckoo and hanging out with a lot of bums.

I think it'd be a good thing for me if I broke loose from Bobbie. But he's such a nice guy."

They decided to have an onion sandwich to take the whiskey smell off the breath before going home. While the Chink was making the sandwich Stan said protectively: "Don't get the idea into your head that Anna's a little trollop, she's not. She probably never did a thing until recently."

"I didn't think she was."

"The point is she might well be if she don't watch out. She'd go to hell awfully quick right now just celebrating being away from that little runt of a husband. You should see him. He's terrible."

The Chink pushed their plates along the marble counter. "I wonder if Stan'll give me her phone number," Harry thought. He hesitated because Stan was feeling too protective. Probably the crossword puzzle story, whatever it was, bothered him. Later on he would be in a generous humour.

"How are things going in the yard, Harry?"

"All right. There's a guy there named Nash. A swell fellow just there for a month until he gets something else. We get on good together. He's been around a lot. You ought to meet him."

"What's so good about him?"

"Oh, I don't know. Just his way, that's all."

"Have you had a run-in yet with that guy Hohnsburger?"

"No, but I can feel it coming."

"I'd hold my horses if I were you, you know."

They drank the coffee and went out.

At home they smelt coffee. Mrs. Farrel and Vera were sitting at a bridge table with plates of cake and sandwiches. Pleasant and comfortable. Harry grinned at Vera. She looked directly at him, smiling happily, glad to see him.

The Farrels left and Harry helped Vera do the few dishes. She washed and he dried them, talking casually because he was deliberately thinking of Anna. Her soft laziness, the effortless swing of her big body. It was possible to think of her without getting her mixed up with his wife. His curiosity for her had no relation to Vera. Stan would say it was on a technically different basis. He looked at Vera, drying a plate carefully, and laughed out loud. He went on thinking of Anna, though she wasn't good enough to hold a candle for his wife. He thought vaguely of Anna.

6

He had dinner in the Chinese Café at the corner with Jimmie Nash, the fellow working in the yard for a month or two. Harry liked Nash; he got enthusiastic so easily. He was enthusiastic about Harry and had talked of the University and a Catholic professor who had been a good friend. He had been out of college for two years but had gone back to take a degree last term, though he had no idea why he wanted it except that his mother had been very anxious, and had cried when he had chucked it. He had worked on the boats and had been a magazine salesman, now he was sure he would be able to get on a newspaper. He talked engagingly, understanding most of Harry's thoughts, creating an impression of being agreeable, considerate, though having many strong opinions which were modified by his habit of finishing, "Still, I don't know, I don't know." It left room for further conversation.

They were walking back from the café to the yard. Men sitting on the sidewalk, backs to the brick wall of the yard office, did not look up at them. Harry knew they thought him a slave driver, but they kept out of his way and that satisfied him. Turning into the yard they punched the time clock, ten minutes early. They walked out into the yard and found a shaded alley between piles of lumber, and made pillows with their coats, stretching out, smoking. Harry was telling how he had often dreamed when a boy of owning a houseboat, sailing up and down the Mississippi. Sailing, not bothering about the time. He talked eagerly, feeling that the story in some way, off-set Nash's greater travelling experiences. He used to lie in bed, thinking of the houseboat. Sometimes even now, looking away beyond the piles of lumber when things were going slow, he thought of the Mississippi, though there was no reason for selecting that river in particular, probably because he knew nothing about it and it was wide and long.

Jimmie shifted the conversation to women. He had some good stories and told them as if curious to see how Harry would react. One girl, a married English woman, quite willing, couldn't figure out why he was interested in her. "She's really a frost and so is her six-foot husband," he said. "I think he tells her what a big bad guy he is."

"You want to watch your step, Jimmie, he may be."

"I really don't want to be bothered with her at all," he said. "The big guy's only hobby is making simply splendid beer. I go up and drink his beer until I get woozy-eyed. Out of respect to the beer I'm polite and even distant to the lady."

"How does she take it?"

"Awful."

"I guess she likes loving," Harry said thoughtfully, thinking of Anna.

"Does she? Do I like mushrooms?"

"Do you like mushrooms too?"

"Dooze I, I should say I dooze."

"I think I like them more than anything."

"Me too, more than anything."

"I like a pan full, fried in lots of butter and gobs of them in my mouth until it's so full I can hardly close it."

"Hell, with toast. We used to have them in the back garden."

The one o'clock whistle blew. They moved briskly. Harry looked up at the unbroken grayness of the sky. A boxcar had to be loaded with six-by-ones before the rain started. It was a sultry-hot, and sticky day.

He got the gang working hard. The air was so hot in the kiln it was hard to breathe. With three men he went into the kiln to push out the big pile of lumber piled high on the steel rollers.

It was easy going into the kiln because you just had to lift your feet carefully, keeping close to the wall but you had to step gingerly pushing the pile out, watching not to trip on the beams and the pipes on the ground, keeping your legs away from the roller. Harry and Jimmie were behind the pile pushing. The Swede and Scottie and the three Italians were pushing from the side of the kiln.

"Heave ho, let 'er go?" Harry yelled, bending his back, and Jimmie bent his back and they heaved steadily, the rollers moving slowly. Harry, pushing, looked along the narrow space between the pile and the kiln wall, over bent backs of men to the streak of daylight near the doors. The pile was hardly moving. Harry knew some of them weren't putting their backs to it. "For the love of Mike, push," he yelled, getting sore, pushing hard and sweating. Jimmie was pushing hard, but two of them couldn't do it. "You're not a cripple, Scottie," Harry said quietly. The pile moved slowly and Harry knew the big wop, Tony, was only half trying. The lousy skunk, holding things up. Tony, his body pressed flat against the pile, pretended he was shoving. "You'll push or get the hell out, Tony," he said. The pile moved slowly out from the dark kiln.

Harry looked grimly at Tony, who stared back stupidly, leaning against the pile. "Jees', it's hot, boss," Tony said smiling.

"Get in the car, Jimmie," Harry said. "You get up on the pile, Tony. We got to get this done quick."

Scottie and the Swede adjusted the rollers so Tony, on top of the pile, could swing a board loose, onto the rollers sloping down to the open door of the boxcar.

The men worked rapidly. Harry saw that Tony was working all right; things were going smoothly. It would not rain for maybe three-quarters of an hour. He turned away from the pile and took a step forward. Someone yelled, he ducked and felt a sharp hot cut on his heel that became a dull ache. A board from the top of the pile had fallen on his heel. He knelt on the ground on one knee. Jimmie Nash jumped down from the boxcar.

"You better rub it."

"Holy smoke, it's stinging."

"It might have hurt your leg for fair."

"Jees' ya, how on earth . . ."

"It swung over the rollers."

Harry got up, limping around on one foot, biting his lower lip and swearing softly to himself. Scottie looked at him stolidly. Tony, up on the pile, put out the palm of his hand, to see if it had started to rain. Saws in the milling plant screeched, tearing through wood.

Harry knelt down, fingering his heel tenderly. He heard Tony say in hardly more than a whisper, "bastard."

He looked up quickly. Tony's head was turned away toward the sloping roof of the flour elevator.

Harry started to climb the pile. Tony, kneeling on his hands and knees, looked down at him, staring stupidly. He got up suddenly, stepped over to the other side of the pile and dropped down heavily. Harry dropped down. Going around the pile he saw Tony standing opposite the kiln, watching him doubtfully.

"I'll get ya, ya skunk," Harry said.

Tony backed into a pile of loose lumber, tripped, sprawled, got up quickly. Harry moving in a circle, edged around, backing Tony into the kiln. He'd get him, smash him. Tony stood still, wetting his lips, staring obliquely at the ground, shaking his head slightly, his mouth opening as Harry crouched, ready to spring.

Tony took one step backward and Harry poked him three times in the jaw, shooting his head back each time so the chin stuck out horizontally. The big wop fell sideways and tried to crawl away from the kiln. Harry jumped on him, his knees hitting him on the chest and swinging his fist to an ear. The wop shook his head, rolling until they banged against the kiln wheel-track, and sank his teeth into Harry's shoulder, trying to smother him with his arms and big shoulders. Punching and gouging Harry worked loose. Get his head against the rail, bang it, hang it, the skunk! Harry got up on one knee. The gang stood a few feet away, watching silently. Two men from the milling plant were standing with them. They should have stopped it but stood there, not caring what happened. Harry rubbed his heel, looking indifferently at the big Italian who moaned, trying to get up on his knees.

Hohnsburger, the superintendent, came hurrying along the platform. Harry brushed his overalls with his hands and straightened his shirt. He waited for Hohnsburger to speak.

"What's the matter, Trotter?"

"Tony threw a board at me and called me a bastard."

Hohnsburger looked at Tony sprawled clumsily on the ground, then his face got red.

"Don't you think the car's got to be filled? Don't you think the job matters?"

"I know that."

"Sure you know it."

"Well, for heaven's sake man."

"There's no use talking here. Come on along to the office."

Harry felt a raindrop on his cheek. He wiped it away with his finger. There was a muddy smudge across his cheek. His shirt was torn open, the buttons ripped off down to his belt. A bruise on his left cheek. The men, whispering, watched them, the Swede and two Italians feeling happy. Jimmie Nash leaned against the boxcar. Big Tony got up slowly, squatting on a beam, holding his head in his hands. Harry limped badly, following Hohnsburger along the platform to the office.

In the office Hohnsburger sat down heavily, tilting back in his chair. He wiped his forehead with a large clean handkerchief, tipped his straw hat on the back of his head. He sneered at Trotter.

"You're a hell of a foreman," he said, working himself up slowly.

"Now listen, why don't you try and get things straight. I tell ya Tony threw a board at me. He might have broken my leg. What in hell do you think I am? Would it have done any good calling you?"

"Don't shout at me, I tell you."

"I'm not shouting."

"You are, I tell ya."

"All right then, let it go at that."

"Let it go at that. Not on your life. Why should Tony throw a plank at you! Why the hell didn't you fire him and let it go at that?"

"That wouldn't have done me any good."

"Well, I'm fed up. In the last six months since you took over the foreman's job we've had about six compensation cases, men getting hurt and so on, if you're not thinking of yourself, you're trying to kill the men. You're going to quit."

"You're damn right I am, Hohnsburger, I wouldn't work around you again for a million dollars. You're low. You're rotten. You're the guy I should poke."

Hohnsburger stood up, six feet and solid. They looked at each other, hating.

"I got to give you a week's notice," he said. "But I'll give you a week's pay instead. See? I'll fix it up at the time office."

Harry stepped out of the office, slamming the door. Oh, the lousy-livered rotter, if he could just sock him right on the nose. He walked along the platform from the office, his hands in his pockets, his shoulders hunched up. He was glad to feel the rain on his face. The gang near the boxcar had taken shelter in the kiln, and though he couldn't see them, he knew they were watching him. The lumberyard often smelled good in the rain, the fresh lumber. Some lumber had a bad smell. Jimmie Nash was standing alone in the rain near the boxcar.

"What's up?" he said quietly.

"I'm quitting."

"What's the matter, trouble with Hohnsburger?"

"He's low. I'll see ya again," he said in an offhand, friendly way.

Harry walked over to his compartment in the warehouse, to change his clothes. He dressed carelessly without thinking of being neat and tidy, his thoughts disordered. He was breathing heavily. He stood up straight, without moving, thinking of Tony, and holding himself in. His heart pounded. He felt his hands on Tony's head. He thought of Hohnsburger and began to dress slowly, trying to feel cool and practical. He tied a tight knot in his dark blue tie. He slipped on his coat quickly, but before stepping out of the warehouse he took out his penknife and began to clean his nails carefully. He hadn't asked Farrel for Anna's phone number. Many thoughts came to him but he knew he was really thinking of Vera.

On the streetcar going home he imagined himself explaining the fight to Vera. He hung on to a strap, leaning forward, brushing against a woman who had on her knees a big basket of fruit. In his nostrils was the faint perfume of pale flowers and the smell of funerals. He looked around but could not locate the scent. His father and mother had been buried, with the same smell in the room. His father had died first, two years before his mother. He remembered his mother's funeral, the odour in the room, and her face small and pinched but very calm. He tried to remember her face from years ago, when he was at public school, and for the first time, seemed aware of having lived in the same house with her for years, without actually looking at her. The woman with the basket of fruit got up and left the car. He was sorry for himself and wanted sympathy. Slightly bewildered, he wished his mother were alive, so he could go home to her.

He went past his car-stop, having made up his mind to go downtown, and home later at the usual hour.

7

For two days he did not tell Vera he had lost his job. In the morning he got up at seven o'clock, as usual, very serious, thinking only of deceiving her. He tried three lumberyards in the city, each time imagining what he would say to her if he got the job, but he did not look like a first-class foreman, nor come highly recommended. In one yard he could have got a job without authority attached to it, at a small salary, but would not take it.

On the third day, Saturday, he left the house at seven and was home at one-thirty. They were to go on a picnic in the afternoon, the two of them, out east and up the railway tracks in the country to a wooded ravine with a slow twisting river. Two or three times a month in the summer Vera packed a lunch and they took the streetcar out east, and stayed in the ravine till twilight when night noises in thickets and occasional sounds of someone moving on the hill scared her, and then they climbed the hill, to walk slowly along the tracks and down the street to the city terminal three miles away.

They got out to the city limit at four o'clock in the afternoon. Vera walked on ahead while Harry went into the Greek's confectionery store on the corner and bought two large bottles of lime juice, and took six straws. The road was not paved beyond the city limit. The cement sidewalk ran on for eight blocks. Harry carried a Boston bag with the lunch, and two bottles under one arm. Vera carried the coats.

At the eighth block they turned north. The street, a few houses on each side, ended at the railway embankment and barbed-wire fence. Harry hoisted up the lower wire, Vera crawled underneath, then Harry went under it and they sat down on the bank till Vera changed her shoes, for it was no use trying to walk along the ties with high heels.

They followed the tracks between the hills until the bank on the right flattened out and they stood at a steep path looking down the dark ravine. They walked on to the next path, Vera strutting happily on the ties. She took a handkerchief from her pocket and knotted it at the four corners. She caught up to Harry and tried to put it on his head.

"Go chase yourself," he said irritably.

She giggled, slyly putting an arm around his waist, and kissed him until she slipped the handkerchief on his head. He put his arm around her, lifting her on to the track, balancing her as she walked.

They went down into the ravine and followed the river to a shady place under a low tree where there were no sounds. Vera spread the coats and lay down, taking out a book from her bag. Watching her stretch out on her belly, skirts far above the smooth curve behind her knees, Harry made up his mind to tell her about the quarrel with Hohnsburger. She seemed so happy he felt aloof from her and depressed. She paid no attention to him, taking it for granted he was enjoying himself. He got up and walked slowly away among the trees, following a cow path that twisted over a piece of swampy ground, ending in the river. Ahead, a wooded hill sloped up to the skyline. A farm house was on the skyline. He decided not to mention anything to her until she had had her good time. He stood still, thinking of her lying in the shade back near the river, her slim hand stroking her face, and didn't want to say anything that would alter her feeling of satisfaction. He went back to the shady place under the tree.

Then they played ball until they got hungry. Harry, standing across the river, tossed the tennis ball, and she hit it with a small branch he had broken from a tree. She hit some far across the river, yelling happily watching him chase the ball.

After lunch they lay down on the coats, Vera went on reading, Harry smoked, turning over in his mind words and thoughts which would make the conversation run smoothly.

Sitting up suddenly, curling her arms around her knees, she said quickly: "Have you thought any more about me becoming a Catholic?"

"Not once, Vera. What difference does it make?"

"Not much I guess."

"Then why bother about it?"

"Sit up and listen, put your coat around you, it's getting cool down here in the ravine."

He sat up, looking at her solemnly.

"I met one of the girls today, and she told me the most wonderful story about a priest." Vera told the story carefully. This priest was a plump man of fifty-six with snow-white hair. In his house were two younger priests, and an old housekeeper. This priest was a jolly man who loved life and at the same time was extremely religious. "He didn't get excited about religion," Vera said. "There was just something about him. It was his way. You got to know that he was religious."

"The way he walked, eh?"

"No, this is serious. He was the sort of man you'd expect to make the perfect father. Or a wonderful husband."

"Well, what was preventing him?"

"Nothing was preventing him. Only something else was holding him. Something else holding him and taking up all that part of him, see."

"I guess he had other things to think about. He knew when he was well off."

"He couldn't have looked at it in that way. I mean when you think of getting and begin married, you can't help thinking of marriage nights and so on, isn't that right?"

"Maybe so, I guess you feel better about it in the night. Things don't seem so practical as in the daytime and your own thoughts work with you."

"You just drift easily with your thoughts, that's it."

"That's it all right."

"Well, listen to this. The old priest's housekeeper found out something. About two o'clock one night she heard someone moving around the house, and standing on the stairs she could see this priest, and he had a coat wrapped around him and his slippers on and he was going downstairs. It was a warm summer evening."

"She followed him, eh?"

"Yes, she followed him out the door and across the lawn to the church. He went up to the altar and knelt down and prayed, 'Hail Mary,' like that. All alone in the big white church at two o'clock in the morning."

"What got into him? Something worrying him?"

"Not really. The housekeeper found out that he did it three times a week. It never bothered him during the daytime. See how it works out?"

"What are you getting at, Vera?"

"It was like keeping a date. Don't you see?" she said, excited a little. "There in the cathedral at night he kept a date. It all took the place of something and I just bet that was the reason why he seemed such a happy contented priest. Somehow or other the idea makes me feel like becoming a Catholic."

"Applesauce, Vera."

She was not listening, staring over the river. The sun sank away behind the hill. It was getting dark quickly in the ravine.

"Is it very important to you?" he said slowly.

"Why ask that?"

"Well, there's something pretty important I want to say."

"Aren't you interested in what I was saying?"

"Yeah, only this touches us closer."

"Well, why on earth hesitate then?"

"All right, I've lost my job at Pape's."

She looked at him steadily, then smiled.

"Don't be silly, Harry."

"It's the straight goods, Vera. You don't think I'd kid you about a thing like that?"

"Harry, Harry, in heaven's name, Harry, what's the trouble, why did it happen? What did you do?"

"I didn't do anything."

"Was it Hohnsburger? You must have done something. You should have watched yourself."

"Yeah."

"Today?"

"No, two days ago."

"Then it wasn't fair to come on a picnic today and pretend to be happy. It isn't fair to me."

"For God's sake, Vera."

"You'll never get another foreman's job. No, I didn't mean that, I mean there aren't many places in the city. Don't get sore, Harry, come here, I'm sorry."

She put her arm around his neck. He shook his head jerkily, feeling a little sick. He waited for her to become sympathetic. She started to cry, then he felt sympathetic. They could hear a train coming along the tracks up over the hill across the river on the other side of the ravine. They could not see it, only sparks shooting into the sky, then a line of car tops and lighted windows pale in the half-light, swung into view.

"It's going pretty fast," he said.

"It's out of sight now," she said, vaguely interested.

"You should have told me before. You know I love you more than anything else in the world and that the main thing is we'll get along anyhow."

She began to talk rapidly, caressingly, excited, till he wanted her to shut up. He was not a ten-year-old kid needing to be mothered. At the moment he wanted to encounter something stubborn and unyielding that would test his strength. He did not want to listen to her talking like that.

"It's kinda dark down here," he said. "Maybe we'd better go. I'll tell you all about it on the way up."

They took a shortcut up the hill to the tracks. Halfway she insisted on sitting on a fallen tree where they had sat a year ago, making love and writing their names on fungus. He explained very quickly why he had quarrelled with Hohnsburger. He tried to settle it, give an air of finality to his explanation of the matter. He said definitely there was no room for argument.

The wire fence was low at the top of the hill. Harry put his foot on the top wire and Vera stepped over and they went down the embankment and along the tracks. They hardly spoke to each other, having their own thoughts.

Harry heard voices on the bank above the tracks. A young fellow and a girl had come up from the ravine and were climbing the wire fence. Harry wondered vaguely what they had been doing down in the ravine so late. The young fellow tossed a coat and leather bag and book over the fence before helping her over. The girl had riding breeches under a long coat and black band around her head. They didn't see Harry and Vera. Harry saw that the fellow was very mad about something. He was swinging the bag at the tall weeds. The girl kept looking over her shoulder at the boy. She tried to put her arm across his back and when she couldn't, started to tease him. It was dark and there were no stars in the sky.

It started to rain a little. The girl up on the embankment had snatched the fellow's peak cap and put it on her head, the peak to one side. Harry let his arm rest on Vera's shoulder, then draped a coat around her. They didn't mind the rain.

Up on the embankment the fellow had chased the girl and catching her, was trying to put her over his knee.

"Those kids are having a lot of fun," he said to Vera. He was determined to avoid talking about the job. The Kingston Road radial car away to the south-east hooted mournfully. The track became a ridge on the level ground.

By a cow-guard on the track, a path went down the bank to the end of a street. "Listen, Vera, let's not talk about the damn thing any more," he said.

"Of course we won't."

"That ain't what I mean. I mean I don't need to be cheered up, see? I don't need sympathy."

Vera, slightly hurt, went down the path. Harry stood for a few seconds looking at the fellow and girl going along the track in the rain, the girl with the fellow's hat pulled over her ear. Harry turned up his coat collar and found himself thinking of Farrel and his self-satisfied good-nature. Things were getting rotten. Then he thought of the fellow and the girl trudging along the tracks. He was disappointed about something, slight weary. Vera called, "Come on." He ran down the path. It was raining hard.

8

It was tiresome hanging around the house for days, and always going downtown in the morning for a paper as soon as it came out, to look down the column of "Male Help Wanted." In a week he had tried three lumberyards in the city and could have had a job without authority but would not take it. Every time he tried to get one of the good jobs, he imagined himself going home and telling Vera he had been successful.

Days passed and he couldn't get a decent job in the city lumberyards. No matter, he was determined never to take another job under three or four managers. For a time, to get over a difficult period, he might take such a job, but finally he would become his own boss. Vera advised him to be practical and pointed out that he had had no training for a difficult position. He got sore; was there one man sitting pretty in the industrial world who had had a college training, shorthand, a correspondence school course in big business? He said. She insisted she was simply being sensible; he wasn't a professional man. He yelled at her, thanking God he wasn't a professional man, so she reminded him of responsibilities till he sullenly answered hardly at all, looking at her moodily, his hands in his pockets.

In the evenings he stayed at home a good deal, though he occasionally saw Jimmie Nash. Sometimes he thought of phoning Julie Roberts, but he had lost confidence in himself, and didn't want to talk to her. She was interesting to him as long as he was strong and assertive beside her, and even then it had been difficult, when she smiled. The idea of meeting her again became embarrassing. Instead of going out by himself he expected Vera to amuse him. He said to her, "Well, what are we going to do tonight?" and when she suggested a show he invariably said, "I don't want to go to a show," so she shrugged her shoulders and said she couldn't be expected to please him all the time.

He told her about the thought of his mother, that afternoon he had left the yard for the last time, and explained she was an exception to all women, who should have interested him long ago. In an easy chair in the sitting-room he was comfortable and with eyes half-closed, talked of incidents he remembered from years ago, illustrating his mother's ability and energy. "She would have been a remarkable woman, if she had had a little more education." Vera didn't appear interested in the stories about his mother, so he spoke sharply to her, and got up and left the room.

He sat alone in the kitchen, sullen and discontented, feeling that he had quarrelled violently with Vera. Afterward he went down to see Farrel and in a roundabout way got from him Anna's phone number. He phoned her. She was sweet, and he went around to her apartment for two or three drinks and told her about losing his job and feeling on the rocks, but she was so cheerful it was hard to remain sad, so he made love to her, his difficulties becoming unimportant, till he was beyond them, husky and laughing, untouched by any single job. The visit to Anna's apartment so impressed him he was eager to tell someone she was the most remarkable woman he had met in a long time. He couldn't tell it to Farrel, who, out of envy, would have tried to make it unpleasant. He talked about her to Jimmie Nash, who was like her in many ways. She was the most natural woman he had ever met. She liked eating, drinking and loving in a splendid good-natured way, never thinking twice, going ahead, and talking about it as she would talk about a bottle of good whiskey. She had absolutely no idea of morals, but was straightforward, and he couldn't imagine her playing him a dirty trick. Lovemaking with her was free from most of the complications usually attached to it. All she asked for was a good time, although he didn't like the cheerful way she talked about other fellows who had loved her, because she related all the intimate details that had appealed to her. Nash was eager to meet her but Harry was indefinite about it.

He liked thinking of Anna, and all day held aloof from Vera, feeling lonely, restless, cut off from days he had enjoyed. Sometimes, watching Vera working around the house, he felt close to her and worried about getting another job. She was urging him to take even a teamster's job till he got something else, for they hadn't saved money. He agreed. She had always helped him. They talked pleasantly and seriously and afterward he was sure he wouldn't see Anna any more, but next day he was irritable after being out all morning looking for work, and he didn't want to be agreeable. He phoned Anna from the corner drugstore.

Weeks passed, and thinking too often of the yard and Tony's big back bending over the tap, he seemed to have lost a part of his life. Vera was sympathetic and patient and so anxious to avoid a quarrel that he tried to irritate her simply to disturb her, to find himself aroused and passionately insistent upon attaining something far beyond his reach. Walking along the street in the evenings he imagined neighbours, sitting on verandas, stared at him, aware that he was no longer of any importance. Every morning he dressed carefully, standing before the mirror, shaving, pausing a long time, his thoughts drifting easily.

He refused to go to parties with Stan Farrel for fear of meeting people who knew him. He wanted to be alone, taking long walks, thinking always of himself, at times walking rapidly, his hands clenched. One Sunday evening he wandered into the Labour Temple and was at first amused at the meeting, then imagined himself making a speech on the platform. Most of the fellows in the audience were the kind of working men he could control and direct. He knew how to handle these men. He could become important among them, and the idea pleased him, and he mentioned it to Vera, but she was not interested. She suggested she would be willing to go out working to make it easier during the hard time. He spoke sharply to her and shook her, calling her a stubborn woman. She looked so surprised he was bewildered, wondering what had enraged him. He cursed himself and tried petting her, till she cried in relief and they went upstairs to bed. Lying on the bed, he told her stories of himself as a child. His father believed that a boy should work hard and have very few opinions, and rarely, if ever, go to parties with the fellows at school. When his father got religious he had to feel it too. He had been allowed none of the freedom of other kids. If he had been happier at home he would have got along much better later on; by this time would have achieved some distinction. Vera agreed that his life had probably been misshapen by childhood experiences, and in the evenings, when there was nothing to say and he was sulky, she led him on to talk about himself. He saw that it was a good story and told it to Jimmie Nash, elaborating upon some of the details. "I was different from other kids," he insisted. Nash encouraged him to talk, half interested, half believing, a little embarrassed.

Finally he took a temporary job driving a milk wagon. He knew nothing about horses but liked driving to the route from the dairy, making the horse go as fast as he could without tiring it. The milk route was in the east end of the city, over the river on the other side of the park. He got used to the route and cultivated the milkman's habit of knowing which of his women customers stayed up very late at night. There was a basement apartment where a light burned nearly all night. Usually dark blinds were drawn over the windows but on some nights he could peep through the blind into the front room. A plump, kittenish lady of thirty-five had a different man in the apartment nearly every night. He got accustomed to going up the alleyway quietly. He heard the woman laughing. The woman, handling herself well, always two jumps ahead of the man. After peeping a few minutes, he rattled the bottles loudly. The startled look on the man's face amused him.

Twice he drove to Anna's apartment which was on a street off the route and on the way back to the dairy, and stayed with her an hour.

None of his acquaintances saw him going to work. He wore old clothes on the job, but in the evening, when going out with Vera or Jimmie Nash, he had on the form-fitting coat, tan shoes, his fingers manicured and nimble. He got up at two o'clock in the afternoon and went downtown. Sometimes he played pool, trying earnestly to win, very disappointed when he lost. He got into the habit of going to cheap movie shows in the afternoon until bored. Feeling disappointed, or unhappy, he went into one of these shows to forget it by watching the picture closely, his thoughts carried away. After looking around carefully, he sometimes rubbed his knee against the knee of a strange woman a few feet away from him. He did not want to know the woman. He never even tried to see her face. His knee rubbed against her dress and his thoughts raced eagerly. He was almost disinterested as far as any particular woman was concerned.

The milk route was only a temporary job and he was laid off in three weeks. It was the early fall and the nights were getting cooler and Vera was saving up to take her fur coat out of storage at the furrier's. Harry went to the Labour Temple on Sunday evening. The Sunday evening meetings in the Temple were not crowded because it was too early in the year and street meetings were being held, but he was interested in the lively way speakers talked of direct action, solidarity, mass action, good strong words that aroused him. He walked home after the meeting, feeling stronger and more confident. He imagined himself lining up forces within the Temple. He thought of himself, a leader, striking out, supported by a militant working class.

The following Sunday he went to the Temple and sat near a white-haired old man, who mumbled to himself during speeches, waiting eagerly for the fifteen-minute period for questions. A man could get up and ask a speaker a question. The old man tried to turn a question into a speech. The crowd applauded him eagerly when he spoke during the discussion period, and the fierce way he snapped out big words excited Harry, who clapped vigorously. Listening to the man speaking and other fellows yelling, "Go on, Pimblett, give it to 'em," he felt that his restlessness had come to a point where it could be turned into energy. He wasn't interested in what Isaac Pimblett was saying but the words sounded good and made him feel alone and attacked. After the speech he felt aggressive.

Isaac Pimblett noticed how attentively Harry listened and how enthusiastically he applauded. They walked together for a few blocks after the meeting, developing a friendship. The old man was hard and caustic and happy to be an outsider. He attacked the life around him, and Harry, eager to agree, was glad to talk to him, though he was not really interested in politics.

He left Pimblett on the corner opposite the cathedral. He phoned Anna from a soda-fountain parlour down the street a block. He walked out east to her apartment and made love to her. They had a good time, and she made some coffee, and they danced to the phonograph, and on the way home he had a feeling he was determinedly going his own way.

He told Jimmie Nash about the Labour Temple, but Jimmie would consider only the political side of it and was cynical of Harry's talk of strength. Vera was not even interested. Harry quarrelled with her because she would not promise to go with him to the Temple. Respectable people did not go there, she said. They quarrelled and he said she was preventing him from living in his own way. She said that if he would be happier alone she would go out and work and he could please himself.

Then he was sorry he had provoked her and wanted to love her, for he couldn't think of her changing her life and becoming strange to him. He wanted to be sure of her at least, he said. Her ankles and hands and hair were always there for him, something unchanging, and feeling lonely, he said that everything he wanted, everything that pleased him, the strength of life, and wind, and trees, and streets deserted in the night were all inside her. It took a long while to tell it to her and at times he was embarrassed for she cried after the quarrel, but he fumbled for words and she seemed to become more important to him. He could not express his feelings satisfactorily but felt that at all costs he must keep her.

He tried next day to get a job in one of the big department stores but there was much unemployment in the city and he was unsuccessful. Jimmie, who had quit the lumberyard, though he hadn't got the job on the paper, advised him to go out canvassing. A man could always earn a living selling magazines, he said, and offered to go out on the road with him. Harry agreed that if something did not turn up in a week he might just as well sell magazines as do anything else. Magazine salesmen went out in crews and had a swell time drifting from town to town flirting with old women and daughters, or getting arrested and given twelve hours to leave town. It sounded adventurous and they talked as if they had made up their minds to go through with it, but Harry had an idea something else would turn up.

He stayed at home a good deal in the evenings. They were not spending much money. They had paid a month's rent but had to spend carefully for they were drawing money from the bank. Harry played checkers a lot with Vera. He got into the habit of looking for the checkerboard immediately after supper. Vera played well but by concentrating he could beat her.

PART TWO

1

*O*n Sunday evening at half-past seven o'clock he walked down Yonge to Albert Street. He had on his straw sailor and no coat though the nights got cooler in the middle of September. At corners, streets with no traffic, intersecting Yonge, evangelists talked to small crowds. The evangelists had chalked huge squares on the pavement and scrawled gospel words. Some evangelists talking on corners where there was a steady flow of traffic got much bigger crowds. He walked down the street wondering how Vera would get along by herself if he went out on the road selling magazines for three weeks, just to get some money. It was possible to make sixty or seventy dollars a week at it, if you had the goods. He might stay at it longer, all fall, and watching his step, be ready to go ahead with something important in the Spring. In the crowd across the street a high-pitched voice grew louder and more powerful and became a wail of despair. Slightly startled, Harry stopped but did not cross the street. He had walked as far as Albert Street and stood at the corner, looking along the street. He hoped to find old Isaac Pimblett in one of the crowds. It was nearly dark. The city hall tower stuck up over the roof of the big department store. An electric furniture sign flared on Yonge Street opposite Albert. On Sunday night the city was quiet but many loud voices cried out on Albert Street.

He stood on the corner, his hands in his pockets, his straw hat tilted back on his head. He put one thumb in the armpit of his vest. He stood there, feeling important but not thinking of anything, though listening to the Salvation Army man making a speech to the meeting on the corner. He was looking directly at the speaker but wasn't hearing a word. He took out his watch, twenty minutes to eight, a little late to get Anna on the phone on Sunday evening. Someone else would be there. He wondered if she told other fellows, too, about his efforts to arouse her. The Salvation Army man's voice sounded far away. Anna might be willing to go out on the road with him selling magazines just for the sport of it.

He was standing in the Salvation Army circle, which had become larger, and he moved along the street to the crowds where Pastor Henderson was shouting defiance at the Communists further down the street. Harry listened to Pastor Henderson who was proving by biblical prophecy that the English were God's chosen people. The pastor, a small wiry man with a little round head and a narrow ten-fifteen-cent-store, sporty spring tie, turned and issued a challenge to the Agnostic Association, holding a meeting a few paces away. Harry stood on his toes, craning, looking for Isaac Pimblett but not sure he wanted to find him. Sometimes Isaac seemed a little nutty. Harry felt hungry and thought of going into a drugstore for a sandwich. He listened mechanically to the Agnostic who lisped in a sharp voice of contempt. He went on thinking of Isaac who had hinted he had something in mind, a kind of an organizing job, hardly worth listening to because Isaac was rarely allowed on the platform in the Labour Temple. "Too radical I guess," he thought. He walked further along the street to the Communist group. Morris Grimmel was speaking.

Morris Grimmel leaning out from the soap box, his arm flung wide, his hair tossed back. Morris Grimmel shaking his fist, his lips drawn back from the gums, teeth clenched, eyes blazing, heavy ponderous words rolling, then becoming analytical, coldly repressed, though trembling with excitement. "The war that would end war," he screamed, along the street.

Harry could not find Isaac. He followed a fat man, hatless, his long gray hair combed back neatly, away from the communists. This man carried his coat under his arm and mopped his head with a handkerchief though it was cool. Harry followed him from one crowd to another, standing at his elbow. At each crowd the fat man got into an argument. He made it clear that he was dealing with a lot of silly people. He turned and smiled encouragingly at Harry who grinned. "I'd like to push my hand in his fat face," he actually thought. A lean woman dressed in military fashion came up to the fat man and talked about a mission that had held a meeting last night. The fat man listened attentively. Harry listened. At the meeting a coloured woman had spoken, the women dressed in military fashion said.

"Ah, yes, I was there, sister," he nodded. "It was a disgrace. She is a coloured woman and can have no message from the Lord for white people. When Mrs. Gibson, who held the meeting, saw me there last night she flushed up to the ears thinking I would be critical, but I never spoke once, just let the Lord speak through me once to give a message. But you understand," he said turning to Harry, "I didn't open my mouth once, though they knew what I thought of the coloured woman. Do you see, sir?" he said to Harry.

"Absolutely."

"Was I right?"

"You hit the nail on the head."

Harry, looking around, saw Isaac Pimblett walking away from the communist meeting toward the agnostics. He walked slowly, limping a little, his body held erect. Harry caught up to him. Isaac smiled, his lean face puckered and wrinkled. He wore no hat, his white hair was combed neatly. He had on a black coat, neatly pressed, and a black bow-tie tucked in under his collar.

"Hello Mr. Pimblett."

"Harry, I was thinking of you last night."

"That's fine, what were you thinking?"

"Shall we take a little walk down near the waterfront?"

They walked toward the corner. The Salvation Army man yelled "Peace on earth, good will to men."

Pastor Henderson, who was praising the large English fleet, cried out, "Peace on earth, good will to men." The little Agnostic stopped speaking, grinned and sneered, "Peace on earth, good will to men." They turned the corner and loud voices rose and fell and as they went further down the street, grew fainter.

"I don't like much the way Morris was talking tonight," Isaac said, "too much of a categorical negation."

Harry didn't understand Isaac when he used too many big words. "What's on your mind, Mr. Pimblett, what about me, I mean?" he said. They had reached Queen Street. Isaac had explained one time why he liked talking with Harry about the movement. He hadn't been spoilt by bad talk, he said. Too many young men had notions about things that didn't amount to a hill of beans and they couldn't get rid of them. Harry was young and healthy and in a way ready to get started right. Last night he had thought about it and realizing he was too old he had wondered if Harry mightn't be the fellow he was looking for to organize the movement. They turned east on Queen Street and were a block away from the cathedral. Isaac was explaining he had never been able to command enough respect, probably because so many people were aware that he had been a labourer, and was now running a shed dealing in second-hand plumbers' supplies, second-hand old baths, toilets, etc. His wife for example could never understand what he was talking about.

"You got to get educated," he said to Harry.

"Yeah, but how is it going to work out?"

"Things must begin with a young fellow, build on a young man, a strong man. See?"

"Well, I'm husky, I'll get guys doing things if I can only get hold of them."

"I saw you one night in the Labour Temple. I hoped you would ask a question, to get a line on your educational background." He talked slowly, with a fierce swagger. "They talk of Marx and of Engels and prophets and leaders, without any appreciation of a philosophical interpretation of history. Study history."

"I know some now."

"You got to know more."

They were opposite the cathedral. The carillon bells chimed out rapidly. Isaac stood on the sidewalk staring at the cathedral spire. A full moon was in the sky. His wide mouth opened.

"That's what you're up against," he said.

"How do you mean?"

"The ultra-respectable class, the cathedral and so on."

"What's the matter with it?"

"What's the matter with it? I think too much about it, that's all. It's personal, too. Once in the Labour Temple, just across the road from the cathedral, I was making a speech on the platform, a good speech. In the middle of it the bells chimed out and I forgot what I was going to say."

"Not so good, eh. Kinda tough, eh."

"It just struck me that you can't get away from it. It's right in the centre of things. I think too much about it, that's all."

They walked down Church Street and smelled fruit, and bad odours from warehouses. They kept on walking down to the waterfront, crossing the railroad tracks. Leaning against a dock rail, Harry told about losing his job and his restlessness and inability to get going again. The water lapped on the piers. He talked slowly and carefully, for it seemed to have become important that old Isaac should understand it.

"Now I think too much about Pape's and the job. Something like the way you are about the cathedral," he said.

"At your age you should be restless."

"I want to step out, get going in a big way. I'll be damned if anybody'll ever boss me again. I'll get going again, you bet your sweet life."

"I never got going. When I was your age I picked up a girl and lived with her almost a year. I couldn't think of anything but her and when she got sick and died I lost all my energy. I got married six months later, but even now, I go to the cemetery and think of that girl. Of course my wife knows nothing about it. She has a bitter tongue."

Harry looked down at the dark water, discerning faintly the light wave line, following it till it lapped against the pier.

Then Isaac said, "A young man should live alone. That's the main thing."

"I guess so, it doesn't matter much. Not to me anyway."

"It does matter, I tell you."

"It never bothers me thinking about it, I mean."

"Look at it in this way though. If you're living with a woman she usually gets in the way when you really want to do something. You know that much, don't you?"

"I was thinking that the other day."

"That's funny. That's interesting."

"No, it's not funny. I had just had a quarrel with the wife."

"Your wife?"

"Sure, my wife."

"God bless my soul!"

"What's up?"

"Why didn't you tell me you were married?"

"What's the matter with being married, it's nothing to get excited about, is it?"

"No, it's not exciting. It just means your settled."

"Not on your life, I'm not settled, I tell you."

"Sure, as far as I'm concerned, Harry. I'm awfully sorry too. You couldn't amount to anything the way I want you to. A married man has to go home at night and the bed creaks, and the wife has her tongue sharpened if you're late. And you've got to stick to the groove. That's all I mean."

"And you think I'm all shot because I'm married?"

"Not at all. I'm just saying that a wife gets in the way of a man's bright ideas," Isaac laughed sarcastically.

"Maybe so, only it sounds like a lot of crap to me."

"I'm not saying you won't get along. You'll just have to fit in. They all have to fit in where they belong."

"Is that so, eh? Well, if you think I'm doing any fitting you got another think comin'. You think I'm just one of the guys that go the same old way home, eh. Yeah, like hell I am. See. Settled down, eh. You're all wrong. Married? Sure, but just let me get the breaks and I'll have everybody eating out of my hand. Get that straight."

Isaac shrugged his shoulders. There did not seem to be anything to say. Harry looked down at the water. He was sore. He didn't want to speak, he was so irritated.

They turned and walked away from the dock. Isaac walked a pace away from Harry, walking silently. Harry was disappointed. At first he had resented the way Isaac had spoken to him, now he felt restive and cut off from something that would have been fine and satisfying. He wished suddenly that he wasn't married.

When they were opposite the cathedral again they both looked at the spire. Harry would not mention it.

"You'll find fellows on the lawn there looking for men. When they get caught they appear in the police court. Rotten at the base. That's it," Isaac said.

They shook hands at the corner of Bay and Queen. Harry smiled sociably at Isaac, who didn't have much to say. He smiled queerly, not that he had expected much; he had simply hoped for a thing and it had slipped away. Harry looked up the street to the clock in the city-hall tower. Half-past nine.

"Come on home with me, Mr. Pimblett," he said suddenly. "Meet the wife. I'll bet a dollar you'll like her."

"I don't doubt it," he said. "I've got a wife, I must be going home."

Harry watched him walking slowly along the street, his body erect. "Maybe he's a bit cuckoo," he thought. He waited for a streetcar, and waiting thought of the way Isaac had talked about his wife. No use going on, simply because he had a wife. He was not sure what Isaac really wanted him for, though he realized vaguely that he was expected to become a leader, acting on Isaac's advice until they became a political force. Maybe Isaac was right about marriage. But he had been happy with Vera. Until recently they had worked together beautifully. Now they annoyed each other. She opposed nearly all of his ideas. He wondered how he would get along by himself, out on the road with Jimmie Nash selling magazines, away from her and feeling stronger, alone until he got on his feet. Now they were bickering too much. He got on the car and sat opposite a girl with slender legs who had her knees crossed. He looked at the knees and thought of Anna. He never felt like quarrelling with Anna. Everything went smoothly, loosely, good-naturedly, his way. Vera was narrow, tight, too often holding herself in. Anna let herself go easily, lots of life in her. She was a big husky girl, loving a good sprawly time. She never expected anything and you didn't need even to think about her unless you wanted to. It was easy to think of her, nice thoughts, only Vera was bothering him again. She was always with him. Maybe that was what Isaac meant. She was with him day and night. Every time he wanted to do anything important he thought of Vera and what she would say about it. He got off the car, remembering Isaac, with his heavy ponderous words, shaking his fist at the cathedral. He wasn't anxious to get home, but there was nothing else to do.

2

At home there was no light in the front room, but along the hall he saw the kitchen light. Vera was not in the kitchen. He went into the front room. She was lying on the chesterfield in the dark. He sat on the chesterfield. She did not speak and he didn't know whether she was awake or not. He put his hand on her hip and thought of telling her about Isaac Pimblett and the walk down by the waterfront, and then he heard her giggling. She was awake, waiting for him to say something.

"I thought you were asleep," he said.

"No, it's only ten o'clock."

He wouldn't be bothered telling her about Pimblett. "Look, Vera get up and play me a game of checkers?"

"Aw no, I don't want to."

She got up and followed him to the kitchen. He got the board and checkers from the cupboard and they sat down at the end of the table.

He glanced at the board, holding his head in his hands, watching her getting ready to make a move. She made two false moves in the corner of the board but didn't take her hand off the checker. He leaned forward each time she made a false move and straightened up when she withdrew. They played the game steadily until of eight checkers on the black and red squares, six were Harry's. He grinned eagerly, confidently. Gradually he had driven her into a corner. Wherever she moved he had her. His organization had been perfect. Not a single false move and now he had her. Wherever she moved she was bound to lose one checker. She studied the board. He leaned back, grinning, making a swaggering motion with his hand. He had her.

He looked at the six checkers he had manipulated perfectly, each one having a definite part in the trap he had set. Playing carefully, he had at first sacrificed five just to get rid of five of hers to bring the game quickly to an interesting point. Now he had complete control of the game's course. Things going his way. Every move thought out and making absolutely sure he couldn't be beaten. Vera moved reluctantly and he quickly jumped her, removing the checker from the board. She had only one left and the game was practically over. He considered the board and the checkers, ready for the last move, but in reality thinking of the board as his own life and the life around him, his interest reaching a high pitch until it became for him no longer a game of checkers. He had the issue, the opposition, in the hollow of his hand. He felt fine.

Vera moved, and the game was over. She swung her hand petulantly across the board, knocking aside checkers, losing reluctantly.

"You didn't do so bad," he said, groping in his pocket for a cigarette.

"You're always lucky. That's the trouble."

"Lucky?"

"Sure, lucky. Or you get away to a good start."

"Play me another game then."

"No sir, not on your life."

He puffed the cigarette rapidly, his thoughts far away. He was looking at the board. "Play me another game," he said.

"No, Harry, I've got some work to do. Now you've beaten me you ought to be satisfied. You've beaten me often enough haven't you?"

"Well, you're getting to be a better player."

"I'm not playing any more anyway and that settles it." She got up. "Go on and play Stan Farrel. You're getting on my nerves."

"You get on my nerves too, don't you?"

"Not in the same way you get on mine."

"No?"

"No."

"All right, go to the devil, I'll see if Stan's in."

He kicked back the chair and went out to the hall and downstairs. The trouble was he had played Stan the night before three long drawn out games and had won them. He liked playing with Stan because he tried so hard and got worried thinking each time he might be beaten. He would rather beat Stan than anybody. They had argued the night before, and Harry had yelled at him because he had taken his finger off a checker after a false move. They had argued and he had wanted to hit Stan, who talked pompously. Vera had advised them to play ring-around-a-rosy, they were acting like silly kids. He rapped on Farrel's door.

"Come on, have a game a checkers, Stan," he said.

"What, tonight, too?"

"Sure, why not?"

"I'm not too keen. Don't you ever do anything but play checkers?"

"Come on, Stan. Just a game."

"Aw hell, I'm getting sick of that game."

"Come on, just a game."

"All right, you're the doctor, but not more than an hour. I guess I can beat you in an hour."

They went upstairs to the kitchen. Vera was sitting in the kitchen.

"I just beat Vera," Harry said. "She's getting better."

"I'm off my game," she said. "I've gone stale."

"Come on, let's get to it," Stan said.

They sat down facing each other. Vera went out and came back carrying dishes. Harry grinned cheerfully and rubbed his hands, not concealing satisfaction in having Farrel face him across the board. Farrel moved first, carefully. Harry's thoughts didn't wander from the game. He was getting all the satisfaction he might have got from fine and buoyant thoughts. He concentrated, playing the game. It was important, requiring all his energy. He was excited but confident. Stan Farrel, his neighbour, a friend of his, his antagonist, someone to hold off, someone to beat, then twist aside. Stan sitting opposite him, his white pudgy hand dallying with a checker, head drooping, three fat chins lapping over a gates-ajar collar, and grinning, easy jests on a ready tongue, his agreeable good nature marking his assumption of superiority, his distinction as a professional man. They were playing a game but he was matching himself against Stan, the strength in him against the strength in Stan.

Stan lost one to Harry. "Life's pretty serious, isn't it?" he said. Harry grinned, aware that Stan was a little sore. They played on without talking, the serious way Harry was playing becoming annoying to Stan who pretended it did not matter who won. He wanted to sneer. He was forced to approach the game seriously. He took one of Harry's checkers, jumping him.

"Chess is a much better game," Stan said affably.

"Try checkers. It'll hold you awhile."

"I'm enjoying it."

"So am I."

"Let's see you move then."

The play was even until the board was nearly cleared. They weren't speaking to each other, eyes on the board, no longer trying to conceal anxiety. Vera came into the kitchen and stood at Harry's shoulder. He was happy. He wasn't winning but had the feeling of winning. He would win. He had won every time he played Farrel. This was the moment when he became Farrel's superior, sitting opposite to him, watching his forehead wrinkling as he concentrated and worried over the result of each move.

"It's pretty even," Vera said.

"Please keep quiet, Vera," he said sharply.

Inwardly excited, he took two from Farrel. The game progressed till he got the breeches on him; whichever way Farrel moved, he had to lose one.

"No use going on," Farrel said, getting up.

"Not a bad game, eh?"

"I've played too long as it is, I must be going."

"Say Stan, is there anyone else around here who plays checkers? How about the people who live next door?"

"Don't know anything about them. I'm going, so long. So long, Mrs. Trotter."

"So long."

Harry stood at the kitchen window and looked out in the backyard wondering if Mr. Gingras, who lived next door, would be offended if asked to play a game of checkers at such an hour. It was dark out and he could not see much of Gingras' backyard, but he knew the lawn was trimmed beautifully and bordered with flowers. Gingras was a cranky man and if a baseball were hit from the ballpark into his yard, he always kept it. Along the top of his fence at each side and at the back of the yard was a barbed wire that made it impossible for kids to climb over after a ball. He decided not to ask Mr. Gingras to play checkers.

"Where are you, Vera?" he called, turning away from the window.

"In the front room."

He went into the front room. She was sitting near the reading lamp. She looked up from the book. "Listen, Vera," he said. "Do you think Jimmie Nash would come over if I phoned him?"

"Don't ask me."

"I think I'll phone him."

"What'll you do, if he's in?"

"Maybe go for a little walk, or maybe have a game of checkers."

"For heaven's sake Harry, he won't want to play checkers."

"Why won't he, how do you know?"

"I don't need to be clever to know it. Just the other night you played him game after game till he got blue in the face. People will get tired of you. You don't want to do anything else but play checkers. What's the matter with you?"

"What's the matter with me?"

"Yes."

"What the hell do you think's the matter with me?"

"That's what I'm asking you, and you don't need to be too tough."

"Well, what's the matter with you?"

"For heaven's sake Harry, go and lie down."

"Oh gee, I can't even hold a conversation with you."

She did not answer him. He stood in one spot while she got up and went over to the sideboard. She bent down, then straightened up. She bent down again. His eyes followed one spot on her back. He felt foolish standing there, waiting for her to say something. He turned and went out of the room. In the kitchen he looked indifferently at the checkerboard, then walked along to the bedroom. He turned on the light and looked at his watch. Half-past eleven, too late to go out. He didn't feel like talking to anybody. He tried thinking of Anna but her image in his thoughts kept fading away and he knew he didn't want to see her. He lit a cigarette and stretched out on the bed. He smiled a little, thinking of the game with Farrel, and then of fellows who might want to play checkers. He remembered beating Jimmie Nash, and the fine feeling. Jimmie had yawned and said checkers was simply a matter of concentration requiring no great skill. They had gone for a long walk afterward and sitting in an ice-cream parlour had talked of the magazine job and Pape's lumberyard, and the new foreman, a wiry little guy called Billie who had a wife that cost him a lot of money for operations.

Lying on the bed, his ankles crossed, he thought of the compartment he had made for himself in the warehouse. At five o'clock, washed up and clean, he walked along the platform, feeling fine, his shoes shining. He passed Hohnsburger and punched the clock sharply without speaking to anybody. He was becoming restless and uneasy and tried to stop thinking of the yard. He got up and stood before the mirror, looking at himself closely. Isaac Pimblett had taken a fancy to him. The trouble had been that he was married. Such a damn fool notion. Isaac was really funny when he got talking about the cathedral. Even at that, he probably had some good ideas about marriage.

He walked into the front room. Vera was reading the book again. She didn't look up when he stood beside her. He went back to the kitchen, got the checkerboard, opened it and placed it on the table. He arranged the checkers on the board and went back to the front room.

"Vera."

"Please let me read, Harry."

"Come on and play checkers, Vera."

She closed the book abruptly. "I don't want to play checkers," she said positively.

"Well, I do."

"I can't help it, I want to read."

"I want to play checkers and you've got to play."

"I don't got to at all. Put that in your pipe and smoke it."

"Come on, I tell ya."

"No."

He grabbed hold of her, hoisting her out of the chair. She kicked, squirmed and pulled his hair. She saw that he was carrying her into the kitchen and bit his neck. He shook her roughly and she let go his neck. He placed her on a chair at the end of the kitchen table. She looked at him, breathing heavily, her eyes moist. "You big fool," she said.

"I want to play checkers," he said indifferently.

She leaned back, crying a little. "I said I didn't want to play."

"Come on Vera, be a sport, just one game."

"All right, only you're a big bully, a big bully."

"All right, I'm a big bully."

They played checkers. She played indifferently, he, cautiously. She was not trying and he insisted she make every move carefully. "You're not half trying," he said. She got slightly interested but could not beat him. Playing skillfully, he beat her badly, getting a good deal of satisfaction out of it.

The game was over and he grinned cheerfully. "Not so bad, Vera old girl, eh," he said. He was in good humour. She smiled at him. He pushed the board away, reached across the

table and took hold of her. He kissed her until he didn't want
to kiss her any more.

3

He lay in bed and could not go to sleep. He turned toward Vera
and put his arm around her to assure her there was no reason
for disagreement, but could not do it because the words he put
together to shape his thoughts seemed silly. There was no reason for assurance. He had no explanation of his restlessness.
They argued, tried to agree, felt sorry for each other. He was
wide awake. He heard Vera breathing lightly and, listening
carefully, felt far away from her though he could have put out
his arm and touched her. He listened to her breathing regularly, curiously detached, aware merely of a woman lying
beside him, and he thought of her as Vera, but she had no further reality for him. If she awakened and argued with him at
that moment, he knew he would be neither angry nor irritated.
He would listen to her unmoved, hardly interested. They simply weren't getting on together. It wasn't her fault, it wasn't
his fault. He wanted to be away from her though he loved her.
"She'd be happier by herself," he thought. He lay on his back
imagining Vera living by herself with enough money so she
would not have to work, going the orderly way of her own life,
having her own enthusiasms, possibly becoming a Catholic.
Often she would maybe think of him, and he would think of
her, if away from her, and she would like thinking of him.
Later on they might decide to live together again but not out
of necessity. She would find friends of her own. He wondered
if she would allow a man to love her. He didn't like thinking

of it. Perhaps they could come to some agreement that would permit him to go away for a time, then she would likely keep away from other fellows, though he knew she wouldn't hesitate to give herself to a fellow if in love with him. Anyway, if he went out selling magazines, he would be away all week, coming home over the weekend, and it would be easy to form a habit of not coming home at all.

He was looking up at the ceiling. The room was dark but his eyes were accustomed to it and he saw clearly various objects in the room. He turned his head on the pillow, looking at the back of Vera's head. He put his hand on her shoulder and shook her gently till she stirred uneasily.

"Vera. Vera."

She was awake. Half turning her head she said: "What do you want?"

"I want to talk to you."

"I'm too sleepy."

"Listen, Vera."

"What?"

"Have you been thinking of being by yourself?"

"I don't know, I'll tell you tomorrow."

"Vera."

"What?"

"This is important."

"For heaven's sake, what do you want, go on to sleep."

"Listen, Vera, if I go on the road with Jimmie you won't see much of me for some time." He talked slowly, hesitating. She was awake and listening. "What do you mean?"

"I'll be away."

"You'll be in regularly, won't you?"

"Listen, Vera."

"I'm listening I tell you."

He looked down the length of the bed. His toes stuck up under the sheets. He saw a tip of the moon through the windows at the foot of the bed. The conversation was not going the right way.

"We haven't been getting on well together," he said, feeling his way.

"Not exactly. Things really don't seem to be going right, but we haven't been watching ourselves have we?"

"No, we haven't, but what's the use watching yourself?"

She put her hand on his shoulder, then touched his neck gently with her fingers.

"Don't do that," he said sharply.

"What's the matter with it?"

"You don't own me."

"Oh, don't be silly."

"I'm not silly, I tell you."

"You're too silly for words."

"I tell you you don't own me. That's clear ain't it? That's what I'm getting at, see. I mean we get on each other's nerves. We irritate each other. We probably need to be alone a long while till we get going again, instead of wasting time getting in each other's way."

"Say what you mean, Harry," she said quietly.

"That's what I mean. We need a long holiday from each other," he said rapidly.

"Well, what are you going to do about it?"

He lay there, looking at the side of her face out of the corner of his eye, wondering what she was going to say.

"Well, you know I'm going away on the road with Nash," he said.

"I know that."

"I don't think we should bother each other. I want to be alone and not have to think about anyone. I want to drift wherever I feel like. I don't want to be tied to thoughts of anyone."

"Well."

"I don't want to quarrel with you. I don't want to do anything to make you different, just leave you going your own way."

"I suppose I'll always feel the same, eh?"

"Yeah, I'd like to think so."

"And what would I do, stay by myself while you had a good time running around with any little hussy you can pick up, gadding about from town to town? Not on your life. If you want to do that, I'll find my own company, and I won't go slowly either."

"That's up to you."

"You're crazy, Harry."

"All right, I'm crazy."

"You're crazy as a loon, I tell you."

"Maybe so."

"Suit yourself, then, only you'll have to give me money."

"I will."

"I tell you you're mad, mad as a hatter. Harry?"

"What?"

"Harry."

"Don't, Vera. Stop. Don't touch me. I tell ya I don't feel like it."

He got out of bed and in his bare feet walked over to the window. He looked out over backyards and fences and trees. On the other side of the ballpark a light was in the front room of a house. A tree was in front of the house and the light shone through the leaves of the tree. He half turned. Vera was not moving. Then he heard her crying softly. He was waiting for her to cry and wanted things to get beyond that point. She was crying much louder and sniffing. "Harry," she said. He did not answer her. He looked steadily out of the window. The new moon was bright in the clear sky. Patches of light were on garage roofs and long shadows in yards. Over the roofs of houses, downtown, he could see an electric sign flashing intermittently, and though he watched carefully, couldn't spell it out. He wasn't thinking of anything, just watching patches of light on the ground and on bushes in Gingras' backyard. A few years ago the ballpark had been a hollow. The hollow had been filled in. He and his brother had had a lot of fun in the hollow under the big willow tree. The brother, now in Michigan, had come home ten years ago for his mother's funeral. He hadn't heard from him since, though he had wanted him to go back to Michigan with him. The light in the window behind trees across the park went out. It would be a good idea to write his brother, he thought, and see if there was anything doing in lumberyards over there. Everything quiet outside. The sky getting lighter. He could make out fences, shrubs, clothes props in backyards. He heard a streetcar rattling over an intersection at the corner, then going smoothly until he could not hear it. He stood there, thoughts no longer coming easily to him. Next week the league that played in the ballpark would be through for the season. He listened and couldn't hear Vera breathing; she had stopped crying. He felt like waking her, explaining he was sorry. It wouldn't do any good in the long run.

He walked over to the bed. She was sleeping, the night light from the window touching her features so she looked strangely foreign. A long time ago she had said there was a bit of Russian blood in her. He got into bed carefully so he would not disturb her.

She was up before him next morning. She got breakfast and they did not talk of the conversation of the night before. She was agreeable. They talked pleasantly. She asked what he intended to do in the evening. He said he had nothing to do. She suggested he have Jimmie Nash come over. She was so agreeable he did not want to start an argument. All morning he was around the house, reading papers. He felt much better, having explained to her the way he was feeling.

In the afternoon he went downtown, as usual, to get a paper and look for a job, but didn't bother much, now no longer anxious to discover a job, suddenly having made up his mind to go out canvassing.

In the evening, at half-past eight, Jimmie came over and they sat around the house. Vera was friendly with Jimmie. He liked talking to her. She liked him because he talked so easily and agreeably, always aware of her as a woman rather than the wife of his friend. They were sitting in the sunroom. Vera, looking out, saw Stan Farrel and his wife standing in the backyard.

"The Farrels are going downtown tonight," she said.

"No place where he intends to enjoy himself, I'll bet," Harry said, "or he wouldn't be taking her with him."

"That guy's got a way all his own with his wife," Jimmie said.

"How do you mean?"

"Don't you notice how he patronizes her?"

"That's an old story."

"I don't think she's used to being taken seriously," Vera said.

"He's got it all worked out," Jimmie said. "He explained it to me just about the first time he met me."

"How come?"

"He told me never to marry a clever woman, then he quoted some venerable Frenchman. The point was that if you marry a clever woman you are more or less responsible for everything she says. People take her seriously and you are handicapped. On the other hand if you marry a rather dull woman, everybody sympathizes with you whatever she says. Get the point?"

"Mr. Farrel explains himself," Vera laughed.

"He likes explaining why he didn't marry a clever woman," Harry said.

"He makes me tired," Vera said. "Who are the Farrels anyway? I've heard his father drank heavily and his family simply didn't count for anything."

"Well, don't hold that against him," Harry said.

"I'm not holding it against him. Just pointing out that his family weren't up to much."

"Well, whose is for that matter around here?"

"Don't forget my old pioneer stock," Jimmie said jovially.

"Pioneer stock?"

"Yeah."

"Say, I'll tell you a story about pioneer stock and my grandfather," Harry said.

"What's it about, Harry?" Vera asked.

"Go on, tell us about Grampapa," Jimmie said.

"The old boy was a real pioneer in these parts, only he died rather young. He used to be the skeleton in the family closet. He was a great drinker. My father once told me that he could drink more than six ordinary men, so he didn't have an ordinary end." He told how his grandfather had been drinking nearly all day at a tavern a little way up Yonge Street, now the main thoroughfare. In the evening someone had offered to help him on the way home, but very dignified, he wouldn't hear of it. He got lost in the dark on the way home and didn't get home all night. They went looking for him and found him all right. He had fallen into a horse trough, and too drunk to get out, was drowned."

"A beautiful story of pioneer life," Jimmie said.

"Harry, that's a rotten story," Vera said. "Your own grand-father!"

"Why is it?"

"It isn't the drinking part that matters, it's the idea of the thing. You had no business telling it."

"But Mrs. Trotter," Jimmie said, "most of us are of pioneer stock around here. We all have these pioneer stories, epics of the clearing of the land."

"It's funny all right, but what good does it do telling it?"

"You're getting damn straight-laced suddenly. What's the matter with you?" Harry said.

"Don't be silly, Harry."

"You spoilt the story."

"It wasn't worth spoiling, silly."

"For heaven's sake, stop telling me not to be silly." He glared at her. She looked at him stubbornly, then glancing at Jimmie, who was pretending not to listen, her expression changed. She looked as if she might cry. Harry was uncom-fortable. He knew Jimmie was uncomfortable. He had nothing more to say. He wanted to shout at Vera, but was ashamed. He bit his thumbnail and stared at her irritably.

"How about a little walk, Harry?" Jimmie suggest mildly.

"Come on, let's go," Harry said, getting up quickly. Jimmie said goodbye very pleasantly to Vera, but Harry didn't look back.

Going along the street Jimmie said: "Where are we heading for?"

"I don't care."

"Well, I don't want to just walk, let's go some place."

"Let's go down to Angelina's then. I want a drink."

4

They took a Carlton car and transferred to Bay and got off at Queen. They walked over to Elizabeth, the street of Chinese merchants, chop-houses and dilapidated roughcast houses used for stores. Some cafés were of new tan brick, with electric signs. Chinese men sat on steps or stood in groups under street lights. No women were to be seen. They crossed over from Elizabeth Street by the Registry office, the new white stone building oddly out of place in the neighbourhood, and walked up Chestnut Street to Angelina's, a brick house with a store front and big white letters on the plate glass, "Italian Restaurant." It was dark and no lights were in the windows.

They went around to the side door. Harry knocked gently. A square panel opened. A woman peered at them.

"How's Angelina?" Harry asked.

"Jimmie Nash and Harry Trotter," Jimmie said.

The door opened and Angelina stood there smiling at them, a plump Italian woman with good features, not too fat. She had nice plump legs. Harry tried in an offhand, friendly way to put his arm around her waist, and she grinned, remov-

ing the arm seriously. In the front room there was no light.
Along the hall they heard voices.

"Many people upstairs?" Jimmie asked.

"You boys don't want to eat?"

"No, just a drink."

"How are the tricks?" she said playfully.

"Fine, how are they going with you, do you still love me?"

"Sure, Mr. Trotter. Be nice boys now."

They passed Angelina's father sitting at the cash register.
A dining room was on the right along the hall. Many people
eating noisily, but laughing quietly, glanced at them as they
passed the dining-room door. They stood opposite the kitchen,
while Angelina spoke to one of the chefs. She was proud of
the chefs and the kitchen. The cooking was done publicly,
only a rail between the hall and the kitchen. Two chefs,
whiskered, plump, were roasting ducks, turkeys, chickens,
legs of pork veal, or fried steaks. The cooking was a perform-
ance. A chef wiped a pan with a piece of garlic, and the steak
on the hat pan sizzled. One chef smiled, acknowledging the
rich odours.

Angelina led the way upstairs to the front room.

"Who's upstairs, Angelina?" Jimmie said.

"Nobody you know, Mr. Nash."

The front room was well lighted, the blinds drawn down,
heavy curtains over the blinds. It was early, not many customers were at the round tables with white tablecloths. More
people would come in after the shows. They sat down in a corner. Harry's elbow brushed against a curtain, shifting from its
position the blind that fitted snugly into the window frame.

"Be careful please," Angelina said, adjusting the blind so
no light could be seen from the street.

"A single Scotch," Jimmie said.

"A double Scotch," Harry ordered.

Harry heard girls laughing in the front room Angelina used for nice people who really wanted to drink in a bootlegger's. "After all, Vera likes nice people," he thought. She might even get to a point where she would give him a pain in the neck. He drank the double Scotch quickly. He thought vaguely of Chinamen standing on Elizabeth Street, wondering if it were true they had a peculiar way of making love to white girls. He thought of it nearly every time he walked up Elizabeth Street.

He discussed the matter with Jimmie, and they got interested, and when they had exhausted the subject, they exchanged interesting opinions about lesbians. Then Jimmie told of an aunt who had greatly impressed him when he was very young, and whom he would like to know now he was older. She had gone away, to Mexico, people thought, and no one had heard from her since.

Harry listened, his eyes closed, assembling interesting facts about his father that had occurred to him since he had been thinking of home in the old days in Maydale, before they had moved to the city. "I never got along very well with my old man," he said. "I liked my mother better, but he was an interesting guy, though I couldn't see it in those days." His father had always worked too hard. He got into the habit of working hard when he was a boy on the farm and kept it up until two weeks before he died. He wasn't very big, a thin man who always wore a coat too tight for him. After they moved into the city his father couldn't get a job and had driven a coal wagon. The bags of coal were heavy, and he got thinner and very wiry, but he kept the job for six months. Sunday was his favourite day and early in the morning at about half-past six he got up and walked up the ravine to do some sketching. The city limits didn't extend as far north in those days, and the ravine was a natural park. The sketches, as he remembered them, were awkward, the lines blurred from too much rubbing, but the old man kept at it and finally turned to painting.

At this time he was a cutter in a suit and cloak factory and was saving up to pay off a mortgage on a house he had built. He had had such a hard time as a kid, he was afraid of being poor and so began to deny himself many comforts, walking to work every day, in the evenings working on the house. At first his wife tried to get him to rest but saw that he was happier going along his own way. He kept on painting, and the canvases got bigger, gradually covering the walls of the front room and dining room of the new house. He looked forward to having some of his pictures in the annual exhibition at the Art Gallery, and sent five good ones to the committee, who wrote a long letter about how remarkable it was such work should be done by a man with absolutely no training. It was a sincere letter and they suggested he should take some lessons that would only cost a few dollars. He absolutely refused to pay for any lessons. His wife cried a long time one evening because it was really his only pleasure in the world and she knew he had been very anxious to have his pictures on the walls of the Art Gallery. He went on painting and working, and walking, and working in the garden, even when not feeling well. He insisted it was taking every cent he had to put his son through high school and if he lost his job there would be years of poverty. At fifty-five he owned his house and had three-thousand dollars in the bank. Then he got pains in his legs one day. He stayed home from work but insisted on painting the front veranda. He got gangrene in his leg and died after two weeks in bed.

"It was funny," Harry said. "My mother died two years later. I was working at the time."

"Your old man was rather tremendous in his way."

"I guess he was but my mother was different."

Angelina was standing at the door and Jimmie beckoned to her, coaxing her to sit down at their table, but she shook her head sadly, waved her forefinger at him and grinned, showing her good teeth.

"It's funny the way you see your mother from a different angle years after, isn't it?" Harry said.

"I guess it is, I don't know. My folks are still very much alive, and the old man has definite ideas about work."

"I mean I got an idea my mother was something like I am."

"Like you?"

"Yeah, she was rather wonderful in her way. I can see how I used to like her, and never realized how much."

"A good way to feel, only go easy, or I'll break into tears."

"It hasn't anything to do with sentiment, Jimmie. Just something happens and for the first time you see your mother as a woman. I can see her quite plainly going around the house, and at night, getting into bed with the old man. I slept with my mother until I was nine years old."

"Well, that's not so good."

"What's the matter with it?"

"Simply, that being a great psychologist, I don't approve of it."

"Stop the kiddin' Jimmie, this is serious."

"And so am I serious. I'm trying to tell you you are too interested, it isn't good for you."

"Why?"

"You're really falling in love with your mother."

"Oh well, the only rotten thing about it is that I don't remember what she looked like when she was younger."

"Sit there and think about it, old socks," Jimmie said. Harry tilted back in the chair, frowning and disappointed, because Jimmie was so practical. Then he felt lonely and remembered how his mother had loved fall weather when trees were bare and the winds got cold. She was probably very good-looking when younger, he thought.

"Here comes somebody I know," Harry said.

"Who?"

"Bob, I think you've met him."

"Sure, met him one night when we were out with Farrel."

"He's looking bad."

Bob and his friend, a fat man with a short neck, sat down at one of the tables. Bob was looking thin. He looked as if he had not had any sleep for a long time.

"A double Scotch," Harry said mechanically to Angelina. He watched her straight body moving out the door. It wasn't likely she loved only her husband, Angelo. Young Italians were hot stuff, though old ones were no good. She was a beautiful bootlegger.

He grinned at Bob who waved back. The fellow with him nodded graciously, a sot with something respectable about him.

"Let's go over and sit with Bob," Harry said.

"Why do you want to?"

"I feel sorry for Bobbie."

"What's the matter with him more than usual?"

"Nothing more only he's all shot. He's getting worse. He's got no friends now. Farrel's breaking off with him. He seems just naturally sad. His wife goes looking for him a lot and tries to help him but he's always tight and she can't do nothing. The best thing he could do is to tell people she's his wife and go and live with her."

"I never saw the guy he's sitting with."

"Oh well, that doesn't matter."

They went over and sat down at Bob's table. Bob was a little embarrassed, wondering if Harry knew Farrel was leaving him, and if he knew he had been on a four-day drunk. They were introduced to Mr. Harris, who was in real estate. His collar was dirty. He needed at shave. He had a slight English accent and an asthmatic wheeze. They all had a single Scotch, and were about even so far, because Bob and Mr. Harris had had a few drinks before coming to Angelina's. Harry was feeling good, everything clearing up for him, and he thought easily and clearly of Vera, who would be getting into bed. She had got on his nerves once too often. He was thinking of her and sore at himself for having to think of her. Day and night she was there forcing his attention. All around him. He looked at Mr. Harris who was staring ineffectually at the rim of his glass. The crown of his head was bald, a fringe of hair, a retreating line around the bald spot, a small mat of hair on his forehead.

"Let's switch to beer," Mr. Harris said genially.

"Suits me."

"Me too."

"Why not?"

"Four bottles, Angelina."

The beer came. In the room was a hum of low talk. More people were coming in. An occasional loud laugh was followed by a sharp warning from Angelina. The beer on top of the Scotch made Harry feel like elaborating upon his thoughts.

He felt himself becoming expansive. He was trying to avoid talking about his wife.

"You all look so dumb," Jimmie said.

"Sure, I'm sad," Harry said, feeling sorry for himself. He thought of something insulting to say to Jimmie. Jimmie was not married and was laughing up his sleeve. Jimmie was grinning happily and he was uneasy. Then he felt sorry for Mr. Harris who was trying to hold on to himself. Harry thought of himself as being neat, quick, dexterous. He began to talk bitterly about being married. He wanted to tell in detail a quarrel with his wife, but found it something he could not explain.

"His grandfather happened to be a pioneer around here," Jimmie explained.

"My father was a squire," Mr. Harris said importantly.

"Thank God I don't know anything about my grandfather," Bob said.

"Don't take it so hard, Bob. Buck up, Bob."

"Cut that stuff, Jim."

"Furthermore, my father was a squire," Mr. Harris explained.

There was a disturbance at the door, Angelina preventing two Italian girls, bold strapping wenches, from entering the room. One of the girls pointed angrily at two girls sitting with two fellows at a table. Angelina was shaking her head resentfully and whispering to the girls, backing them away from the door. The girls stood at the door, watching sullenly.

"They been cut out I guess," Harry said, accurately measuring each word.

"They'll be thrown out," Mr. Harris said.

Harry watched the girls and Angelina, and listened vaguely to Mr. Harris whose father was a squire in the old country. When he got tired of the Italian girls he concentrated on the salt shaker in the centre of the table, a tall salt shaker, with a dinted silver top. He was not interested in what Mr. Harris was saying though he heard him quite plainly. "I'm all set to get going good," he was thinking. He wouldn't go home tonight, nor next morning. He would leave Vera absolutely alone a while. Later on he would try and fix things up with her, but at present they were getting in each other's way. She agreed with him but made it clear he was wrong. "Me and me brother were not much good," Mr. Harris was saying. "We came to this country fifteen years ago. Father gave us the money to come out. Father was a squire." Harry winked at one of the Italian girls who was leaning against the door, trying to get her eye. She looked as if she would have lots of pep. He didn't want to go home. He seemed to have lost his pep simply from hanging around the house. He had gone stale. He was out of his stride. Tonight he felt like having a good time just for a change. In a little while he'd suggest going to a dance hall. Jimmie would be willing, the most agreeable fellow he had ever met. Bob, of course, was agreeable, but in a very unsatisfactory way. Then he listened attentively to Mr. Harris, who was talking slowly, carefully. "Freddie, the brother, and myself ain't been doing much since we came out here but drink, but we never forgot we came from a family of real importance. We sent letters home, fine letters that said we were doing well and were prosperous. That would make father feel first rate. He had faith in the Harris boys though they had been a bit wild at home. That's what he always said in the letters."

"A decent sort, Mr. Harris."

"A fine old bloke. He wrote he was coming out to see how we were prospering. That put the wind up us, men, but we were the Harris boys and we wrote him to come. We hired a swell flat for all the time he was here."

Harry, sipping beer, caught a glimpse of Angelina's head in the door. A lovely head, a lovely neck. Splendid legs. Maybe she'd go dancing. They had always been rather friendly. Two weeks ago he had pinched her and she had giggled. She had forgotten herself and giggled, for she was really a businesswoman. Splendid legs. Still, Vera had good legs.

"It took all we had to fix up a flat but it was worth it, wasn't it? There's been nothing doing in real estate for a year, you see, and I'm missing the little there is anyway. The old man liked it though. He was proud of us and surprised and happy that the Harris boys had turned out first rate."

"Great idea, wasn't it?" Jimmie insisted.

"Wonderful," Bob said.

"Very interesting, Mr. Harris," Harry agreed.

Harry took a drink of beer and shook his head. He didn't want any more beer. He wanted to get out of the place.

More noise at the door. Angelina had taken the Italian girls by the arms and was attempting to push them downstairs. Angelina's face was flushed. One of the Italian girls had caught the eye of a young fellow sitting with the girls, and smiling, was exhibiting her bust, her hand on the curve of her hip. Angelina was angry.

"The wops are getting snotty," Jimmie said.

"Are they?"

"Yeah, you were saying, Mr. Harris . . ."

Harry, whispering to Jimmie, didn't want to offend Mr. Harris, but he kept thinking of the dance hall. It would be better to pick up a girl there and not bother taking one along.

"I wonder what time it is, Jimmie?" Harry said.

"When the old man went home we were broke," Mr. Harris went on. "That wasn't so long ago either. And Freddie, me brother, went on a spree. Freddie was a bit of a nobleman in his way but he drank too much. He didn't know the meaning of the word restraint, Mr. Nash. But there was something grand about him. Think of straightening up like that when father came out here. A Harris all right."

He took a big drink of beer. "Mr. Trotter, Freddie died," he said. His red-rimmed eyes bleared with tears. "They said he died of del-er-ium tre-mens," he said it slowly, to be accurate. He took the salt shaker from the table and began to caress it with both hands. "That wasn't so long ago either," he said.

"Then it was up to me to do the right thing," he said. "I had to send Freddie home for a decent burial. That's what father wanted. I got a letter from father saying he would meet the corpse at New York. Bob, you will understand that I had to assume responsibility," he said with great dignity, straightening up in his chair. "I had the undertaker do the right thing by Freddie. I had a dress suit put on him. A full dress suit on Freddie in the coffin."

They all turned and looked at Angelina who was walking over to the fellows and girls at the table. It was getting late. Everybody was going. "You'll have to go some place else with the girls," Angelina said distinctly. "It's all right to meet them here but you'll have to go some place else." Angelina glanced once or twice at the door, afraid the Italian girls were waiting on the stairs.

"It's getting late," Harry said.

"Freddie looked simply splendid in that dress suit," Mr. Harris said very seriously. "I met the old man in New York. He shook my hand very warmly and then we went to look at

Freddie in the coffin. The old man looked at him and he was so proud I thought I'd cry. 'Fred was a gentleman,' the old man said. 'He looks like a Harris.'"

Mr. Harris was squeezing the salt shaker till the bones stood out white in his thin hands. "I been here since supper time," he said. His chin dropped to his chest. "No good," he mumbled. "No good." Lifting his head he said eagerly: "Do ya think, men, I'll look that good in a dress suit? Will he say that about me?"

"He sure will, Harris," Bob said enthusiastically.

"Do you think so, Mr. Trotter?"

"You got nothing to worry about."

"We'll be stepping along," Jimmie said, getting up. They shook hands. They went out. Harry looked for the Italian girls on the stair. They had gone.

"I was getting kind of tired of that guy, Harris," he said.

"I kinda liked it."

"It was all right for a while but I wanted to get moving. Come on and let's go to Arcadia and dance."

"It's late, we'll only have about an hour."

"Come on anyway."

They walked over to take the car. Harry was thinking of Bob back in Angelina's.

"I guess Bob's about done," he said.

"He looks all in."

"Why on earth did he marry her? Other guys have married Jewesses and got along all right."

"It ain't that. It's the way he handled things. He can't get out of it now. He's just a bum now."

They took the streetcar to Arcadia, the biggest dance hall in the city, dancing every night in the week, the snappiest orchestra in town.

5

In the dance hall lavatory young men elbowed each other away from the mirror trying to comb back sleek hair and brush dandruff from shoulders. The hot-water tap was running. Paper towels were used, crushed and tossed on the floor. Nash waited at the door while Harry combed his hair.

They went upstairs and bought tickets at the wicket. The music had stopped, a dance was over and the crowd sauntered off the floor through gates and into alcoves.

"There's two peaches over there. What do you say?" Jimmie said.

"The fair one's a kind of a frump isn't she?"

"Well, what do you expect for your money, gravy on it?"

"Lemme have the dark one then."

"Sure, they both look alike to me."

"Just a minute, Jimmie, take a look at that egg over there. He gets on my nerves."

A slim, elegant fellow was hemmed in by three or four girls who looked at him eagerly liking his arched eyebrows, lips lipsoled and lightly rouged cheeks. He smiled showing his teeth, holding the smile, talking good-naturedly to all the girls, playing no favourites, a duke, a prince. The music started and he didn't ask one of the girls to dance but smiled aloofly, nodding encouragement to other fellows coming up to claim dances.

"Jees, how I hate that guy," Harry said.

"He's on the outside of things," Jimmie said. "You can't touch him. Come on, let's grab off those two kids over there, or someone else will do it."

Jimmie asked the blond girl to dance. She didn't speak or smile, but went on chewing gum, her eyes wandering around the hall. She simply took Jimmie's arm. The tall, hollow-eyed dark girl's heavily arched lips smiled encouragement at Harry. He took her arm, a warm, intimate arm.

"Do you dance here much?" she said as they passed through the gate.

"Now and then," he said, liking the lazy droop of her body and soft swell of breast pressed firmly against him. Too much perfume on her. "I wonder why she isn't here with somebody," he thought.

"I'm not much of a dancer," he said apologetically.

"Oh, that's all right," she said politely.

They danced straight ahead, the old-fashioned jerky strut, though every one else seemed to be doing a variation of the Charleston. One, two, three, on the floor, swish, swish, swish. *Yes sir, she's my baby, and I don't mean maybe, yes sir, she's my baby doll,* sang the saxophone player on the platform. In slow, twisting eddies, the dancers moved around the floor, legs swinging, soles beating to the insistent rhythm of the Charleston.

"I'm sorry I can't Charleston," Harry said.

"Oh, that's all right," she said generously.

He looked down at her. "Oh go to hell," he thought, annoyed by the monotonous vibration and sound of soles swishing on the floor. He bumped into somebody. A flying heel barked his shin. He looked around. Everybody happy. Everybody grinning. His girl very serious, the heavily arched red lips on the powdered pale face never wavering. She had a straight nose, a better nose than Vera had. She was hardly interested in him. He wondered what she was thinking about, "I wonder why she breathes so heavily," he thought, watching her nostrils dilating. He squeezed her and thought of the darkened alcoves where they could sit down. Her legs were long silken legs, brushing against him, moving easily, seeking something. Then he felt he didn't want to think any more about it. The saxophone player stopped singing and lifted his instrument, handling it expertly. "Hot papa," the girl said suddenly. The dance was over.

"I wonder where Jimmie is?" Harry said, mopping his face with his handkerchief.

"Oh, Mabel'll be along," she said.

"Can we have another dance?"

"Oh, I guess so. I can stand it if you can," she said, friendly and smiling.

"We get along all right, eh?" Harry said. She was worth taking out after the dance. She had class and looked like a peach, though she probably lived with the other girl in some hole in the wall.

Jimmie and the fair girl sauntered over.

"'Lo kids," he said.

"How'd it go, Jimmie?"

"Fine as silk. Me and the girlfriend, and the girlfriend and me are going to stick together," Jimmie said affably. "How about you two?"

"Might as well, I guess."

"We got along fine," the dark girl said.

They stood near the ticket booth, Jimmie doing most of the talking, with an easy assurance pleasing to the blond girl. They were watching two girls who were a little tight kidding each other, three fellows urging the girls to get more enthusiastic. One of the girls who was a little tight had a heavy masculine jaw and a snub nose but looked good-natured as she swung her body indolently, snubbing the girl friend with an air of grotesque respectability. The girlfriend's short thin coat showed big, round knees and bow-legs when she swung into the light. Harry looked out of the corner of his eye at his own girl, her arm linked in his, a pale pink scarf knotted in a sweetheart bow at her neck. Hollow eyes she had and lazy limbs and a drooping weariness. She was better-looking than Jimmie's girl, who was whispering to him and giggling.

The slim elegant young man with the rouged cheeks passed, casually nodding his head to Harry's girl. She smiled cheerfully, waving her hand. His short coat, snug at the hips, irritated Harry. He was a duke, a prince, he was on the outside looking in.

The bow-legged girl who was a little tight was laughing out loud. She couldn't stop laughing. The girlfriend slapped her on the back and she started to hiccough and her face got red.

"I think it's time the bouncer threw those bums out," the blond girl said to Jimmie.

"Let 'em be, let 'em be," Harry said.

"The dear girls must have their fun," Jimmie said.

The hiccoughing girl and her friend went off to the ladies' room. Harry grinned at the dark girl, taking more interest in her, preparing to suggest a rest in one of the alcoves. In the old days in Arcadia refreshments had been served in the alcoves, but the idea had never been successful, and now fellows sat in easy chairs with girls on their knees, on the watch for the bouncer in the balcony, who kept an eye on the alcoves.

"Too many Jews here," Harry said suddenly.

"Some Jews are pretty nice," the red lips moved, she spoke broad-mindedly.

"Yeah."

"Yeah, you said it."

"Oh well, let's stick together the rest of the evening, eh?"

"Oh, I don't know, I don't know. I don't know what Mabel'll want to do."

"Leave that to Jimmie, sweetheart."

"I guess it's all the same anyway."

Music started. Harry fumbled in his vest pocket for tickets. She gave him a coy smile and a long sincere glance.

They were dancing better this time. He knew the song and hummed it, strutting. The orchestra was doing a pantomime, the crowd surging slowly toward that end of the hall, dancers jockeying for position so as not to move very far away. Harry bumped into someone. Turning slowly, he again bumped and was annoyed. His girl looked up mildly. He grinned but was irritated. He was bumped and this time he bumped back, holding the girl firmly. He looked around grimly. The elegant young man with trimmed eyebrows passed gracefully, a nice Jewish boy. Harry tried to get going but was hemmed in, dancers balancing, bodies swaying with the music. Again he was bumped and he turned sharply, elbowing the fellow away. The lipsoled young man, holding the smile as long as possible, was plainly disgusted and deliberately bumped him again.

Harry stuck out his arm and pushed him away. His arm was pushed aside. Suddenly hating, he swung his open palm and caught the young Jew across the mouth. He felt his girl pulling away from him. She pushed her way among the dancers until he could not see her.

He was slightly puzzled to find himself standing alone on the floor and the music going on. A little Jew with oiled hair dived at his legs. He dropped his knee, catching him on the forehead. The music stopped. The little Jew lay on the floor swearing. The slim boy with the rouged cheeks looked at Harry, hesitating. Girls, screaming, backed away. A big Jew with wide heavy shoulders jumped on Harry's back, and feeling his knees sagging, Harry dropped quickly to his knees, swinging his body, getting one leg around the fellow's middle. Someone hit him in the eye. He yelled and hung on tight and kicked out, and his toe hit something soft. He smelled sweat. The big fellow was sprawled across his face. Someone was on top of him, punching. The Jew started to cry and rolled over. Harry tried to get up but someone punched his head.

"Get up, Harry," Jimmie yelled.

Harry got up on his knees. He rubbed the back of his head with his hand. He blinked his eyes, then gently massaged his left eye. He got up slowly.

"How are you feeling?" Jimmie asked.

"Fine."

"Like hell."

"You look kinda tough."

Jimmie's mouth was bleeding. They got off the floor, walking along the aisle. Two bouncers had hold of two fellows by the neck. "Come on, let's go down to the lavatory," Jimmie said. Three sympathetic fellows followed them to the lavatory.

In the lavatory Harry looked at himself in the mirror, and fingered his swollen eyelid. "Boy, what an eye you've got," Jimmie said. Harry daubed his eye with a paper towel soaked in hot water. He didn't turn away from the mirror. His tie was pulled away from the collar, his coat-sleeve torn at the shoulder. His fingers twitched at the torn sleeve. His thoughts got all mixed up and he glared at fellows jammed in the doorway, regarding him silently.

"I didn't get him either," he said to Jimmie.

"Who?"

"The little Jew with the coat."

"Forget him. Let's get out of her quick before the cops come."

Steam from hot-water taps clouded the room, making the air heavy and moist. Fellows crowding at the door were a little afraid of Harry, but wanted him to see they admired him, one of them, only bigger and stronger and carrying them along with him. One of the boys suggested they talk it over there in the lavatory and go after a bunch of Jews outside. They talked excitedly, watching Harry standing there erect and husky, mopping his lean face with a steaming handkerchief, his forehead sweating, his fair hair wet and curling. He looked around obstinately, only half-hearing, and breathing deeply, lifted one hand to his shoulder, toying with the rip. He straightened up suddenly and leaped toward the door.

He went upstairs, three steps at a time. He stood still, looking around deliberately. Two or three couples were dancing, many people were talking. He saw the lipsoled young man in a corner alcove, surrounded by three Jews and two girls. They saw him coming. Somebody hollered. The slim man darted out along the aisle and ran. Harry ran, and someone tossed a floor lamp at him as he passed the alcove.

He followed around the aisle, gaining rapidly. He knew he could catch him. Hurt him, deep and tight, the little show-off. The form-fitting coat snug at the hips flew open and the slim boy jumped, tripping on the rail, stumbling on the dancing floor. Harry vaulted and caught up to him. The little Jew feeling him close, dropped on the floor, turning flat on his back, and flung his feet at Harry, using the small of his back as a pivot base. Harry took the heels in the belly as he flopped down, driving his fist against the scared face.

Then he heard shouting and pounding on the floor and yelling, and someone jumped on his back. He swung his elbow, but the weight got heavier until he could hardly move. Then the weight was lifted off. The slim boy was lying very quietly on the floor. He got up quickly. Jimmie was wrestling. The fellows from the lavatory had rushed the Jewish boys and were beating them up. The saxophone in the orchestra started to play, and stopped suddenly, and the orchestra men jumped down on the floor. "Here come the cops," somebody yelled, and the cops came, two abreast, two wagon-loads through the front door smartly, in double-quick time.

Harry got off the floor and went up to the balcony by the back stair. Jimmie followed. The balcony was crowded, girls were yelling and craning necks to see the floor. When the cops ran out on the floor, there was no yelling in the balconies. Everybody kept quiet. Harry, looking down, saw the cops going into the alcoves and roughly pushing fellows. Girls were filing down from the balcony to the check-room, the line moving slowly.

The police inspector ordered everybody to file out quietly. He took the matter philosophically.

They lined up and got their hats from the check-room. They had to line up to get out. They watched the two girls who were a little tight earlier in the evening, and who now seemed quite drunk. The crowd hemmed in the girls and the officers. Harry kept well back. The girls were having a hard time getting into their coats. A policeman shook one of the girls roughly, giving her a push. The girlfriend with the heavy jaw and snub nose, putting her hands on her hips, wagged her head. The officer shoved her away and her helmet hat dipped down over one eye. The inspector told four policemen to put the girls in the wagon.

Harry followed the girls and the officers to the street. He forgot about getting away and was sore at the cops who had hold of the girls. The girls were walking quietly but the tall girl with the big round knees and the bow-legs got excited when she saw the wagon. "Put them in," the inspector said. Two cops took hold of the taller girl and she jumped at them with her knees, but they got hold of her, lifting her off her feet. In unison they swung her at the open wagon door. Her feet skidded along the wagon floor but her head crashed against the iron doorframe and she lay still, her head hanging out six inches. One of the officers pushed in her head. They did not have so much trouble with the other girl, whose hat was tilted more rakishly over one eye. She was scared sober, though she fought when they pushed her down on top of the girlfriend. The wagon moved away, and she was hollering: "Get your knee off me you bastard, do you hear, get your feet off me."

"We'd better pull out of here," Jimmie said.

"The poor little tarts."

"No use worrying about them, they'll simply wake up tomorrow and wonder what it was all about."

"I know, but still, all right let's go, up to your place, eh?"

"All right. I'll fix up your eye."

They moved away quietly. Looking back, Harry saw the cops dispersing the crowd around the dance-hall door.

They turned north, walking along without talking. Harry's eye was feeling bad. It was getting worse. His collar, torn away from the front button, was held in place by his tie. He rubbed his eye with his hand. Jimmie looked all right. His shirt had been torn but you couldn't notice it. They kept in step and Jimmie started to whistle. Harry grinned, then they both laughed out loud.

"Holy smoke," Harry said.

"How you feeling?"

"Good enough."

"Me too."

"All right, let's cut up the street here."

The street was quiet, no lights in the houses. It was nearly two o'clock and a milk wagon turning the corner swayed, the bottles rattling loudly. The horse jogged up the street, hoofs beating steadily on the pavement. "I'm glad I'm not going home," Harry thought, watching the milk wagon go up the street.

They turned another corner, and the neighbourhood was poor, now mainly ramshackle old houses, fifteen blocks west of the centre of the city. Along the street the city-hall tower and the big clock stuck up over the roofs of houses and small stores downtown. They walked two blocks without seeing anybody, but when they were crossing a street they saw a heavily loaded truck six doors up from the corner. They walked on about fifty feet, then Harry said: "That truck looked kinda funny there."

"Booze, I guess," Jimmie said.

"Come on back and let's take a look."

"What's the use?"

"They may be unloading."

"Sure, they probably are, but what of it?"

"Come on, let's watch them."

They turned, walking on grass close to the wall of the corner house, and at the end of the wall they looked up the street.

"There's a guy standing on the sidewalk near the engine," Harry said.

"I can't see him."

"No, the truck is between us and the sidewalk but I saw his head move twice."

A man came out of the alleyway. Harry watched the man intently. He lifted a case off the truck and went back along the alleyway. Harry leaned against the wall. He didn't speak to Jimmie for about five minutes, watching for the man to come out of the alleyway. The man worked steadily. They watched him take six cases along the alleyway. He rested for the seventh case, leaning against the truck, talking to the fellow near the engine.

"A pretty big bootlegger," Jimmie said.

"He takes his time. That truck's worth a lot I bet."

He took hold of Jimmie by the arm. "It's worth a lot, I bet," he muttered. His legs were getting cramped and he straightened up. "Lord, Lord," he whispered. He moistened his lips, turned and looked at Jimmie, but could see only the side of his head.

"What's up?" Jimmie said.

"I'd like to take the load. I'd like to take the whole damned load."

"Take the load where?"

"Sell it, some to Angelina, anywhere."

He didn't look at Jimmie. He heard him breathing but he was watching the man getting his arms on a case. "It's a hell of a chance to take," Jimmie was whispering. Accustomed to the darkness now, Harry could see one of the men distinctly as he walked toward the alleyway. He had on a dark sweater. He had big shoulders. His neck was thick.

"It's a chance," he said.

"What do you want to do?"

"We've got to cross the road without the guy at the front of the truck seeing us, and then we got to bluff them, see Jimmie, we got to bluff them."

"All right."

"Come on then."

"Go on."

Pressing against the wall they went around the front of the house. The man came out of the alleyway again and stood on the sidewalk, cutting a plug of tobacco. He straightened up, putting the plug and the knife in his pocket, and rubbed his hands. He shot a stream of tobacco juice out on the road. Then he took another case from the truck, said something to the other fellow and went back along the alleyway.

They were directly opposite the truck across the street. "You're sure you can drive it, Jimmie?"

"Sure I can."

"When we hear the guy coming down the alleyway, we'll duck and try and get on this side of the truck before they see us."

They crossed the street, not moving fast but treading carefully, their heads bobbing up and down as they moved on the balls of their feet. They made it. They got across the street without making a noise. They leaned against the truck. On the other side of the truck a man scraped his feet, then thumped his heel on the pavement. Along the alley the other man moved coming out to the street. Jimmie moved toward the back of the truck. Harry took two paces toward the engine. Looking across the driver's seat he could see the back of the man's head. He straightened up and said quietly but distinctly: "Put up your hands, both of you." He heard Jimmie at the back of the truck say: "Put up your hands." The head turned quickly, trying to locate the voice, and backing away from the truck. "Put them up," Harry said harshly. The hands went up slowly. Harry took three steps around the engine. The man saw him coming and his hands sank slightly, then shot up quickly.

"Turn around," Jimmie said. Both men turned slowly, their hands up. "Get into the car, Jimmie, I'll watch these guys," Harry said. He heard Jimmie getting into the car, fumbling with the controls. He kept his eyes on the backs of the two men. The head of one was swaying. The engine ran smoothly. "Keep them up," Harry said, getting into the car, one foot on the mud-guard. The truck jerked forward. One of the men ducked toward the alleyway. The other turned and fired three shots. A light came on in the front room of the house. The truck was going fast.

Harry got on the seat beside Jimmie. His heart was beating very rapidly. He put his hand on the spot, rubbing it uneasily. Jimmie was undisturbed. As they turned the first corner another shot was fired at them.

"I can't get the lights on," Jimmie said.

"Lemme see."

"Right here."

Harry fumbled with his fingers. They turned another corner. Jimmie bent down and groping with one hand turned on the lights.

"Now for Angelina's, eh?" he said.

"Let her go."

They drove downtown, avoiding main streets. They went down University Avenue and behind the Armories and along to Angelina's corner. A police station was only a block away but they felt safe. Angelina was very friendly with the police, who didn't bother her. No lights were in the building.

Jimmie stayed in the truck while Harry rapped on the door. Angelo came to the door and they talked. Then Angelina came down and at first shook her head, shrugging her shoulders, but Harry coaxed her till she said she might take a little, and when he pointed out that they truck was half unloaded, she said she might as well take it all at that price.

Angelo helped unload the truck. They carried the cases into the backyard. Harry offered to help carry them down the cellar, but Angelo said he could look after that himself. They went into the house and Angelina, a dressing down wrapped around her, sat down at the little table in the hall and wrote a check. She grinned cheerfully at Harry. Angelo grinned.

Outside Jimmie said: "What are we going to do with the truck?"

"Can't we keep it?"

"Like hell we can. We'd better park it some place and beat it."

"Any place up north then."

They parked the truck on a side street north of Bloor and walked back to a car-stop. They waited twenty minutes for a streetcar and Harry got sleepy and leaned against the post, his eyes closed. The night had been long. He wanted to lie down. He wasn't going home. He wanted to lie down and be away from home.

"I'm going down to Anna's," he said when the car came.

"Suit yourself, it's none of my business," Jimmie said.

On the car they were both sleepy and didn't talk much. Harry promised to meet Jimmie at eleven o'clock the next morning and Jimmie got off the car. Harry went further east to

Sherbourne Street and walked down to Anna's apartment. There was a light in the hall of the apartment house. He pushed the buzzer that had Anna's name over it and went upstairs and rapped gently on the door. She opened the door and said, "Oh my heavens!" and he went in. She was surprised and excited and glad to see him.

He made love to her, then she slept, but he couldn't sleep. He had never been in trouble with the law. He didn't even like knowing cops. Trouble could come from cops and the law only if you were poor and a failure. The satisfaction he was nursing made him feel he was going in the right direction. A man who was feeling so exultant and expectant couldn't have a bad conscience. If you did a thing, and after it had been done you had this feeling of elation, it meant the thing you had done had been right and good for you. He could tell he felt great because already little things that had been troubling him, things he couldn't name that had been making him feel lonely, were getting lost in his new sense of ease and satisfaction. He fell asleep. He had a happy dream. He was in the woods making his way painfully through some thick tangled underbrush to a sunlit clearing just ahead. It was a gold-lit clearing. People were gathering there, waiting for him with presents. They were preparing a table for him. Then he heard an angry voice and he looked back. His own father was there; he was in his shirt-sleeves; he had been in his chair reading the newspaper. The quiet, docile, white-haired, blue-eyed little man whose head came up to his son's shoulder was shouting with fierce authority, "Come back here, Harry. Come back, do you hear?"

It was a bad dream. He woke up suddenly, his heart pounding. He didn't know where he was, or when it was, and he thought his father or mother must be very sick and waiting to hear from him. Minutes passed before he could convince himself that a lot of time had passed and his father and mother were dead. It was astonishing that such a dream could shake him. It was a joke. It was news to him that he had ever had any real respect for his old man. His mother used to say, "Harry needs a strong hand now. You talk to him," but the old man, the serene blue eyes on him, would say quietly. "He doesn't want to hear anything from me. You're the one he listens to," and go back to reading his newspaper. And the old man had been right; how could you respect a clever-talking man who accepted the fact that he was never to make more than fifty a week and was content with his little house and his garden and all the sketching he did and the daubing in oils? A man who didn't even know he was such a little guy wasn't entitled to any real respect.

It was not yet dawn. A gray light was widening on the ceiling. Feeling lonely and restless, he got up quietly and went to the window. The street lights were still lit. While he stood there the sky changed, the street lights went out. The daylight brought him a new morbid excitement. It was a feeling of not knowing what was going to happen next. He liked this feeling. He had always wanted to have it. While he could keep this feeling he was sure he would never hear anyone crying out, "Come back here, Harry."

PART THREE

---◆---

1

*A*ll winter Harry and Jimmie were developing into good
bootleggers, living together in two rooms and a bath in a
rooming house overlooking the Normal School grounds,
opposite the Young Women's Christian Association. There
was a window in one room affording a view across the street
into two or three Y.W.C.A. rooms. In the evenings, with nothing better to do, they sat at the window hoping to attract the
girls' attention. Business developed slowly and Jimmie was
unsuccessful when he tried to get a job in the Customs Office,
so at night they sat down at a table in the room and carefully
studied the Act, provisions for exporting and for local con-
sumption of liquor. The elaborate and difficult wording of the
Act bothered Harry, but Jimmie, in an offhand way, made difficult points quite simple: the breweries were allowed to take
orders for foreign shipments and consignees could provide
trucks and take delivery at the brewery so long as it was
intended for foreign shipment. The night they developed the
idea and decided Jimmie should go to Niagara Falls and phone
in an order, they slapped each other on the back, shaking
hands warmly. It was a time to get drunk, and they went
around the corner to the English Cooking Café and made a
date with two waitresses for an hour later. They had a modest
party in the room, but one of the waitresses, a tall Swedish girl,

got sick early on beer and they put her to bed and while she was sleeping, Jimmie, sitting in an easy chair, his feet hooked up on the dresser, insisted on reading in a loud whisper various speeches from Shakespeare's comedies.

By the time they took their first deliveries from the brewery they had become confident of each other's ability. Sometimes Jimmie's enthusiasm made Harry uneasily aware that Jimmie knew too much for him, not in Stan Farrel's pigeon-hole way, but in a manner so simple and direct it enabled him to dismiss things casually, leaving an impression of absolute sincerity. At first it bothered Harry that Jimmie was mentally swifter, his better education giving him an advantage, but as days passed, he learned that Jimmie was too lazy to carry out his splendid ideas, and lying awake in bed one night, staring out of the window at the moon over the roofs of the school, he felt that Jimmie depended upon him to carry out even the simplest plans. It made him happy to realize it. Lying awake in bed he was eager for more strength and influence and money. He felt surer of himself, more confident. He hew he would never be bothered again by an uneasy thought of Jimmie. Though Jimmie ordered most of the liquor, Harry actually called at the brewery with the truck. They never wasted time storing liquor but drove directly to speakeasies and unloaded at once. Angelina, a good customer because they sold cheaply to her, had made possible the development of a trade supplying eight small bootleggers in different sections of the city. The business was on a solid basis and Harry was anxious to go home and explain to Vera that he was becoming successful, the business developing, his influence increasing, until he would soon have his own power and his own importance. He was eager to talk to her but knew he would not go home and it became a foolish dream of power. It was as if she were an essential audience for him and there was no use trying to interest any one else in the same way.

He talked about Vera to Jimmie, who was sympathetic without being sentimental. He reminded Harry that he had left Vera deliberately, and now was fairly happy, going along his own way, and besides it wasn't likely Vera would be glad to hear he was running liquor. Such a thought hadn't occurred to Harry, who had taken it for granted she was eager to be with him no matter what he was doing so long as he was successful. But he couldn't argue about it. He said, "Is that so," and started a conversation about ridiculous laws. A long time ago they had agreed they were not breaking laws in the old way like plain crooks, and all the silly laws on earth couldn't make them crooks. Jimmie wanted the point to be distinctly understood, the night they had walked for hours along the lake front talking till midnight, and he spoke profoundly about theories of law, and individual freedom, problems uninteresting to Harry, but encouraging him to go ahead with the business. He imagined himself talking like that to Vera but knew he could not explain the matter so clearly. He sent money to her every week, enough for rent and her own living.

For a few weeks he enjoyed living alone, sleeping alone. There were no difficulties after the day's work, but he became conscious of a new responsibility, a new kind of awareness, forcing him to be alert even when in a restaurant, or walking along the street. He developed a habit of glancing slyly at people who passed him. A head turned. He walked on, half looking over his shoulder.

In two months they had enough money to dress expensively and went together to a haberdasher's and bought clothes; three suits apiece, ties, shirts of English make. They were buying ties and Harry watched Jimmie, who was uncertain whether he liked a particular colour. Holding a tie of weak, indefinite colour in his hand he said, "That is about right, eh? Neat and not elaborate, eh?" It occurred to Harry that Jimmie was afraid of his own taste in colours, and he said good-naturedly, "Oh, that's terrible, Jimmie, try this." And while in the haberdasher's he was a little patronizing to him. Jimmie had often taken too much for granted, and in the store Harry couldn't resist being helpful carelessly enough to make it plain he had good taste naturally. Something that couldn't be developed from now to doomsday.

They left the store and walking along the street Jimmie felt obliged to defend his taste in colours. He explained patiently that there was a scientific basis for good taste. He was argumentative and talked about primary colours, colours of the spectrum. "What an awful lot of bunk to help a guy buy a tie," Harry said, but Jimmie went on indignantly explaining mechanical rules used as a basis for securing harmony in colours. Harry took it quite peacefully. "I've got Jimmie's weak spot," he thought.

The easy money from buying slowly and selling steadily encouraged them to live more elaborately. Harry took a flat in the good apartment district up on St. Clair. A decorator furnished it in splendid style. Then he bought a grand piano. He couldn't play the piano but liked coming into the room at night and looking at it. He was lonely in the apartment. He ate all his meals downtown and merely slept there. He told Jimmie that the apartment lacked something, a kind of stability. "Get a servant, old boy, get a servant," Jimmie suggested, adding that a Chinese cook with a valet's talent would be okay. The idea appealed to Harry. "That's a beautiful idea," he said. He thought about it for three days, then advertised for the Chinaman. He got one all right, but for two weeks was not comfortable with him in the apartment.

He had many parties. They were able to get some fine-looking women but usually picked up little tarts and had a merry time for a few hours. After one of these parties lasting all night he thought remorsefully of Vera and made up his mind to send her a definite sum of money each week.

He was unhappy when he thought too much of her. He hadn't definitely decided never to see her again but thought vaguely of living with her later on when he had made more money. He was growing tired of picking up women and got into the habit of making love to Anna constantly. She was satisfying and no bother at all. He promised Anna they would live together in the apartment as soon as he could buy a swell car.

He didn't buy a car for a month because it was necessary to move slowly and avoid treading on the toes of men like O'Reilly and Al Cosantino, and two Jews, Simon Asche and Steve Weinreb, who divided the Jewish trade. O'Reilly was influential in three wards, owned a few bawdy houses and a hotel. Cosantino had most of the Italian trade, delivering from door to door, and had men out taking orders all the time. He had supplied Angelina until she dropped him for Harry.

He met O'Reilly out at the Sunnyside Palladium one night in January. O'Reilly waved to Andy Collins, alderman in Ward Three, sitting with Harry, Jimmie, and Mike Regan, the lawyer. Jimmie had known Collins for years. Regan was afraid of Collins. Collins waved to O'Reilly and went over to his table, and then he came back with O'Reilly. "You men should know each other," Collins said.

They shook hands all around, and O'Reilly sat down to have a drink. He was friendly. He told some jokes, but Harry watched him alertly. Everybody in town knew O'Reilly. All the policemen liked him. Police-court interpreters liked him very much, he was so good-natured and employed so many foreigners. After the second round of drinks O'Reilly said, "So long," cheerfully and left them.

Harry said quietly to Jim: "I don't like that guy."

"That's one bird you got to like," Jimmie said.

"I don't like him anyway."

"Why, he was nice wasn't he?"

"Maybe so, but I'd like to push his fat face."

"We're going to be damn nice to him," Jimmie said emphatically. "For a while anyway."

"All right, I got nothing against him, I guess."

He didn't understand his dislike for O'Reilly. He had resented the respectful way Collins spoke of O'Reilly. He didn't like the way everybody shook hands with him. "I guess I want the centre of the stage myself," he thought, shrugging his shoulders.

They were making money though it was awkward using the apartment for so much business. Harry agreed they ought to have some kind of a small place for the sake of respectability, and Jimmie suggested a store downtown. He agreed, knowing Jimmie had for years wanted to own a bookstore.

Well-dressed, they interviewed publishers and agents, talking with easy assurance, commanding credit, assistance and good will. After an interview they walked along the street, talking rapidly, laughing, each insisting his manner had more impressed the publishers. They finally selected a store downtown on Adelaide, just a block away from Yonge Street.

The windows in the back of the store faced a lane and the stage-door entrance of the Olympia Burlesque Show. Standing at the windows at half-past one in the afternoon, Harry could see chorus girls walking up the lane to the door. These windows became office windows. A mahogany desk, many pens, an imitation oriental rug, a swivel chair and three plain chairs gave the office distinction. He got as much pleasure from furnishing the office as Jimmie got from the bookstore, done in orange and black, prints on the wall, etchings, watercolours, bric-a-brac on tabarets, gifts on small tables. In the evening he sat in the swivel chair in the office, his feet on the desk, fine and pleasant thoughts amusing him, till he got up and went into the store to look at Jimmie, one leg over the corner of a table, reading attentively.

"I'm getting used to that office," Harry grinned.

"Yeah."

"Of course it isn't so much right now."

"Yeah."

"But when I get more money I'll get different woodwork, see?"

"Yeah."

"Really swell woodwork, eh?"

"Don't bother me, do you hear."

Jimmie swung his arm, the corner of the book grazed Harry's forehead. Ducking, Harry grinned, and sliding in, thumped him on the ribs lightly.

"Cut it out," Jimmie said.

"Go on, read your damn book then."

He went back to the office. Jimmie was happy, not that he was expecting to sell many books, but rows of shelves made him feel good.

They hired a girl to look after the store in the daytime. They hired five girls in two weeks before getting one who was satisfactory to Jimmie. Eva Lawson was slight and dark, wore her clothes well and had a surprising way of twisting a knot of hair on the back of her neck. She was twenty-three, and liked books and pictures, and after she had worked in the place three days Jimmie took her out to dinner. They became friendly and seemed fond of each other and sometimes worked together in the evening. Harry liked Eva and was disappointed when Anna, who met her at a dance out at the Palladium, had some nasty remarks for her. He didn't quarrel with Anna over it. Anna didn't like women anyway. He simply shrugged his shoulders, pinched Anna's waist, and said: "Good old Anna." He told her very practically that Jimmie liked Eva and had talked of marrying her later on, and so she would simply have to be friendly with her.

In the office at the back of the store they kept their accounts, records of sales and of prospects. They kept the accounts carefully and the business steadily improved and they decided it was foolish to risk arrest driving a truck. They hired a returned soldier, Joe Atkins, a lean man with a wife and two children. They offered him a salary of fifty dollars a week. He understood his work and became reliable. He talked frequently of his wife and children. Fifty dollars a week made him happy.

A week after hiring Joe, Harry heard that Julie Roberts had actually married Augustus. He saw their pictures in the paper, and a note on Augustus and his well-known skill with the violin. He looked at the pictures a long time and thought of going to see Julie at once, simply to show contempt for Augustus, but got sore, and threw the paper away.

2

At lunch time, feet up on the desk, he yawned, tilted back in his office chair, just a block away from an armchair lunch place at the corner. And there was no reason why his easy chair shouldn't become a wheelchair, well-cushioned and comfortable, to eliminate the necessity of moving even for lunch, when Joe Atkins could simply wheel him out of the store, across the road to the armchair lunch, call for him later, and wheel him back to the office. It would be necessary to have a movable arm on the chair to hold the lunch. He grinned and yawned, very lazy. In the old days he had to get up at half-past five to be at work in the yard by seven o'clock, and now whole days slipped by unnoticed or without recollection of having done anything. In the afternoons he looked forward to evenings with lively parties that were usually successful, though one Thursday night, in the apartment, he had a crying jag and Jimmie, Eva Lawson and Alderman Collins had to promise to take him to Vera before he would lie down. It was unfortunate because he was enjoying himself immensely at this party, and it had become a big crap game with the women winning, and this man O'Reilly, who had good-naturedly come to the party, was ugly-tempered because he was losing. This same O'Reilly tried to change his luck by singing a bit of a hymn just before rolling the bones, and since it didn't help he might have got sore, only the song interested him, and they all stood up and sang. There were more songs, the best one was:

Von Tromp was an admiral brave and bold.
The Dutchman's pride was heeeee—
And he cried, 'I'll reign on the rolling main [very rapidly]

As I do on the Zeider Zee. As I do on the Zeider Zeeeeee.'
[slowly now]
And Von Tromp had a broom at the mast. [Their voices
blended well on that.]
'I've a broom at the mast,' said heeeee,
'That the world may know, where'er I go
I sweep the mighty sea.'

They were dealing with Blake, the English admiral, who
had a whip at the mast, their arms linked, chins lifted, then
their heads lowered gradually to take the low notes. They
shook hands at the end of the song and were delighted till
Jimmie said: "What a simple pair of admirals! They had no
dignity. One wants to fight with brooms and the other with a
whip, just like a couple of stable hands." There was some truth
in what he said, they agreed, though Alderman Collins, who
was talking vaguely, suddenly said the remark wasn't in good
taste, and there might have been an argument, but Harry insisted on telling them about his little wife. He was very sad,
and wanted their sympathy so they promised to take him to
her while he retained some dignity.

Next morning he was ashamed, and assured himself he
would never again mention her name when with other people.
He left the house without eating breakfast, wandering aim-
lessly downtown, walking miles without getting tired. For the
first time he wondered why he had left Vera, and the thought
of the whole business of bootlegging and the parties discouraged him. He walked along the street, realizing only vaguely
that he had left her and had been away for some time, and his
life of the last few months seemed to have absolutely no reality. He crossed a street corner, disregarding traffic lights, so
restless and uncertain of himself he wanted to run and feel

himself lurching along, his feet thudding, going on, further away from all thoughts that had bothered him. But instead, stopping on the opposite corner, he leaned against a post, suddenly tired and hungry and unimportant, so that his thoughts seemed trivial. He had lost all identity, nothing he did was of any consequence; he had shoes on his feet, his left shoulder was itching, he scratched it slowly, then sucked in his lips and went into Bowles Lunch to have a chopped steak sandwich and a cup of coffee. The coffee warmed him. He felt like a fool to have been wondering about other days when he was now alone, unrestricted, with no one to bother him.

But the next morning he was restless again and got up hastily to walk downtown, simply to keep moving. It was Sunday morning and he walked by the Labour Temple, opposite the cathedral that had had a big fire the week before. He was walking slowly, eyes on the charred beams, all that remained of the cathedral roof. The walls were still coated with ice from the water that had streamed over them. Then he stood still, slightly confused, for carillon bells were ringing. He looked up at the tower and saw smoke coming from the windows, and guessed the carilloneur was up there with a stove, keeping the bells ringing in spite of the fire. The sound of the bells had surprised and aroused him again, and, walking up the street his thoughts flowed rapidly, the old thoughts of Vera he had been trying to avoid.

He went home to dinner and forced himself to be cheerful with Anna. He didn't think of Vera all next day and by the middle of the week he wondered why he had been so uneasy about a few old thoughts.

The weather was bitter cold, the streets covered by a heavy snowfall, when he bought a coon-skin coat. He wore the coat

whenever possible and in the office took it off solemnly, expos-
ing the lining, hanging it up slowly. At the time he got the coat
they hired two more men. Sam Martin, an army man, hard-
boiled, was an old friend of Joe Atkins, who had tried for years
to get reestablished in civilian life. He explained he hadn't
worked steadily because he had been gassed at Ypres; the gas
came back on him when he lifted heavy loads. And Atkins
hired Eddie Thomas, a sentimental fat man, a perfect shot with
a gun. Both were awkwardly out of place the first time coming
into the store. Harry talked about an appearance of respectability, and in a few days they got used to the shelves and looked
like decent customers. They were paid every Saturday though
merely helping Atkins make deliveries on the truck.

In the daytime Eddie Thomas loafed around the store. He
had a sleepy stupid expression in his eyes, but was alert. He
had long black hair falling over his eyes. He got used to hanging around the store and grinned at Eva Lawson. She told
Harry and he asked Eddie to be in the office after the store
closed. Then he told Eddie to keep away from Eva, and when
Eddie grinned stupidly he hit him three times, twice on the jaw,
once just above the belt. When it was over, Harry was nice to
Eddie, explaining he should be sensible enough to realize he
was getting more money working for him than he could get
from anyone else. Eddie had simply made a mistake and was
sorry, insisting he would rather work for Harry than for anyone
else on earth.

Three weeks after hiring Sam and Eddie he got the car, and
Anna moved into the apartment. The car and the apartment and
Anna made him feel comfortable, at times so comfortable he
wondered if he was getting soft, and he wanted to test his
strength. Down in the store one night he challenged Jimmie to

weight-lifting contests and danced around him, shadow-box-
ing, but only occasionally did Jimmie respond sufficiently to
interest him. They danced around each other till Jimmie got
tired of it. Harry wanted to keep it up and took off his coat but
Jimmie impatiently insisted they had come down to the store
to talk business. They hadn't touched the hotel trade. They
hadn't even touched the big money.

Most hotels in the city sold beer over counters, getting it
straight from the breweries, and bars were crowded and hotel
men getting rich. Jimmie said if they had their own chain of
places they could get rid of hotel opposition for a time at least
merely by informing, or paying policemen more than hotel-
keepers paid. "You've got to work fast and stick up for yourself," he said. Harry agreed they were marking time, not getting anywhere in particular mainly from lack of money.

They sat in the office and argued about the possibility of
doing an exporting business. Jimmie insisted they didn't have
enough money to offer any serious opposition to O'Reilly, the
biggest exporter in the city. They checked up accounts. Some
small bootleggers were behind in payment. Harry damned
them and smoked a cigar and kept asking Jimmie if those guys
thought it was a charity bazaar. "We got to work, don't we?
We got to take turns running across the border and phoning in
orders and getting stuff from breweries, don't we?" He was all
for having their own places in different sections of the city.
Waving his hand, he developed the idea further, talking
eagerly. Eight or nine trucks getting liquor from breweries,
and at least sixteen houses in different sections of the city.
They could pay salaries to men managing houses and still sell
cheaper than anyone else in town. All the cops on the beats
would have to be fixed, a big salary list, but worth it.

"You don't think other guys are going to let us get away with that?" Jimmie asked.

"All right, what's stoppin' us?"

"They'll do their damndest, won't they?"

"So'll we do our damndest, won't we?"

"Don't forget Cosantino. Angelina was telling us about him."

"Oh, that little squire don't amount to nothing anyway."

"Well, he lost a good customer in Angelina."

"But he don't amount to anything, I tell ya."

"And he told her he was good and sore."

"Aw hell, I'm sore too."

"Have it your way then."

"Listen kid, let's hire a taxi and take a round trip and look over some places right now."

"It's too dark."

"It's not too dark. We won't want to inspect the plumbing or anything like that. Just look at places from the outside."

"Have you got the price of the taxi"

"I guess so."

"'Cause I haven't."

"All right, come on then."

Jimmie waited while Harry put on the heavy coonskin coat. He took a long time with the coat, then asked Jimmie to hold a sleeve. They put out the lights, went out and walked over to the corner and got a taxi. Harry told the man to drive up University Avenue slowly. They sat back in the car. "Some of the places should be just joints, and others swell places for a high-class trade," he said to Jimmie. They didn't have the money to make the plan a reality, but they drove along side streets in the western section of the city behind the Arcadia dance-hall and up through the good apartment-house district just west of the University, driving for an hour and a half. Afterward they stood under the street light in front of Harry's place and Jimmie talked about a Christmas present he was buying for Eva. It was three days before Christmas.

3

The night before Christmas he was lonely and drank wine with Anna in the apartment till she became so good-humoured she stretched out lazily on a sofa and was agreeable when he said he'd take a long walk by himself in the cold air. He put on his burburry coat and overshoes and walked along St. Clair for five car-stops, then took a car downtown.

He got off near the city hall. The store was just a few blocks away, but he walked west along Queen Street. A soft snow was lightly falling and he looked into stores, the snow falling lazily across windows, and remembered how, years ago, he had always felt there would be snow for Christmas. The city hall clock was striking; one, two, he counted, looking at foreign faces passing in the street, and counting clock strokes. He walked along Queen past the heavy iron fence, snow-capped, and the Law School grounds lonely and snow-covered. At the corner of York, he hesitated, confused and losing track of the strokes, and he turned, looking up at the clock. Ten o'clock. He walked down York — unlighted stores, second-hand shops, pawn shops, money lenders — his head down, following a single line of footprints in the snow. The footprints turned round the corner on Richmond, and he kept on, alone on the street.

Away from lights and hearing only heavy overshoes swishing in soft snow on the pavement he was more contented to be alone, but inside him was the old unsatisfied feeling and he was trying to walk away from it. "Why don't I go out and see Vera if I want to?" he thought, but the uncertainty the meeting suggested terrified him and he was sure it would be better to let the evening pass in the old way. He kept on walking south and crossed King Street, passing a policeman on the corner, a daub of white snow on the peak of his fur hat. He looked down the street, glad ro one was in sight, not wanting anyone to intrude on his loneliness, or hear even the sound of someone walking. He turned west on Wellington, the street dark in shadows of unlighted warehouses and no one in sight for blocks. He put his hands deep in his pockets, trying to see clearly in his own mind the life of the last few months, wondering vaguely at the cause of his separation from Vera, her image in his mind while he deliberately thought of other things — the store, Eva Lawson, Al Cosantino and all the conversations about him. The night he had met Cosantino in Angelina's, they had shaken hands and Cosantino had mildly asked how was business. He had grinned at Cosantino, shaking hands vigorously, but had felt that he was bigger than he, could never be touched by him, a small man with a wife and two children, a fruit store, many relatives, barrels of fruit, a fat father — all of it making him grin at Cosantino. They had talked a good deal about Cosantino, who was not as strong as O'Reilly but more important than Asche or Weinreb and making big deliveries all over the city. He had held Cosantino's hand and grinned at him, feeling he would have no trouble with him, a little Italian, nearly bald, rubbing the bald spot gently with the palm of his hand, a worried expression on his face.

He turned south on Simcoe Street remembering there was a bridge a few blocks away and that he could cross the railway tracks and go down to the Lakeside Drive. He walked faster, away from the city and down to the waterfront, telegraph posts, street lights, hydrants passing mechanically, unnoticed, the snow still falling and heavy underfoot. He came suddenly upon the bridge over the tracks, the surface snow unbroken by footprints, and walking slowly, his hands still in his pockets, he reached the centre of the bridge and stood by the rail, looking down the tracks to the engine yards. Clouds of vapoury smoke from engines floated in the dark valley underneath the bridge, and flashes of fire from furnaces streaked with light drifting smoke clouds. An engine shunted under the bridge and he was hidden in smoke. He closed his eyes, he opened them, the smoke had drifted eastward. Fire and smoke and engine wheels grinding on steel tracks in the yard in front of the city excited him and he gripped the railing, trying to look back at the city, but could see only a dark line of buildings. His hands tightened on the railing as he felt himself reaching beyond the line to lights and traffic and policemen on the corners, and dance halls and beer parties and Christmas trees and hundreds of men sitting up waiting for kids to go to sleep — hundreds of men willing to work for him when the time came: politicians, ward heelers, cops, gunmen, businessmen, Andy Collins, alderman in Ward Three, his good friend, and two thousand dollars could always assure his re-election. Andy Collins with his big body, heavy face and thick drooping moustache. Lawyer guys like Regan protecting him, three or four students worrying over cases. His hand dropped from the rail. He kept on looking at the city, his skin warm and tingling, and he glowed with a splendid self-satisfied feeling. In a year or two he could become the biggest exporter in the country, shipping liquor across the border — launches on the river, men on the railways — and in the meantime he was cleaning up thousands of dollars in the city.

He hurried across the bridge, anxious to get down to the lakefront and walk east, so he could face the city, looking up long streets and at electric signs on the skyline.

Another train passed, and watching it moving westward he suddenly thought of jumping a boxcar and going as far west as Sunnyside, then walking up to the street not far from the lake and seeing Vera. He stood still, looking at the train gathering speed. He knew he wouldn't try and jump a boxcar. He turned away from the bridge and the cloud of white smoke from the engine, walking on uneven ground frozen under the snow.

He walked along the drive and in the shadow of the new white warehouse on the waterfront he was muttering mechanically, "Christmas cheer, Christmas cheer," and becoming aware of it he realized he was no longer enjoying the walk. At the temporary wooden bridge below Bay Street, he turned, as he had intended, looking over the bridge up the city streets but got none of the satisfaction he had expected. All of it had passed away, the good feeling was gone. Lights were there, noises, streetcars moving, but he was uncomfortable, definitely unhappy and anxious to get home. Taking long strides he hurried across the bridge.

A taxi driver, looking for customers, leaned out from his cab, moving alongside the curb. Harry called him, gave him Vera's address, and got in clumsily, confused in what he was doing. He sat back in the cab, looking at the man's thick neck. The cab was going too slowly; he leaned forward and said, "Faster, man, faster," then leaned back, taking off his hat and wiping his head, rather bewildered, for his hands were trembling and his forehead feverish. His fingers groped in his pocket for cigarettes. As the cab went further west, he looked out of the window, passing familiar corners, till he realized he was close to the house. He threw the cigarette out of the window and, pounding on the grating, he yelled: "Let me out here. Let me out." The taxi stopped suddenly. He got out and paid the man, who looked at him suspiciously.

He stood there, watching the cab turning, hesitating to move till he was sure of being unobserved. He took a few steps along the street, looking around carefully, observing only big flakes of snow drifting across the street lamp and carried diagonally on a light breeze. A man came down the street, a basket on each arm, and alarmed, he realized he might be recognized, so he crossed to the other side of the street, moving out of the light. He put his hands in his pockets, his chin dipped down in his turned-up coat collar, and walked slowly down the street to the house, without an idea of what to do when he got there. He dallied guardedly with the notion of going upstairs to talk with her casually, but when directly opposite the house he decided not to go in at once, not until he had tried to see her shadow on the window blinds. Her shadow moving on the window shade. Standing opposite the house, he saw no light downstairs (the Farrels were out) and no light in the front room upstairs, though Vera would probably be back in the kitchen anyway. He shivered nervously. "I'll go in and see her," he muttered, though he walked carefully along the side entrance to get to the back of the house. His toe stumbled against a picket in the walk, covered by a thin layer of soft snow, and in the backyard he tripped on the clothes prop leaning against the fence.

A few feet from the rear of the house he stopped, looking up quickly, but there was no light in the upstairs windows. He took four quick steps further away from the house and looked again, then hurried back along the alley-way, for there might be a reflection of light from a window on the wall of the opposite house. He stood still, then learned against the wall, for it had never occurred to him she would be out, and it was ridiculous that there shouldn't be light in the apartment. He thought of a solution that, at the moment, was entirely reasonable. When he had been at the front of the house, she was probably in a back room, and just moving to another part of the house, after turning off the light, as he walked in the alleyway. He hurried along the picket walk, confident of seeing a light in the front room upstairs. There was no light. Crossing the road, he leaned against the lamppost, staring up at the front room.

Suddenly he was angry at Vera. She ought to be moving around in the front room, her shadow on the window shade, and she might just as well be irritating him deliberately.

Someone was watching him, he knew, and turning, he saw a woman on a veranda, her arms folded, looking directly at him, a suspicious character prowling around the neighbourhood. He grew afraid she might recognize him, and feeling guilty, and even detected, he hurried up the street to the corner and stood in the entrance to a grocery store that had just closed. He was waiting for a streetcar, he thought, but one passed by and he kept looking down the street to the corner where the car lines intersected. A second streetcar passed and he didn't even pretend he was anxious to get it. He said: "I'll wait three cars more and if she doesn't come along the street, I'll go home."

A girl on the street, walking gracefully, aroused him, and hesitating a moment, he hurried toward her, then wondered how he could make such a mistake. She didn't really walk like Vera, who carried her neat body so perfectly. Years ago, the first time he danced with her, his hand on her back, he had felt the gently curving groove of her spine and splendid firmness of her back. He wanted very much to see her come along the street.

He walked to the corner, then back and forth. He walked slowly, his feet getting wet in the soft snow. He took off his hat, his gloved finger scraping thick snow from the brim. His feet were very cold. He had no energy, and he looked down the street a last time, taking a deep breath, his face wet from melting snow. He got a streetcar. Not many people on the car. "What a hell of a Christmas Eve," he thought, leaning back on the wooden seat, and angry because not many people were on the car. He wondered why a vague thought of his mother made him feel better.

Anna was asleep when he got home. He went into the kitchen to get a glass of wine. He took off his shoes and his coat and collar. He sat down at the kitchen table, filling the glass again, regarding the bottle seriously. He filled the glass four times. It was good wine and he tilted back on the chair. After the fourth glass he was too lazy to get up and stretched slowly but finally got up. He went into Anna's bedroom. He sat down on the edge of the bed and it creaked. He made the spring creak again, thinking of Isaac Pimblett and the walk they had taken on a Sunday night, months ago. "Old Isaac was right," he muttered, peering at Anna's face, turned away from him on the pillow, eyes closed. "Here I am, getting into bed." He had left Vera and was simply getting into bed with someone else.

He got up and went into his room. He undressed quickly and got into bed. He was drowsy and fell asleep quickly.

Christmas Day was pleasant, not too cold, and they had a good time exchanging gifts. In the afternoon Jimmie and Eva Lawson called and they exchanged more gifts. In the evening they went downtown to a hotel and had a big dinner.

4

For two weeks Jimmie and Sam Martin watched Cosantino. They found out how many trucks he had on the road, and where he made his biggest deliveries, and how many men were usually on a truck. Cosantino had good trucks in four garages in different sections of the city. He was called a fruit importer and had a fruit store in the city run by his father and mother. In the daytime these trucks made deliveries all over the city to regular customers mainly on streets in the centre of the city.

Once a week in the evening three trucks went along the highroad to Hamilton.

In three days Harry had rented eight houses in downtown sections because respectable people and university fellows liked to do their drinking away from home. For the houses he got good men who knew they would be well-paid, if forced to do a stretch in jail. He picked out men with wives and children so they would be more reliable, and promised to pay at the end of every week. It took three hundred dollars to pay a month's rent on eight houses. The salary list was increasing.

They had to make money quickly. Their own truck was making small but regular deliveries, and some customers were behind in payment. They had just enough money to pay store rent and wages for two weeks. Thinking of money worried Harry and he was restless because the houses weren't ready to be used for storing liquor. He hadn't sent any money to Vera for two weeks and was irritable because Jimmie was so happy in the store, talking and laughing with Eva Lawson. Even if the houses were successful there wouldn't be any money for at least a few weeks. But Anna was good company and loaned him three hundred dollars, all she had in the bank. It really belonged to her husband, she said.

On a Thursday evening he was eating with Jimmie and when they had finished he said: "Well, we get Cosantino's trucks tonight."

"I wish like hell I was going with you," Jimmie said.

"I wish you were too, only you got to be on deck in the city here and me and boys'll be enough."

They talked it over on the way home from the restaurant. The January thaw had melted the snow and the streets were slushy.

At half-past eleven it was cold out. The slush on the street had frozen. Snow was falling lightly. Harry, Sam Martin, Eddie Thomas and Joe Atkins drove out to the highway and across the river, where there were hardly any houses, back a little from the road. Lights from a suburb were a few miles ahead across fields in the big curve of the highway and, looking back, they could see a line of city lights curving around the margin of the lake.

It was hard driving in the icy ruts. They drove the last mile without talking. Harry, sitting in the back seat, looked straight ahead, following the glare of the headlights, avoiding thoughts of anything but a suitable place for parking the car. The highway curved by a clump of trees, and they drove the car at the snow bank and into the shadow of the trees, and got out of the car and Joe Atkins switched off the lights. Sam, Eddie and Joe got the sawed-off shotguns from under the back seat, and Joe went back to the road and stood there looking toward the city. But there were no lights on the highway and the snow was falling heavily.

Joe waved his arm when he saw lights coming along the highway, and the others got out of the car again and Joe went further down the road. They knew it was a truck because it sounded heavy on the road and the engine was powerful. Joe came back and said: "I'm sure it's them, all right."

"Are we all set?" Harry said, and the truck came around the bend.

The truck stopped when three men stepped out with the sawed-off shotguns. Harry stood a few feet back from the road. The boys didn't have to use the guns. Three men got out of the truck and stood in the middle of the road. They were Italians and stood there without speaking.

"Tie the wops up, Eddie," Harry said, "and lean them over there by the tree."

Eddie went back to the car and got some rope. He tied them up quickly, their hands and feet, and they sat down on the road. Eddie and Sam dragged them over to the tree and gagged them. Atkins got in the truck and had a hard time turning it around in the snow. Harry talked to him and then watched the tail light of the truck going toward the city.

They waited for Cosantino's second truck. The air got colder and a sharp wind from the lake blew across the field. They sat in the car, huddled together, talking quietly. Harry talked casually and good-naturedly to the boys. They were close together in the car.

An hour later they had more trouble with the second truck. Sam and Eddie stood in the road, but the truck didn't stop and they exchanged gunfire. Joe fired from the side of the road. The truck stopped twenty paces further along. A man jumped from the passenger's seat and ran across the field, twisting and dodging. They ran up to the truck. The driver had been hit in the arm. They had no trouble tying him up. Harry was glad the man had been hit because Sam had also been hit in the hand, not a bad wound, but Sam was swearing softly. They carried the man who had driven the truck over to the tree and leaned him against the trunk with the other two.

Then Eddie got the truck's engine going and, turning around, went back toward the city. Disappointed, Harry watched the truck until it was out of sight. No use waiting for another truck. He tied a handkerchief on Sam's hand and they went over to the car near the trees. They finally got the engine going, but the wheels spun in the snow and wouldn't grip till Harry got out and pushed. He got into the car again.

Sam watched him tugging at the wheel and said: "What are we going to do about the guys under the tree?"

"Let 'em stay there."

"But Jesus, boss, it's cold, they'll freeze."

"What the hell do you care, you won't freeze."

"Yeah, but one guy's hit in the arm."

"Well, you got hit on the hand."

"All right. You know I don't care. I don't give a damn what happens to them."

"Oh, they'll get loose in a few minutes anyway."

They drove back to the city. Once off the highway and on the lighted streets Harry was more contented. The two trucks were heavily loaded. It was over and he let himself think about it. Things could move forward. He drove faster, turning north near Exhibition Park and along Queen, heading for University

Avenue. He was sure a truck would be parked near the corner of Winslow Street. No one could interfere. It had been hard getting police protection. In a week's time they had only four policemen from the beats. These policemen had been useful in getting others who were easier because not many of them wanted to miss anything.

5

At home he took off his shoes, walking in his stockinged feet. He didn't want to awaken Anna. He was tired, and went to sleep quickly.

In the morning he took a cold bath before Anna was up. He pulled on his underwear slowly, then sat down on the bed, arms linked behind his head, and stretched out comfortably. Rays of morning sun fell across his face and he blinked, rubbing his eyes. He scratched his head with both hands. He closed his eyes so he could feel the sun without blinking, lazy and comfortable. Uneasily he remembered how he had always been eager to tell Vera anything that had increased his opinion of his own strength. Often he had thought there would be no fun in doing anything if he couldn't go home and tell her about it, while she listened attentively. For that reason, she insisted on reading all his letters, discussing them seriously even when they were dull and unimportant. Of course Anna was all right, too, and even more direct and simple. He puckered his forehead and sat up on his haunches, stroking the hair on his leg. "I wonder why I was so fond of Grace Leonard?" he thought. In the beginning Vera had said Grace was beautiful, and always, for him, she would be a lovely woman, though he preferred merely to remember her rather than actually meet her again. But her legs weren't nearly as good as Vera's so she wore her skirts too long.

Vera had encouraged him to be friendly with Grace. The three of them were often together and at such times he was happy and very nice to Vera. They went to shows together and danced at the island across the bay. They were over at the island one night, sitting on a bench near the lagoon and there was moonlight and dew on the grass. He had one arm around Vera but, out of the corner of his eye, saw in the half-light and shadow the lines of Grace's face. And then, walking down to the boat, Vera gaily ran on ahead over the damp grass and Grace told him she was going to Virginia the following Monday, and that she hoped he would enjoy himself with the Julie Roberts woman he had mentioned to her. She spoke maliciously. He wondered why he had ever mentioned Julie to her. They walked slowly down to the boat, the three of them arm in arm, and he thought he was very much in love with Grace. She had gone away the following Monday.

In the two women, Grace and Julie Roberts, he had found something to take the place of an old feeling for Vera, and when Grace went away he was miserable for three days. She had reminded him of Vera as she seemed in the early days, only prettier, and he could never think of Julie in the same way. Grace was simply a beautiful thought for him, and so he imagined, in her, all the sympathetic qualities that might have made him happy. She was a part of a background for all his emotional experience, a memory that assisted him in his lovemaking with the big woman, Julie Roberts, and in his practical life with Vera.

He shook his head. The sun felt too hot on his face. Always he got back to Vera. He had left her, and was going further and further away so that now he was without passion for her and was anxious for new experiences in strange places. There was a world where he could be alone in his own life, but now she had become a strong thought, a magnet, and all his new thoughts returned finally to her. He was irritated and got up quickly to finish dressing.

Anna was still sleeping when he left the house to go downtown. On the street he was self-conscious, as though people were turning, looking at him. He had to prevent himself from half turning and glancing out of the corner of his eye at many people.

All afternoon he was uneasy, though he talked and laughed a lot with Jimmie over taking the trucks last night. He didn't say that he had become nervous, and worked for an hour in the office.

At four in the afternoon he went over to the department store to loaf away the hour before supper. He went into the store because many people were there, and he was determined to get rid of the notion of people watching him, and besides he liked the big store in the afternoon, at the magazine counter and in the perfume department. He looked directly at girls behind the perfume counters. He had always been convinced that girls at perfume counters were more apt to be loose and voluptuous than any other girls — the perfume probably did it.

He had a good time in the store. So many people seemed unaware of him that he became more confident and lazily good-humoured, smiling at all the girls who would look at him. A big blond girl in the perfume department was eager to be friendly and he walked down her aisle twice, enjoying himself.

He went back to the office and phoned Anna to say he wouldn't be home because there was a hockey game. Jimmie was taking Eva out to dinner, so he ate by himself.

After supper he had an hour before the hockey game, so at the newsstand on the corner, where he had established himself as a customer, he bought some papers, read the magazines and saw a mystery story, "The Gaunt Stranger" by Edgar Wallace. He had read all the good mysteries that Eva had picked out for him, but the cover on this one looked so interesting he bought it and hurried back to the store. In the office he took off his coat and vest, scratched himself under the right armpit, slipped his suspenders over his shoulders, lit a cigarette, then taking the book by Edgar Wallace, he made himself comfortable. Breathing easily, he read: ". . . it is impossible not to be thrilled by Edgar Wallace, and Premier Baldwin, who has the affairs of an Empire on which the sun never sets at his fingertips, was seen purchasing two copies of this author's book before getting on a train." Two copies of the one book, or two books by Edgar Wallace? he reflected, looking around for some place to throw his cigarette. He dropped it on the floor and put his foot on it. Who cares, he thought: somebody had said Winston Churchill, too, liked Edgar Wallace. Important English politicians, and someday possibly his own picture on the cover of one of these books!

Now he was seriously interested in the book, following "The Creeper" in London fog, a finger pushing his soft collar down from his Adam's apple. In the contact of finger against neck, he discovered a hangnail on his right index finger, and though his thoughts remained entirely with the story, he tried to seize with his teeth the hangnail, which persistently eluded him until his mind wavered between it and the story. When

Vera would see him biting at his fingers she would pull his hand away from his lips. He didn't like the thought, but abandoned the finger which he held between his legs underneath the book.

The story was exciting and yet not as thrilling as one he had read two nights ago in bed, and he got up to wash his hands. The only time to read mystery stories is in bed, when there's a wind in the streets, and windows rattle and you listen for small sounds.

He put his coat on quickly so there would be time to walk over to the arena. Outside, his flesh tingled in the winter weather. He jerked his fur collar up to his ears. Standing under the street light, looking at a red traffic signal, he was vaguely aware of feeling fine; there was so much satisfaction in being alone.

He was a little late for the game, but had a reserved seat in the fourth row, in the centre of the arena. The usher preceded him down the aisle and his satisfaction increased because people were staring at his fur coat. To reach his seat he had to walk on some people's toes and brush closely against knees of good-looking girls, and even, he hoped, tickle their small faces, in passing with the fur of his coat. Finally seated and quite happy he looked at the ice, then at the rows of faces, the skin on his back tingling when he heard a great shouting, and took a deep breath before concentrating on the ice. Canadians, of Montreal, playing the local team. Canadians in flashy red sweaters, the best team in the world, and for no reason he jumped up and yelled, "Come on, Morenz" and the people around him yelled: "Sit down, you ham."

He yelled for the Canadians, their graceful skating and neat stick handling arousing him as they swept down the ice, three abreast, Morenz in the centre, taking the pass, hurdling the sticks of the defense to get the shot on goal; the local team, checking stubbornly, defending, attacking clumsily. He roared with the crowd, then they tied the score near the end of the first period.

The second period was livelier, and he slapped his gloved hands together and stamped his feet. The score was tied. Morenz, the Canadian centre player, skating recklessly, rushed, sidestepping, feinting with his body, split the local defense, but missed an open goal. He started at his own goal line, a marvellous dash, zigzagging up the ice, his face absolutely calm, hair flat on his head, held back by the fierce speed of the rush. Harry jumped up, yelling "Come on Morenz," and howled derisively when a local defense man bodychecked Morenz, swinging against him heavily, spinning him flat on the ice.

The referee swung his arm and the defense man skated off to the penalty box. It looked like a stiff but legitimate body-check, and the crowd, convinced the officials were discriminating against the local team, booed and yelled, and many newspapers were thrown down on the ice. Harry fumbled eagerly in his pockets, finding eight coppers, and standing up he yelled at the official, who smiled cheerfully while dodging newspapers and a few pop bottles, "Oh you lousy skunk," and threw the pennies down at him. The crowd around him liked it and cheered. Other people began to throw coppers at the referee. The coppers stuck on the ice and at first the officials, down on their knees, tried to dig them out of the ice, and the crowd laughed, but they couldn't pick them all up and the game was stopped while attendants cleared the ice. Two policemen walked out on the ice to quiet the crowd. The crowd yelled in unison, "Left right, left right, left right," while the policemen walked.

A hard-boiled little man, near Harry, grabbed hold of him by the arm and said: "Boy, how would you like to sock that sap of a referee? Did you ever see anything like him?"

"Brother, you said it."

"What I wants to know, mister," the little man continued, "is how much d'egg has on de Canadians?"

"Yeah, he's got his shirt on them," Harry said, standing up suddenly and letting out a long, loud, "Boo-oo-oo-oo." "Listen, Mac," he said confidentially to the little man, "another thing I want to ask, is did that guy out there stop the punishment they were handing out to Morenz in the first period?"

"Morenz, huh?"

"Sure, Morenz."

"Canadians, huh?"

"Sure, Morenz."

"For the love of Mike, sure they're handing him punishment, making him like it. I hope they kill the bastard. What's the matter with birds like youse, don't you want your own boys to win? You might as well be refereeing this game, brother." He stood and yelled: 'Kill Morenz."

"Lay down, you smell," Harry said.

"Say, Mac. Me smell, eh? Who the hell do you think you are, a performer? I was playing this game when you were so high, see."

They were playing the game again, but three of the home team were in the penalty box and the Canadians quickly scored two goals. The crowd booed mournfully. For Harry, the figures in coloured sweaters on the ice were now simply arranging themselves into a series of patterns and he was thinking of the little man saying he had played the game years ago. Harry remembered playing in the high-school league. He had been a good stick handler, though a rather clumsy skater, and was always getting hurt. Over his left eye he rubbed his fingers, feeling the slight indentation that remained from stitches that had been necessary one afternoon after a high-school game. Three fellows had pulled him on a toboggan to the doctor, then pulled him home and lifted him onto the kitchen table. He remembered how glad he had been that his mother was out that afternoon. The doctor had stitched the wound over his eye and taken him up to bed. When his mother came home, he was asleep, his head bandaged. He heard her crying and she was kissing him, and the doctor was assuring her his sight wouldn't be affected. The worst part of it all had been lying on the toboggan, the fellows pulling him home, in his mind a picture of his mother's misery when she should see the hasty bandages over the eye. And she hadn't been home. Sweat was on his forehead now, for he had been drawn back into that afternoon and suddenly had the feeling he should get up, leave the arena, and go home and see his mother. Leaning back, he was only pretending to watch coloured sweaters moving on ice. Really he was experiencing the uneasy restiveness that had been bothering him whenever he thought of his mother. Thinking of her he was happy but nervous, then a little sad and eager to do something that always eluded him when he thought too hard about it.

People on the seats behind him shouted angrily as he got up slowly and moved along, banging against girls' knees, but not noticing it this time. "Sit down there, you sap in the coat," they shouted. He hardly heard them. The game was no longer interesting. He preferred his own thoughts.

Outside on the street he walked south, intending to go down to Childs on King Street and have something to eat, for in his present mood he definitely didn't want to go home to Anna. He was sad, a few flakes of snow were falling lazily, drifting under the street lights. The air, no longer damp, was brisk. He walked on, becoming disappointed, for he couldn't think clearly of his mother, other thoughts — of the game and the little man who had spoken to him — coming into his head, till he finally got a clear picture of her again, and the lonely feeling was agreeable to him. He walked slowly, indifferently, old memories comforting him. In a way he was happier than he had been in a long time. He muttered to himself, crossing the road, that he ought to be able to do something about it, then was angry with himself for breaking the flow of his thoughts.

He went down to Childs, where young people and some good-looking actresses go after the shows, and ordered a plate of kidney beans. He looked around, heard many voices and laughter and realized he was entirely satisfied to be alone. "It's funny the way I'm getting to like being alone," he thought.

6

Late in March when the snow had gone from the streets and the river had overflowed the Don Flats and the lumberyards and gravel below the first bridge, the body of Joe Atkins, the legs tied and caught on the branch of a tree, was found by two boys. He had disappeared early in March when the snow was on the ground. The truck he had been driving and two men with him had disappeared. He had been driving the truck out west at eleven o'clock in the evening.

Sitting in the office in the early afternoon, checking up the payroll, Harry tried to forget Joe and yesterday's funeral and the long talk with Mrs. Atkins. It had been a poor funeral. He looked at the payroll, counting, multiplying, making mistakes. Words he had said to Jimmie were still in his mind, words for Cosantino running through his thoughts. He didn't want so many words to come easily to him. Later on he would think of Cosantino, but now, in his mind was the monotony of newspaper facts, insistent and simple, forcing his attention.

The late Joseph Atkins was survived by a wife, two children and a sister. Hearing the dreadful news that followed closely upon a previous communication filled with a detailed account of happy enjoyment, the sister wasted no time in useless lamentations. She instinctively knew her duty and followed it out willingly and with dispatch. She had the grief-stricken wife and children brought to her home where Mrs. Atkins, with extraordinary fortitude, recovered her composure sufficiently to be interviewed. Mrs. Atkins declared that her husband had no enemies. He didn't belong to any lodges, though at one time he had been a member of the Episcopalian Church. The wounds in the back of the head of the murdered man, and the fact that his feet had been tied, led the police to suspect a deliberate killing with bootleg vengeance as a possible motive. The theory of the police was that he had been taken to the bridge in a car and tossed into the water. This was the third killing of a similar character in the last three months. If her husband had been a lawless man, there was no suggestion of it in the face of Mrs. Atkins, or in the eyes of the little children, for the gray-haired mother had wept when she told how her husband had come back from the war. The two children, little girls, Alice, aged eight, and Pansy, nine, held on to their mother's skirt and cried.

Harry rubbed his hands through his hair. The figures on the page bothered him, and he had read the newspapers too much. He looked steadily at the page and by concentrating he avoided all thoughts of Joe. He scanned the column of names closely, for he had been writing many checks for fellows operating the houses. "There are too damned many cops on this list," he thought. Thousands of dollars a month for cops and lawyers. Still, they were doing well, with twenty houses in the city, and they were supplying many independent bootleggers, the thought of it giving him a fine feeling. He tilted back in his chair. Fifteen powerful trucks, the best on the market, and yet it was hard to supply the customers' demand for liquor. About once a week they took one of Cosantino's trucks. He grinned, thinking of Cosantino, then was nervous at the thought that came into his head — something he had been avoiding for hours.

Through the office doorway he saw Eva Lawson in a black silk smock, waiting on a customer. Again he rubbed his hand through his hair, patting the top of his head. Then he hitched up his trousers further above the knees, so the creases would not be spoiled. Nothing in the world like a first-class suit, and the ones he had at home, fifteen good ones, had lots of class. He always enjoyed thinking of buying a new suit. He turned and looked out of the window to the lane leading to the stage door of the Olympia Burlesque. It was about half-past one in the afternoon, the show started at two-fifteen, and he watched girls walking along to the stage door. Some girls had much nicer legs than others. Most of the girls wore funny-looking shoes but he liked the way chorus girls walked, their thin dresses clinging to their shapes, their backs arched, walking defiantly, proud of their silk-stockinged legs, even the hard-boiled ones walking independently. The muscles at the back of the leg were too highly developed on some of the girls. He wondered what Anna would look like walking down the lane. He imagined Vera stepping along with some of the girls. He got the old uneasy feeling and tightness inside him thinking of Vera. He stared out of the window, though now there was no one in the lane.

Jimmie opened the door. Jimmie was putting on weight. He had a small paunch. His face was much fatter. He sat down on the edge of the desk. "What's worrying you, the poison ivies in the lane?" he asked.

"You're getting fat, Jimmie. I just noticed it, you're getting fat."

"Me fat? Fat! Just normal, and eating like a gentleman."

"You're getting fat anyway."

"All right, I'm getting fat, but you're a sad-looking guy."

"I've been thinking too much about Joe."

"Joe? Why, we talked about it last night until we were blue in the face."

"I know."

"Now let Cosantino worry about it. Listen, Harry. I'll bet a dollar you're sitting there mooning about Vera."

"Who the hell said I was thinking about Vera?"

"I shudder to think of it, but I did."

"The wise guy, eh?"

"You're not sore are you?"

"No, I'm not getting sore, you're just a wise guy, that's all."

"You're rather bright yourself, you know."

"Yeah, only you know things, you've been there."

"Ah shut up. I don't care what's bothering you, only try and get some manners."

"Manners, eh?"

"Sure, manners, and while you're at it, come down to earth and try and be civilized."

"Oh, don't bother me, you never have anything to say."

"No?"

"Listen, when are you going to cut this out?"

"Sure, I'll cut it out, I just asked what was wrong with you."

"There's nothing wrong, Jimmie, only it's hard to get used to being away from a person you've been with a couple of years. See? Off and on it gets your goat and you feel punk."

Jimmie sat down and crossed his legs. Harry grinned at him, offering a cigarette. Jimmie took the cigarette.

"Well, I may be dumb but I can't see what it's all about," Jimmie said finally.

"What's what all about?"

"I mean, why on earth did you leave Vera then? What got into you?"

"Nothing got into me, I tellya. We were getting on each other's nerves."

He listened to Jimmie talking and tried to place definitely in his mind the particular quarrel that had been the cause of separation. Old words he half-remembered, but the unpleasant words seemed unimportant. He couldn't think of them for any long time, and his thoughts drifted till he was talking to her, the unimportant little details of their life together pleasing him, and though trying to justify leaving her, he found himself holding on to thoughts of happy moments they had both enjoyed. Jimmie was talking but he didn't hear him, half-remembering the way he had balanced Vera on the tracks walking up the railway ties in the summer, before going down the ravine.

"I don't want to waste any more time thinking of Vera," he said.

"That's the stuff. If you want Vera, go and get her. If you don't, then stop thinking about her. See?"

"I see all right."

"Only it don't mean a thing to you."

"Not a damned thing."

"Suit yourself," Jimmie said, offended. "Don't mind me. Go to hell if you want to, it's none of my business."

"Don't get sore, Jimmie. No use getting sore."

"I'm not interested, let alone sore."

"Aw, be a good guy, Jimmie. I mean I want you to do something for me. Go around and see her, willya, just to get a line on things? Not that I want to see her again, but if I'm happy thinking about her, then I ought to go on thinking about her. It don't do me any harm."

"Why not go and see her yourself?"

"It can't be done. Jimmie, you know it can't be done."

"Sure it can. Shoot her a line. Tell her you've become a first-class shoe salesman.'

"Stop kidding, Jimmie. Later on but not now."

Jimmie tilted his hat over his eyes. Harry couldn't see his eyes.

"If she wouldn't stick with me, whatever I was doing, she could go to the devil," Jimmie said quietly.

Harry was unhappy. He wished Jimmie wouldn't tilt his hat over his eyes. He heard Eva talking to a customer, chatting gaily.

"That's all right, Jimmie, only this is a little different." Really it wasn't different, he thought, but from another viewpoint was probably different absolutely.

"Do you want me to go and see her, Harry?"

"Maybe you'd better not," he said thoughtfully.

"All right, I won't then."

"No, you'd better not."

Eva came into the office, the same height as Vera, same shape, too. She said: "Did you tell Harry about your friend in here this morning?"

"No, I forgot," Jimmie said.

"Who, Jim?"

"Guess who, Stan Farrel."

"Farrel, eh?"

"Farrel himself."

"What did he have to say?"

"Nothing, as usual. I let him think I was buying a book here," Jimmie said. "He enjoyed me immensely."

"Did he buy anything?"

"Oh no," Eva said, "but some other day . . . "

"Stan himself," Jimmie said, "just as bright and breezy as life itself. Says he saw you on the street one day and mentioned it to Vera, but she insisted you were travelling."

Eva went out. Harry grinned at Jimmie, who was looking at him thoughtfully. "I don't want to meet Farrel," he said.

"Oh, forget that guy. Come on out. I've got to go over to the bank."

They went out to the street and over to the bank. It was winter weather but the air was fine, and wet pavements near open doorways were steaming. Their coats swung open. A great day for a long walk. The sun was bright and many people were on the streets for afternoon shopping. Girls with pretty legs walked with open fur coats showing short bright skirts and a flash of round silken knees. They crossed the road and a man waved at them. He stood in the United Cigar store entrance, lighting a cigarette.

"Holy smoke, there's old Harris, the guy we met with Bob that night at Angelina's."

"Poor old Harris, he's looking bad. I haven't seen him since."

They waved at him and shook hands on the corner.

"You boys are looking fine," he said, wheezing.

"How's the real estate business, Mr. Harris?"

"Bad, very bad, off and on as it were."

Mr. Harris was trying to talk without moving his lips. He smiled. His upper teeth were missing.

"Lord man, who borrowed your teeth?" Jimmie said.

"If someone borrowed them I'd be able to ask for them," he said sadly.

He explained he had lost them somewhere last night. With his old friend Bob he had been drinking at a woman's place and he had taken out his teeth. He only took them out when he felt himself getting a little stupid from drinking a good deal. He had been unable to find them. He couldn't go home to his wife because she would know he had been drinking heavily if he appeared without his teeth, and two weeks ago he had sworn never to touch a drop again, so he hadn't been home all night. At the moment he was going over to Bob's office to find out if Bob knew anything of the teeth.

"What's happening to Bob?" Harry asked.

"He's done, I think," Mr. Harris said. "He's going away."

"Last I heard of he was straightening up. Living with his wife and so on."

"So he is. He did it for a month. Now his wife's trying to look after the office. She can never find him."

"It's a damn shame. He was a good sort."

"He is. I think he's giving up law and going to New York to sell bonds for somebody."

"Oh well, wish him luck."

They hoped he would find his teeth and he left them.

The bank was on the corner opposite the city hall. Jimmie made out a deposit slip while Harry leaned against the marble table. Chinese were lining up at the teller's cage, the bank having most of the Chinese trade in the city. The manager came over to the counter, feeling friendly and respectful, and asked them to sit down in the office and have a cigar. They were good customers and Harry was impressive in the coon-skin coat. Sitting in the office the manager politely stood for a good deal of kidding from Jimmie, then told some jokes rather pompously. Some of the manager's jokes were fair but most of them poor.

Outside the bank Jimmie said: "Let's go down to Childs. Some of the newspaper boys may be there and we'll talk. Chuck Taylor and Bill Rose usually have some coffee about this time."

They went down Bay, passing people standing on a corner watching excavation work for a new skyscraper. The long-necked crane swung the shovel in a wide arc, then dipping down, the jaws gripping earth. The engine at the base rattled, the long arm stationary, then lifting slowly swinging wide, emptying the jaws. Heads moved, following the swing of the shovel.

They crossed Adelaide Street. The Metropolitan Building stood up over smaller buildings grouped around it, the squat tower dark, the sun striking the west wall, tan colouring the bricks, sunfire in the gleaming windows.

Chuck Taylor was in Childs at one of the tables telling a story to a laughing big man and the manager in a white uniform. He waved to Jimmie and Harry. They sat down at the table while Chuck went on with the story about leprechauns and his nine-year-old kid.

"The kid believes I can go along a road, and, whist! Change my coat for a pink one or a purple one, or I can squat in a field and become a pansy, or a butterfly with long quivering feelers. Beautiful, isn't it, Trotter?"

"I believe anything you say, Chuck."

The manager said, "Very good, Chuck, but did you hear this one," and he told a sly story, and they laughed while he walked away to the desk. The manager turned quickly, came back to the table and told another story. He was a good-natured manager. Harry liked talking to these fellows. Often they kidded him about bootlegging but in the same way they kidded boys in the bond business. He poured coffee from one of the funny little mugs, spilling it on the glass tabletop. The manager, bending over the table, said: "Watch the fellow out on the street looking in the window."

A man, poorly dressed and without an overcoat, was looking in the window.

"Watch me," the manager said.

He got up, walking a few steps toward the window, and stood still, looking at the man. The man without an overcoat became aware that the manager was looking at him and moved away guiltily.

The fellows at the table laughed, and the manager came back and said: "That big window's there for people to look in. There's a guilty feeling in nearly everybody. Nearly everybody looks in the window and runs away when they see me frowning at them. I play the trick a couple of times a week. They all hurry away."

For nearly an hour they sat at the table talking agreeably. Chuck Taylor conducted an ignorance contest in classical reading. The man who hadn't read the famous book got a point. "Have you read *Tom Jones*?" "Yes." "No." "No." "No." "How about *A Tale of Two Cities*?" "No." "Yes." "No." "Yes." And the questions and answers became monotonous to Harry, again the idea he had been avoiding all afternoon came back to him, exciting him till he shifted uneasily in the chair, gazing solemnly at Chuck Taylor. "Yes." "Yes." "Yes." "No," then a loud laugh gradually becoming irritating as he moistened his lips, grinning foolishly, thinking of Cosantino. "I'm all right," he thought. "I'll always be all right with these guys." Still there was the thought that he had withdrawn, become more alert, working on the outside. "I got to, I got to," he was saying to himself, and when they laughed and answered "Yes," "No," he felt it was in the same swing. "I got to, I got to." Suddenly he was eager to beat Cosantino with his fists, swinging, hooking, pounding, but became depressed, knowing he was trying to get away from the important thought. "It's settled, settled," he repeated to himself.

"Snap out of it, Harry," Jimmie said.

"You're right, Trotter, it's getting tiresome, and I've got some work to do, let's go," Chuck Taylor said.

"I was only thinking," Harry said.

"Some other day then."

He walked up as far as the store with Jimmie, who said he was going to take Eva home. Harry didn't go to the store but walked over to York Street and got his car out of the garage, one of those buildings six stories high, and he coasted down alternate grades to the street.

<h1 style="text-align:center">7</h1>

He drove up to the apartment on St. Clair, the blue car moving smoothly along residential streets. He avoided streets with heavy traffic, not wishing to force a genial smile of recognition for policemen on corners who knew him, and followed the crescent around Queen's Park — snow and ice at the base of the red stone parliament buildings, trees bare, lights in the windows of Hart House. The snow had gone in patches from the level park ground but was still banked along the curb. Out of the park he drove up Avenue Road. The street lights, coming on, curved up the slope and dipped down, then stretched out on a level run.

He was hungry. The meal would be good, and afterward he might go to a show with Anna — all the same to her unless she had a pain from overeating.

When he got home she was stretched out on a sofa in the front room, dressed nicely, her knees hunched up, the line of her long leg accentuated by silk stockings all the way up to the thigh. She enjoyed sprawling out, showing her legs. Alone in the house she hardly wore anything, no stockings or shoes, and only a slip loose on her full body. She waved to him when he came into the room.

"How's the big boy?" she said, yawning.

"How's the dinner?" he said, sitting beside her and pinching her leg till she squealed. She stretched out lazily and he wondered where she had been all afternoon. He didn't want to ask her, for she would laugh, trying to tease him, and even if someone had been petting her all afternoon, she wouldn't think it important enough to tell. Hardly interesting enough to tell. He had often wished she would try and conceal adventures, rather than pass them off as unimportant. He pinched her again and she giggled, kicking, and he held on to her long leg, loosening the garter. She lay there while he kissed her knee and then she suddenly tickled him and he straightened up, laughing. He felt himself getting excited, wanting to take hold of her tightly so she would never be interested in anybody's lovemaking, pin her down definitely so she would understand she belonged to him, but he was aware that he would leave something untouched, something he was unable to take away from her that prevented him from exhausting her.

They got up and went into the dining room. Watching her sitting across from him, he smiled turning away casually, a thought making him feel sore. "She makes me think she belongs to any guy that's ready for her." It was the way she let herself go that excited him and the feverish thought that she could smile while he offered all his energy. She was big-bodied, but had no intensity, no thin-lipped intensity nervously eager, and he thanked God for that.

The maid, not very good-looking, brought in soup, and for a few minutes they had a careless conversation about the Chinese cook who was satisfactory.

Then he said: "Want to go to a show, Anna?"

"Sure, if there's anything worth seeing?"

"How about *Blossom Time* at the Royal? I can get tickets if you want to, or if you'd rather we'll drag out some wine and sit around for the evening, eh?"

"I'll have both, thanks."

"How come?"

"Let's go to a show first and come back and sit around afterward."

"All right."

"A lovely evening, eh?"

He enjoyed each single dish and was disappointed when he felt his hunger leaving him. He liked being hungry. He was glad Anna had such a fine appetite. He hated people who fasted, or tried diets, or counted calories. Sitting at the table with Anna he was happy. He was unhappy only when he thought too much about her.

"How'd things go today, Harry?" she said.

"Nothing much to talk about, nothin' stirrin'."

"Weren't you thinking of seeing Cosantino?"

"No, who said I was going to see Cosantino?"

"I thought you said so yesterday."

"I didn't. I didn't say anything of the kind. You know I didn't."

"Well for heaven's sake, don't get sore about it."

"I'm not sore, I tell you." He was furiously indignant.

"I just meant, why should you take anything from that wop."

"You don't see me taking anything, do you? What did I say to the little bastard the last time I met him? I told him to lay off me while he had his health."

"And what did he say?"

"What did he say? Same as usual, the old bull, a lot of crap about having it all fixed with Weinreb and Asche to stick together."

"Hmmm."

"But that ain't the main thing."

"What's the main thing?"

He folded his napkin. He unfolded it, and crumpled it in his hand. "Joe Atkins has been worrying me."

"It's kind of late to worry about him, I think."

"It ain't him exactly, it's the idea really," he said slowly. He decided not to talk to Anna about Cosantino and the notion that had worried him all afternoon.

"We've lost a couple of trucks, all right," he said.

"That's terrible, Harry," she said.

"It's lousy all right."

She winked at him. "Spit in their beer, Harry old boy."

"There's only one thing stoppin' me."

"One thing stoppin' you?"

"Yeah, no, nothin's stoppin' me, not a thing in the world."

"Well, what are you going to do about it?"

"Nothing right now."

"Take it, eh?"

"The hell you say so."

"It's hell, I'll say so."

"Aw, forget it."

"Everybody gets used to taking it," she said, putting her plump elbows on the table.

"Stop kidding me, you sap. I won't be kidded, I tellya."

"Whoa, papa."

"I'll 'whoa papa' you."

"Be nice, Harry. Anna's only teasin'. Come let's get up and step out, eh, big boy, what do you say, big boy, come on, let's go."

"Well, lay off me, Anna, see, or I'll start rubbing your fur the wrong way."

"You mean you're really sore?"

"No," he said, thoughts going swiftly through his head. He wanted to have many thoughts, not one, not the one thought that was too important. Anna was sitting there smiling cheerfully, faithful to him, her thoughts faithful, only the woman part of her belonged to everybody on earth. It had been that way when he had first met her in that office of Farrel's. It would always be like that. Vera was entirely different. He shook his head and frowned.

"Through, honey?" she said.

"Yeah, I'm through."

He left her sitting in the front room while he changed his clothes for a dark suit, English woolens, the best fabric in town, the fashionable herringbone stripe complimented by a flashy bowtie with a fairly loose knot, and in the mirror he admired the cut of suit and flash of colour at his neck. Then he walked down the hall. Anna was not in the front room. She came along the hall and he helped her with her mink wrap. The maid was attentive to Anna, patting her gently on the shoulder, smiling, holding her hands together. It interested him the way the homely, masculine girl fussed over Anna, and the way Anna enjoyed having the girl in love with her.

"You look well," he said casually.

"You're a hot-looking baby yourself," she said, taking his arm.

They went out and she walked slowly up and down the front walk while he got the car out of the garage. She got in beside him, shivering a little. The air had turned colder, it was freezing, a fine snow swirling along the pavements. He turned the car around without speaking. It was warm in the car and she straightened up, glancing at him, aware that he was not, at the moment, interested in her, his face somber in shadows, his eyes staring at the windshield. She wanted to interest him.

"I saw Momma today," she said.

"Oh."

"Yeah, I did."

"That's nice."

"No, it wasn't nice, it was funny."

"What was funny about it?" he smiled slightly.

"You 'member me telling you about Ma being divorced?"

"Something, I remember about it, why?"

"You 'member she divorced Pa about three years ago, I said, to marry the guy she's living with now, the hardware salesman, you remember, don't you?"

"I getcha."

"Well, listen to this."

"Go on."

"Pa had been out of the city ever since Ma divorced him, and he came back the other day and went to see Ma and he made love to her, and now Ma's having a new love affair with him in the afternoons while her husband's out to work. What do you think of that?"

"Damn funny."

"It's funny all right, but it doesn't seem wrong to me, I mean there's nothing wrong with my Ma and Pa making love, is there?"

"No, I guess not, only where does the other guy, her husband, come in?"

"I don't know, but he ought to be able to see there's nothing wrong with Ma and Pa making love to each other, and think of the kick they probably get out of it."

He was interested and she was satisfied. They were nearly downtown. A wind was driving the thin snow against the windshield. Half a block away from the Royal they parked the car and walked over to the theatre, and in the foyer he got a good feeling, glad of his coon-skin coat and Anna's mink wrap.

Anna was enjoying *Blossom Time* but he was interested only occasionally. A plump round-faced man sang songs in a sweet voice and Harry liked it because the music helped him to think more clearly. He went to a great many shows because of thoughts that came to him in a theatre. He could close his eyes, listen to the music and think about tomorrow, the pictures in his mind remarkably clear. He tilted his head back, half-closed his eyes, seeing the lips of the round-faced man with the sweet voice, and thought of the two trucks that had been hijacked and the money lost. Then he thought of Cosantino and his eyes opened wide and he was alert, the one idea strong in his thoughts. He didn't answer Anna when she talked. He had lost all interest in the show.

On the way home, and later, sitting in the front room sipping wine and eating biscuits, he couldn't get interested in Anna, the wine, or good jokes. He talked and laughed and she sat on his knee, but his hands were clammy, and when he closed his eyes, kissing her, thoughts flew into his head, probing, eliminating difficulties, the situation directly under his eye, the fruit store, Cosantino, the car, Eddie driving the car. He held on to the kiss and his thoughts went beyond the point he had been avoiding all day. Pressing against Anna, he felt his head hot, he was sweating, but relieved, much more content. It was harder going after a man you knew, and thinking about it for a long time. It was much harder than shooting at someone you didn't even know. He made Anna get off his knee.

"I'm going to bed," he said.

"Heavens, Harry, what's the matter?"

"Nothing's the matter."

"Well, you're not very sociable."

"I know, I'm just tired. I've felt tired all day but this is the first time I've felt like lying down."

He slept alone. He had a good sleep.

8

The newspapers were carrying long stories about a bootleg war. Harry, sitting in the office, was reading a reporter's interview with O'Reilly. There was a picture of O'Reilly and he spoke sadly of unnecessary trouble between exporters, and couldn't understand why there was so much shooting. He himself had a wife and children and didn't want to be carried out on a slab someday because of greed getting the better of common sense. He talked in a straightforward manly way, hoping there would be no more trouble. A picture of Joe Atkins was on the same page. Harry looked at O'Reilly's picture, wondering why he had talked so much to the reporter. "What the hell has it got to do with O'Reilly?" he thought. He closed his eyes, rubbing the palms of his hands up and down his face, restive, but ready for Cosantino. He had become very practical, he imagined. He had been looking forward to this afternoon and now he was ready and waiting. It had become such a simple matter he was ashamed to think he had wasted so much time worrying over it. He looked at his watch. In an hour the business would be finished. In the meantime he simply had to wait for Jimmie and Eddie, then it would be so easy he'd get a big laugh out of it. He tried reading the sporting page but he lost track of words in the column and before he could find them again he was thinking of something else. He closed the paper and looked out through the open door to the store. Eva was bending over a table reading a book. He put his feet up on the desk, observing the shiny toe-caps. He heard the front door open. Jimmie spoke to Eva, then came into the office. Jimmie sat down without smiling.

"Well," he said.

"Well, there's a good story in the paper."

"I saw it."

"What do you make of it?"

"I don't know. The thing that bothers me is why did O'Reilly open up. Is he coming in on it?"

"That's just a lot of bull. He just thinks Cosantino is going to come out right side up. That's all."

"Are you going ahead this afternoon?"

"You bet."

"Listen, Harry, why not let Sam and Eddie do it?"

"Not on your life. It wouldn't be any good. If they didn't bring it off things would be all shot. I'm going along, Jimmie."

"There's no use talking about it then."

"No use at all, we've talked it back and forth enough haven't we?"

"Yes, I guess so."

Harry got up and walked the length of the room. "Sam ought to be here now," he said.

"In a few minutes."

"Listen Jimmie, if anything happens, remember how to straighten out things and fix up Vera. She'll be fixed for life anyway."

"I'll do it, only don't talk about it, let's not talk any more about it."

"All right Jimmie, there's no harm mentioning it, and if I were you and this thing didn't come out all right I'd beat it, cross the border, go to Europe, Paris, see?"

"Say, are you trying to give me a good time?"

Eddie came in. Harry slapped Jimmie on the back, put on a cloth coat and a felt hat and opened the door. He grinned at Eva. He didn't even look back at Jimmie. He got into the car beside Eddie, it moved forward slowly and he said: "It's about twenty after three, what time should we get there?"

"About twenty to four, I think," Eddie said.

He leaned back in the car. Eddie was driving slowly, out west and then north. "It's a swell day, a spring day almost," Harry thought. The snow was gone from the streets, and little kids playing follyta with marbles along the curb shouted loudly. He felt that his breathing was becoming uneven and he straightened up in the car, anxious to have only agreeable and placid thoughts but, unable to think of anything, he became too much aware of his own body, the little itch at the back of his head, the heavy feeling in his shoulder — so conscious of his own being that he felt alone in the car. He glanced at Eddie's profile. What were his thoughts? The car turned suddenly around a corner, he lurched against Eddie, the lurch startling him, and he was suddenly alert, for the first time aware of the hard object in his hip pocket pressing against him. The uneasy restive feeling was gone, his back stiffened, he was ready.

The car was going along residential streets, with old houses, in the district above the Arcadia dance hall. Then they passed Cosantino's store, an old-fashioned fruit store on a corner, fruit on stands on the sidewalk. Across the road was a three-storied vacant house, the windows boarded and nailed. On the other corner was a grocery store and to the left a garage and a lane. Two kids were playing catch in the lane, coaxing summer. Eddie turned the car around the corner for three blocks to the Catholic church and then came back slowly. A woman with a black shawl over her head came out of the store. They passed the corner again going a few blocks west before turning. Harry moved uneasily, rubbing his back against the seat. Cosantino might not come out of the store, he thought. He glanced angrily at Eddie, but they were at the corner and three men were coming out of the side door of the fruit store. Harry leaned forward, the breath whistling in his nostrils; he rubbed his left arm gently, then touched his head, and pulled down the peak of the cap he had put on. The car turned at the corner. One of the men coming out the side door was Cosantino, short and dark. The two men with him were taller and wore caps. Cosantino's overcoat was open, the white scarf flapping loosely over the blue coat. They were on the sidewalk. They were crossing the road. The car passed, moving slowly. Harry fired three times at Cosantino. Eddie fired twice. The car was moving very slowly. Cosantino and one of the men fell on the road. The other man with the cap stumbled, lurched to one side, and staggered across the road toward the lane. The car jerked forward, gaining speed. They didn't speak to each other. At the first corner Eddie spun the wheel, the car swung round, coming back along the street, the woman who had come out of the store screamed and ran, the car passed within a few feet of Cosantino who was sprawled in the middle of the road, his face down, one knee hunched up. The white scarf had got tangled around his neck. His hat had fallen off. The car passed over the hat and close to Cosantino and Harry fired two more shots into the body, and the car leaped forward, swinging around the corner. People running along the streets were yelling. A cop on a bicycle came along but they sped by him and he blew his whistle.

They turned north. "We got the wop," Harry said, "we got the wop." The blood seemed to be surging into his head. He heard the whistle again and laughed out loud. The car turned east, north, west, north, south, zigzagging down to the lakefront. In Exhibition Park Eddie got out of the car and changed the license plate. Harry got out of the car and helped him put up the car top. Then they took off their caps and put on felt hats. Harry grinned at Eddie when they were driving along the lakefront.

"That was a good job," he said.

"The best in the world," Eddie said.

They drove downtown. There seemed to be no noise in the city, everything quiet, and Harry couldn't even hear the car wheels moving on the road. He listened intently, waiting to hear the wheels, and heard a purring sound and felt better. Suddenly he thought of Cosantino standing bewildered on the road, then swaying drunkenly and spinning a little on his heel before going down. Cosantino on the road, his face against the pavement. He closed his eyes, opened them quickly, looking at Eddie. Eddie's fat face had a pleasant expression. Harry wiped his lips with his tongue, deliberately avoiding bad thoughts. He thought of something else, anything that had happened the night before.

The car stopped outside the bookstore. Jimmie came out on the sidewalk and grinned, waving his hand. Harry was suddenly glad to see Jimmie. He put his hand on his shoulder as though he hadn't seen him for a long time. He looked at him as if he hadn't really expected to see him, and had experienced all the disappointment, and then, accidentally, had encountered him again.

Eddie stayed in the car to drive it over to the garage. Jimmie and Harry went through the store to the office and sat down, and Harry told about him about it. He didn't use many words.

"It was going to be me or Cosantino," he said.

"You can bet your boots on that, anyway."

"I know I'm right."

9

The rest of the afternoon he was nervously alert but gradually became confident and sure of himself. Over an hour he sat in the office, expecting something to happen, then got up and walked into the store and talked casually with Eva. He began to talk pompously, turning his mouth down at the corner. He put his hands in his pockets, leaned against a table and grinned. He felt very impressive, and wanted to talk authoritatively to someone. He went back to the office to think of people he might talk to. Remembering Julie Roberts, he slammed the palm of his hand on the desk, for she would be astonished at his self-possession, while he suggested certain facts that would leave her with absolutely nothing to say. Augustus, her husband, was of no consequence, she could get rid of him for the evening. So he looked up the number in the phonebook, found they were living in Julie's cottage and phoned her, and she was first of all surprised, then polite, and finally quite eager to see him in the evening.

He drove up to Julie's house. She opened the door. Standing in the hall he was sore at himself for thinking momentarily of Augustus. Julie took hold of his hand and he sat down on the couch but he moved awkwardly, for he didn't have the old curiosity. He felt he was with a very big woman, wondering what to say easily, and she remained a very big woman. She smiled. Her face was pale, with the cheeks faintly rouged. Her face was round. Her lips moved. She said: "Why on earth haven't you come around before, Harry?"

"Oh, I thought you'd be all wrapped up in Augustus," he said playfully.

She sat down slowly, very heavily, the spring sagging, stretching, sinking, and she leaned heavily against him, her hand on his knee. "Start talking about yourself," she said.

"There's nothing much to say. Jimmie was asking for you the other day. You remember Jim?"

"Yes. I liked him. What are you thinking about so solemnly?"

"I'm not thinking about anything, Julie."

"You don't look happy."

"Honestly, I'm happy, happy. Sure, I'm the happiest guy in the world."

"Kiss me."

He kissed her, without putting his arm around her, then tried to talk rapidly because she was looking at him too eagerly. She got up, moved over to the desk, the size of her startling him, and sat down slowly. He watched her covering completely the seat and back of the chair. She bent over the desk, a curious rigidity to her body, her fingers stroking gently a metal paperknife. "What's so different about her," he thought, as she put both hands flat on the table, interested only, it seemed, in the large green blotter on the desk.

"How have things been going?" he said slowly, fumbling for words.

"There have been times when I would have phoned you, times when I was so unhappy I wanted to sit all day without moving. What have you been doing?"

"Things have been going all right, Julie."

"We used to have such good times together."

"Good times, I liked the good times. They were part of a fine summer and I was pretty happy. I needed to be happy then."

Curious, he watched her, imagining she was deliberately arranging and rearranging words to get a convincing combination, and he was embarrassed, for she no longer seemed so experienced and aloof. In her big body she had apparently felt many of the important sensations that elude most women, he used to think; she had smiled at him, always held in restraint, till he felt like a kid, nervously hoping to touch her. That arousing part of her was gone. He had no words for her. She sat there, still trying to get the right words.

"Have you sometimes felt that you'd like to make love to me?" she said, without smiling. "I'm happy, but I'm lonely, I don't mean Augustus isn't good company but he needs a background. He's individualistic compared with other people but always there must be the other people. By himself, or just the two of us together, well . . . it's very lonesome. He plays the violin for me then."

She was talking quite rapidly and he was interested. She used to talk lazily, now she was trying to convince him of something important to her.

"I don't mean I don't want him. I do, but he's slight, or rather, inadequate. Oh, he'd far rather someone else was interested in me too. Then he wouldn't feel entirely responsible. Do you see, Harry? He's really very nice."

"He's not a bad kid at that," Harry said, stretching his legs, "but just a kid and not very interesting to me, Julie." He felt very generous.

"Of course not, silly, nor would he be offended at you for saying it. He wouldn't be jealous of you either. You two are so entirely different, he'd never feel jealous of you."

He frowned, while she went on talking, wondering why she was trying to interest him in Augustus. The implication was eluding him, and then he decided vaguely that she was attempting to come to an understanding on the basis of their appreciation of Augustus. He started to laugh. He slapped her lightly on the back and laughed. She simply took hold of his hand, holding it firmly, her eyes turned to a corner of the room. He followed the line from her eyes. Nothing in the corner. His hand was getting moist, so he tried to withdraw it gently but she held tightly, her hand trembling. He said good-naturedly: "I've often thought of you, Julie, nine times out of ten, when I get fed up with all kinds of people, and I want someone to talk easily and slowly, making me feel I'm not so wise." He stopped abruptly. She loomed over him, her body trembling. He went on nervously, "I mean sometimes in the evening. Oh, let go my hand, Julie, your nail, ouch." He tried to pull it away but she held on, bending over him, following him, getting up slowly, her lips shaped to kiss him.

He put his arm on her shoulder, the tips of his fingers touching her hair lightly. She smiled, moving to sit down again but he held on to her, his arm slipping around her waist. Her heavy corset, hard under his fingers, terrified him; he let go suddenly and she sat down, the couch-spring sagging beneath her. Never before had she seemed such a huge woman, and he wouldn't sit down beside her. He shoved his hands in his pockets, staring at her round, large knees. Always he had thought of her as a woman with a big body, now she was merely a fat woman of a startling size, years older than he had imagined. He tried to be sympathetic.

"It was good to see you," he said, "but I really ought to go now."

"Sit down a few minutes," she said slowly.

"If I sit down I'll stay." He smiled with difficulty, feeling the lines on his face. "I must go and get home early for I haven't slept for weeks. I just wanted to drop in on you."

"There wasn't much use coming," she said, without looking at him. He was ready to answer genially, but saw only the white part in her dark hair and said weakly: "No, I guess there wasn't much use coming."

"Don't go, be a good scout and stay for a while, Harry."

"I got to go," he said suddenly. He looked at her directly, repeating angrily: "I got to go." She didn't move from the couch and he walked quickly out of the room. He took his hat and coat from a peg in the hall and opened the front door, putting his coat on as he hurried along the street.

The cold air calmed him. He walked slower, drawing on his gloves. "What the hell," he thought, "what the hell. Why did I ever go to see Julie?" Back there on the couch she sat, huge and immovable, encased in steel bands, but walking along toward Yonge Street lights, he was sorry to remember he had once thought her so mysteriously desirable, and though all feeling for her had gone, old thoughts of her weren't very comforting. "I wonder what the hell's the matter with me. I'm sick of everybody almost," he thought. "I got to do something about it." At the corner he went into the tobacco shop and got cigarettes, and talked to the man behind the counter till other customers came in and he was obliged to leave. He wouldn't go home so early, and looked up at the clock on the fire hall — twenty minutes to ten — so he walked north on Yonge Street, standing a while in front of the moving-picture show, reading the bright posters till he said to himself, "I'm getting sick of this whole damned business, what's the matter with me?" For the first time he thought of the possibility of being arrested. There would be a trial, the best lawyers in the city working for him, his picture in all the papers, headlines carrying his name and big lawyers getting an easy acquittal finally. Vera would cry. She would leave the city. She would leave the country and, dressed in black, go from one place to another. But why dressed in black, he thought, moving away from the theater, walking up the street. The streets were slushy, there had been a thaw, and he unbuttoned his overcoat. "I think it's about time I made up my mind about Vera," he thought. "I got to do it sometime." It was just as well his mother was dead. Remembering Jimmie had said months ago that he had fallen in love with his mother, he tried to remember her face at the time they lived in Maydale when she was younger. Someday, later on, when he got out of the whole racket, he would take Vera for a weekend in Maydale, and they would talk to people who had known his mother and father and perhaps go for a long ride in the country. He was entering the underpass and looked around alertly. It was dark in the subway so he walked rapidly, very practical again. Shadows from pillars made him uneasy and he knew he had been foolish to go walking in lonely places. He wanted to run but deliberately walked slower. "Cosantino be damned," he muttered.

At the end of the underpass he shrugged his shoulders and leaned against an iron railing. Here at the end of the dark underpass he was alone. The underpass was at the foot of a sloping hill, car tracks climbing up the other side, a long slope of street lights. He looked up at the stars, was quite comfortable against the railing, and the solitude and darkness were pleasant. No one on the street. Deliberately he sought the thread of his thoughts of Maydale, to walk again in the town, close to his mother. He grinned to himself, imagining Vera beside him strolling very formally along the main street. A streetcar light at the other end of the underpass flashed brightly and the car rumbled noisily. He walked up the hill. In the afternoon he had felt impressive and had thought of talking pompously to Julie about Cosantino, now it seemed a faraway thought. He walked up to St. Clair and all the way home.

He went into his own room and looked at himself in the mirror as if not accustomed to seeing his own image. He leaned forward, closer to the mirror. He grinned at himself. Afterwards, he was jovial with Anna, teasing her, pinching her, but he didn't want to make love to her.

In the morning he read the papers. They carried stories with pictures of Cosantino and the word of detectives that it was a bootleg feud. Later on in the afternoon reporters had more time to be diligent and the papers ran full-page stories with pictures of the Cosantino family. He looked at the picture of Mrs. Cosantino and wanted to cry. She was young and good-looking. He looked at Cosantino and felt sorry for him. "I had nothing against that guy," he thought. "Only it had to be done."

He read about the plan for an elaborate funeral. Thousands of dollars for a casket. Hundreds of dollars for flowers to cover the casket. He read the paper at half-past six in the evening, sitting across from Anna at the table. The police were discouraged because Cosantino's friends wouldn't say whom they thought responsible, but Mike Gerrardi, Cosantino's partner, told a reporter he would willingly meet the murderer and settle the matter hand to hand. Gerrardi's words were impressive and read splendidly. In the paper there was a long account of Cosantino's charities and the articles of furniture in his home and paintings he had bought for fabulous prices and a piano far-famed, the work of a master, and a picture of three of his cars — roadster, touring and family limousine — and estimated values of rugs, mirrors, suits of clothes, silverware, talking-machines, brass, and clocks.

At first Harry resented so much talk of Cosantino's life and said, "Hmm, humph," but the feeling passed away and he wondered at the Italian's influence. He was impressed. He made up his mind to attend the funeral.

It was a big elaborate funeral. Harry spoke gently to the widow, who fainted when the casket was carried out. Thousands of people were on the street. Simon Asche, one of the pallbearers, wouldn't speak to Harry at first, but later on he said quietly: "What are you doing in this house, you son of a bitch?" Harry said: "What's it to you, ya little kike?"

Weinreb and O'Reilly were at the funeral and shook their heads sadly looking for the last time at the face in the coffin. It was hard to get close to the coffin because of the flowers.

Police formed a cordon around the house. From flat roofs and leaning out of attic windows, people watched the hearse go slowly along the street, a long line of cars following it to the cemetery. Jimmie and Harry were in one of the cars. There wasn't much to say. The cemetery was up Yonge Street, at the city limit, a sloping hill and a long valley. The snow had all gone from the side of the hill and the valley, but the warm sun melted the frost in the ground and the hill was slippery underfoot. The long line of mourners followed the casket around the crescent curve of the cinder path, and passing the tombstones, Harry read the Irish Catholic names, O'Donnelly, Fitzpatrick, O'Neil, McDonagh, and a few Italian names on newer tombstones. At the open grave he shuddered and wouldn't look at the casket. Standing there bareheaded, he kept his thoughts on the old Irish names on tombstones, but the softly weeping women elbowing him annoyed him and he looked down the long valley at aristocratic vaults like Greek temples and the whole world seemed to become quietly unimportant, and he felt sad and sorry for Cosantino and himself.

The crowd moved slowly away from the grave. He walked with Jimmie, his head still uncovered. A reporter from the *Star* touched his arm and said: "Well, how's it all going to turn out?"

"I don't know," Harry said.

"You had nothing against him, did you, Mr. Trotter?"

"Not a thing in the world."

"I've been watching to see who didn't come out to the funeral."

"That's a good idea," Harry said, and the reporter went away.

On the way back from the cemetery he was depressed and exchanged only small talk with Jimmie. He leaned over to one side in the taxi and closed his eyes. He thought of the crowd in the cemetery and longed to surround himself with people who would respect him and look up to him, more influential and stronger than Cosantino, himself in the centre of a crowd, at the head of a long table, a political banquet, a party, the biggest party ever thrown in the city, everybody there, ward heelers, big guys, Johnston, the dukes in politics, women and wine and whiskey and food, slabs of it, gobs of it, truckloads of beer, champagne. He opened his eyes and sat up straight. The idea excited him. Later on he would explain it to Jim.

PART FOUR

---◆---

1

The tombstones in the cemetery where Cosantino had been
buried impressed him so that for days after, in idle moments,
he remembered standing on the cinder path, looking at the
crowd around the grave. Tall granite stones, polished and
carved, were beautiful but one large, uncut granite cross, tow-
ering over smaller stones, seemed remarkable for dignity and
strength. He remembered the time he had thought of going to
Maydale where his mother was buried and longed to see a
huge cross over her grave. It was an exciting notion and he
thought of going there at once and was happy and not at all
sentimental, for it was advisable in any event, to go away for
a week. It astonished him to find so much pleasure in such a
simple thought, and he determined not to tell anybody, but
later on, talking to Jimmie Nash, it was necessary to tell him
he would be gone for three days, looking up some of his mother's people in Maydale. He told the same story to Anna.

On Friday morning he took the train, and as it moved out
he wondered why he hadn't asked Vera to come with him as
he had at first intended, but he preferred to be alone, for the
feeling he looked forward to couldn't be shared with anyone,
and besides, he wasn't quite ready for Vera. Still there were
complications in all his thoughts of her. He sat back in the seat,
half-closing his eyes, avoiding any kind of thoughts. The train,

in the yard, moved slowly and the whole movement of his life seemed to have slowed down, and there was a new pleasure in enjoying the vaguest sensations. Maydale was an hour's ride from the city, but he didn't read, though he had two new mystery stories in his bag. He went into the smoking-car and was alone for half an hour, looking out of the window, occasionally counting telegraph poles, contented until two cattle dealers, who had got on at the last stop, came into the smoking-car. He went back to the parlour-car and amused himself remembering that his people had come to the city over this road. Ten years ago he had gone to Maydale for his mother's burial, but he couldn't remember the station or the village, so through the window he followed the bare fields, dun-coloured after winter's snow, and isolated farmhouses appeared too lonely and remote from life. He saw a woman standing at a farmhouse door and a young man walking up a lane, and leaned forward eagerly, glad to see a figure breaking the desolation of the country, and followed the woman with his eyes till the train swung him round a bend.

The conductor called out: "Stouffville Junction. Change here for Maydale." At twenty minutes to twelve, irresolute, he got off the train. He asked a man in the ticket office how to get to Maydale and the man told him to wait for the jitney, or hire a buggy. No trains stopped at Maydale. So he walked down the dusty road to a frame hotel and said good-morning to an old man hunched in a chair on a freshly painted veranda. The man regarded him suspiciously, muttering vaguely. Inside the hotel he pounded on the desk and asked a man in a blue shirt if there was a hotel in Maydale. There was a small hotel in Maydale, the man said, and he recommended one of his own buggies and a horse in the stable.

On the front steps Harry waited till they hitched up the horse. Stouffville was discouraging, no one on the road, only the old man in the chair, wagging his beard. Harry didn't like the road or the colour of the houses. He smelled the fresh paint and liked it, and cheerfully noticed marks of raking on the lawn across the road. The horse and buggy stopped at the curb. The stable-hand said: "She don't need much attention. She ain't as young as she used to be, but she gets there just the same, and that's all you want."

Harry gave him a quarter. Uncertain of himself, he sat in the buggy and said "Geedap." Maydale was fourteen miles away, it wasn't the first time he had ever driven a horse and he liked having the reins in his hands. Carelessly, he tilted his hat back on his head, to show indifference, for he knew the man was noticing him, leaning forward alertly. Out of the town, he drove along the main road, the horse jogging evenly, the reins held loosely. He was in no hurry and though all along the road there was only the monotony of irregular wooden fences to interest him, he drove slowly, for the air was good, and it was a holiday. This road, at a time when he was very young, he must have known well, and he wished there were green summer fields and leaves on the bare trees. For no reason he became very happy and, jerking out the whip from its place, tickled the hindquarters of the beast till it leaped forward angrily, a swinging, swaying gait suggesting its annoyance, and he clicked his tongue on his teeth. The road dipped down between low hills. A line of trees on top of the hills interested him, so he stopped the horse on a bridge over a small stream, wishing the branches were covered with green leaves. Moving the horse to the middle of the bridge he tried spitting into the stream, following with his eyes a piece of white paper on slow-moving water till it was carried out of sight around a bend. He grinned, wanting the horse to jump forward, go charging into the village, down the main street, panting and steaming; instead, they loafed along and he leaned back in the seat, the warm sun and the clip-clop of the hoofs making him drowsy, all the way into Maydale.

The village surprised him. So many houses were of limestone. Then he remembered it was a limestone district. The horse slowed down to a walk on the main street and he looked at the Anglican church and the town hall, and many stone houses. There was more sun than in Stouffville and some people were on the street. The horse stopped mechanically near a small stone hotel. He got down, and in the hotel asked the man behind the desk if he could get a good meal, and a stable for the horse. The man, who had been reading the paper, smiling, kept a finger on the line, pointing at the dining room door. He said the horse and buggy could be left in the livery stable as long as he pleased.

In the dining room he was alone. It was late for dinner and a boy with a clean apron brought him some pork chops. He ate the pork chops and some cake and drank a glass of milk, and went out to look at the village.

People on the short main street were friendly and he nodded agreeably. He had a long talk with the livery-stable man, who directed him to the Anglican cemetery, after insisting he remembered Harry's father and mother from twenty-five years ago. He was a skinny old man with yellow teeth and a habit of listening with his mouth held wide open. He became very positive, as he talked, that he remembered the Trotters. Putting a hand on Harry's shoulder, he stood on the sidewalk, pointing the way to the cemetery — two blocks south and walk down opposite the brown frame house. The Trotters, he said, used to live down the road and three blocks to the left, only a brick cottage was there now, with the lilac bushes on one side.

Harry walked to the cottage and sat on the wide stump of a poplar tree close to the curb, looking at the neat brick house where once had been the old rough-cast two-storied one. Vaguely he remembered the lilac bushes, leafless now and thick at the roots, well trimmed, older than the brick cottage. As a kid he had run around the house, chased by his cousin and a black dog, dodging among the lilac bushes. At twilight three or four kids played around the big poplar, a stump now. With his eyes closed, he imagined the old house was there, but when he opened them the neat brick cottage was an irritating sight; so he got up and walked back to the main street and the road to the cemetery.

The Anglican cemetery was at the edge of the village and beyond the cemetery were a few houses and barns, and then a long stretch of bare field to the horizon. In the afternoon sun the cemetery, after winter snows, was dirty, and a poor place for graves. It was dry on the path, but walking on sod, looking for the family plot, his shoes sank into soft mud. The sod was faded, and some of last year's flowers lay dry and dead on re-membered tombstones. Pretentious stones on well-kept graves offended him, and he was indignant, as though it had become necessary to defend his parents; for he knew he would find a poor stone on the family plot. Two small stones about a foot high were on the family plot — "James Trotter in his fifty-second year," and "Amelia Trotter, beloved wife of James Trotter." The stones were square and dirty. He looked down at the sod, strangely embarrassed before the small stones and last year's grass, and wanting to kneel down and mumble some prayers, his mouth opened a little; he moistened his lips, scraped one foot in the mud then looked around wildly, alone in the desolate place of stones and dried grass and rotten twigs. He looked up at the sky, then at the sod, and walked away quickly, out of the cemetery. He saw no one, there were no sounds; there was sun, but no breeze, and nothing moved.

A little way down the road from the cemetery was a stone cutter who displayed his stones on his front lawn. Small tomb-stones without inscriptions were planted on the lawn, not far from the street. From the sidewalk Harry looked at the stones critically, shrugged his shoulders, took two steps away, then came back and walked up the path to rap on the door. A tidy woman with gray hair came to the door.

"I'd like to talk about a stone," Harry said.

"Oh, just one minute," she said, and called, "Tom, Tom." A man in a brown sweatercoat, smoking a pipe, came along the hall. He had a long red moustache, faded at the tips. "Was it a stone?" he said.

"I want to see a very big stone," Harry said.

"Well, you can't do better than some of those out there," he said. "Those stones are good enough for anyone in town."

"Listen, you don't get me. I want something big, grand."

The man was offended. The woman said, "Every stone there is pretty enough for anyone."

"You don't get me. I want something big and I'll pay for it and I want it at once, see? Raw stone. A standout. My God man, this ain't all the stone there is in the country, is it?"

"Who said it was? Sure, I got some stone. I got stone in the backyard, but a lot of good it'll do us, unless I make you something."

"Lemme see the stone first."

"There's nothing to see. It's just stone."

"Let the gentleman see what you have, Tom," the woman said.

So they went around to the backyard and looked at two pieces of solid granite, each about seven feet long and two-and-a-half by two, rough-hewn and massive, and Tom said it had been there since last fall. They sat on the stone, without speaking, till Harry slapped the man on the back and said what was it worth to make a pillar with the two pieces.

"Don't be silly," the man said.

"Go easy and don't be so damn fresh. I'll pay you money for this. I mean it."

Tom said patiently it was a foolish notion because a pillar wasn't a stone. Harry, deliberately polite, asked if he couldn't take his tools and taper an end for the top, leaving most of the fourteen feet rough-hewn, different from all other stones, and quickly he took out fifty dollars, offering it as an advance, with his own final price later. Tom, slightly flustered, said the cemetery authorities mightn't stand for it. "Promise them anything," Harry said.

"It would take at least two weeks," Tom said.

"I want it tomorrow afternoon."

"My lord, man, it'd take half a dozen men to get it to the cemetery, and I got to do work on it too."

"Hire a regiment, but get it there tomorrow and then send a man down to the hotel for me when I can see it."

The stone cutter scratched his head then remembered there ought to be an inscription, which would cost a little more, and would have to be done later anyway. He agreed to taper an end and have it propped over the grave by tomorrow, but suggested respectfully that he ought to have some money to pay for help. They shook hands, very friendly. On the way back to the hotel Harry whistled cheerfully.

He had an early supper and afterward sat on the veranda, smoking cigarettes, his feet on the rail, and tilting back in the rocking chair. Three men were on the veranda but he didn't bother talking to them. After seven o'clock three young fellows and two girls, walking slowly, passed the hotel. One of the girls was pretty. The young men were dressed carefully, their faces very clean. It was getting dark, the corner light was brighter now. A tall man on a bicycle, peddling slowly, came down the road. Harry heard someone laughing, a girl giggling, and leaning forward, he tried to see her. She laughed again and he jerked his head, staring across the road at the thick trunk of a tree, sure the girl and fellow were there. He smiled happily, positive that he understood everything that was bothering the boy and girl; he was in his own town; a silly notion for he wasn't at home at all but a stranger, and he wondered why he had come to Maydale. He had come because of his mother, but now he didn't remember her very well. A long time ago she used to get excited easily and her voice was harsh and she spoke fiercely, then became nervous and started to cry. She had many arguments with his father, but soon became friendly and tried to pamper the old man till he was good-humoured again. She bought furniture slowly and carefully and the selection of wallpaper always bothered her. When they decided to repaper a room she brought home five or six sample rolls of paper and pinned the sample on the wall, comparing the colours and patterns a long time till satisfied she had selected the finest pattern. She was critical of other people and, of course, Harry realized it for the first time, she would have liked Vera, who was always so neat and tidy around the house, never deceitful, and whose clothes fitted her nicely. He closed his eyes, taking pleasure in an imaginary meeting of Vera and his mother, watching them getting interested in each other gradually, each one coming to him in turn, assuring him of splendid qualities in the other.

Holding this agreeable thought, he got up, left the veranda and walked slowly down the street to a soda parlour for a root beer. Young people were sitting at the wire-legged round tables. He asked the Greek for a root beer, drank it slowly, then walked back to the hotel, thinking comfortably of getting into bed early, stretching leisurely under clean sheets, and reading a mystery story for hours till he dropped off to sleep.

In the early afternoon next day, the stone cutter came to the hotel and asked Harry to go to the cemetery. They walked there together and from a hundred yards away Harry saw a small crowd, and in the centre of the crowd a huge pillar of granite tapered to a point, held up by scantling props. Everybody watched him come along the cemetery path, and he was embarrassed for some of them were smiling openly and others looked at him curiously, whispering among themselves.

The stone cutter leaned against a prop. "The mortar's not dry yet but I guess we can just about take the props down now," he said. "Does it look like what you wanted?"

Harry, forgetting the crowd, concentrated on the pillar of granite, a solid cenotaph among smaller stones, its rugged massiveness pleasing him, and he was ready to enjoy all the sensations he had looked forward to. Deliberately he thought of his mother, groping for the old feeling as he stood there, his hat off, looking at the pillar's peak, but he became very conscious of people watching him curiously. He turned to the stone cutter and said, "Send these hicks away," and Tom said, "It can't be done, sir. They seen me putting this stone up and they've been here an hour."

So he closed his eyes but the dream was broken and he said to Tom: "Well, let's get out of here. Walk down a road a piece. This looks all right to me." A few people followed them from the cemetery but most of the crowd remained before the pillar.

Speaking casually, Harry told the man to put an inscription on the stone as soon as possible, copying it from the small stone. Tom asked: "Just the lady, or the husband too?"

"Oh both, certainly," Harry said.

He paid him generously, asking him to have a photograph taken of the stone and the inscription and flowers heaped around the base. He gave him a city address. They shook hands and Harry walked away.

Out of sight of the cemetery he was happy, not thinking of anything in particular, but content from having done something that had been absolutely necessary for his own good. At the hotel he learned that a train left Stouffville Junction at eight o'clock, so he had an early supper, and afterward went down to the livery-stable to have the horse hitched to the buggy. The liveryman offered to have a boy drive him to the Junction but he preferred to go alone. He drove away from Maydale in the late afternoon when the streets were quiet, a few women on the verandas, and some families having early supper. The horse was going briskly, he held the reins tightly, sitting erect till he got on the road to Stouffville. Well away from the town, he started to sing out loud, then talked cheerfully to the horse, making strange clicking noises with his tongue and lips. The road was good, the wire fences new in this district, and farmhouses clean and of a prosperous appearance. At sundown the sky was red in the west, and stopping the horse he watched for a long time the sun becoming larger and redder, and felt solemn and alone. He listened for some sound to arouse him, and heard faintly a chirping sparrow. He jerked the reins, the horse jogged along.

He leaned back, the horse taking its own time. Someday he might get a place in the country. "That would probably appeal to Vera very much," he thought. He urged the horse along, eager to be back in the city, and thinking pleasantly of Vera now, on the way home. For days his thoughts had been drifting toward her, and he was taking it for granted that he was going back to the city to have a long talk with her. Then he remembered that party he had planned and seriously he thought of Cosantino's friend, Simon Asche, who couldn't worry him except that he was a friend of O'Reilly. "Oh well," he thought, "there are some things that simply have to get cleared away first, then I'll fix it up with Vera."

He had to wait twenty-five minutes for the train to the city.

2

His neck felt uncomfortable in the stiff collar and dinner jacket. He drove Anna down to the hotel, intending to get there half an hour before guests arrived. They drove in the open car, the weather was good, a spring breeze blowing from the lake.

They saw the chef first. On the way down, Harry had told her about the dinner, the cooking, the month-and-a-half spent in preparation, the liqueurs, wines, cases of champagne. He had wanted a whole roast pig and venison, barbecue style, for the hundred guests, but the chef, a silent, sad little man, had objected because his kitchens and ovens were not big enough for the venison. A whole pig, he said, was very tough, and did not look nice, but a suckling, twenty sucklings would be just the thing. The chef went with them to the ballroom. He was polite. They stood at the doorway, looking down long tables, and the chef apologized for being able to get only two bottles of real green Chartreuse, fifty dollars a bottle, forty years old. The chef went away. Harry looked at his image in a long mirror. He straightened his shoulders, waving his hand at himself, "You're there, kid," he thought. Out of the corner of his eye he saw Anna smiling. Turning quickly, he kissed her, shaking her and getting powder from her shoulders on his jacket.

Then he was aware of being practically alone in the big ballroom. He looked around, wanting people to come. For the moment, the idea, the party, the food seemed unimportant, and he wondered how it had come that he was standing there looking at himself in the mirror.

He heard laughing and talking in the corridor, the Negro orchestra getting off the elevator. Grinning, they came over the carpeted floor of the blue room to the ballroom. Then Jimmie and Eva, arm in arm, came along from the corridor and bowed to Harry.

"Great King Harry," he said.

"Damn glad to see you, Jimmie."

"Great King Harry."

"Lay off."

"Good King Harry."

"You two have a head start," Anna said. Eva's eyes were shining too brightly. Her dress was cut low, just a band around her breasts. She laughed happily, patting her hair, pouting her lips at Jimmie, who insisted upon being soberly serious.

"Will O'Reilly come?" Harry asked.

"Said he would, didn't he?"

"I know he did, only that don't mean nothing."

Harry turned to shake hands eagerly with Johnston, who was standing with Collins, the alderman in Ward Three, his hands behind his back. He wanted to impress Johnston, an old-timer in politics, a party man, strong on the stump and in a convention. They shook hands. Johnston was friendly, and made some jokes, suggesting he had a long thirst. Collins and Johnston were interested in some hot-looking babes in the blue room, they said. "He's a nice guy," Harry thought, and feeling happy, put his arm around Johnston's shoulder to lead him over to Anna and Eva and Jimmie.

He talked with Johnston till he saw O'Reilly standing a few feet away, grinning at Johnston. Harry was uncomfortable. He waved his hand. O'Reilly was enormous in a dinner jacket. It was early in the evening but he was hot already, wiping his forehead with a big silk handkerchief. O'Reilly was stroking the end of his nose, which had been pulled out of shape. He laughed, his fat belly bobbing up and down. "It looks as if you're throwing a swell feed," he said to Harry. Whenever Harry talked to O'Reilly he felt apprehensive because he was so much aware of him, his personality, his fat face, the easy money that went his way. Ten years ago O'Reilly had been a bartender out of a job. He had taken a temporary job for two weeks running a hotel for a woman whose bartender was away on holidays. In two weeks O'Reilly impressed the woman so much that she married him, and when her bartender came back there was no job for him. That was the year before prohibition.

He got in a big stock of liquor and did well the first year and had been doing better ever since. His son was on the police force, a sergeant at a downtown station. His brother was vice-president of a local political association.

The orchestra played lively jazz, the ballroom and the blue room coming alive with chatter of many voices. Girls dragged fellows out on the floor to dance. Some men had their own girls, but twenty girls, unaccompanied, loafed around, ready to become sociable. Watching a strapping hussy with broad bare shoulders and wonderful long legs leaning indolently against a table, Harry thought, "The swellest women in town, twenty-four carat blondes, I've got them here." He rubbed his hands together, smiling at whoever was looking at him. The friendly, pretty women amused him. He closed his eyes, his thoughts alive with women — blond heads, dark heads, almost bare bodies, dancing happily. "Wait till things get really going," he thought.

The party sat down to eat, Harry and Anna at the end of the long table. He looked the length of the table. He smiled at Anna. Every time he glanced around the room he couldn't help smiling.

He looked at the real white Czarist caviar he had never tasted before. "It used to be very hard to get," he said to Mr. Johnston, who was sitting three plates away. "Indeed," Johnston said. Harry wanted to tell him the chef's story of Czarist caviar but decided not to. "That would be putting on the dog too much," he thought. Everybody was eating the caviar but Harry didn't like it.

Honest green turtle soup, imported from England, and sherry wine. Bottles of old port wine in the hands of many waiters.

"I had to get the caviar from Paris," he said to Anna.

"I don't like it much," she said.

"Neither did I, only that ain't important. See what I mean?"

"I'd like it if I could swill it," Jimmie said.

Harry drank eagerly the old port wine. He was friendly, anxious to encourage everybody. Sitting down at the head of the table at first he had been embarrassed, now he wanted to laugh out happily. He tried to think of a good joke, something hot to shock the troops, but couldn't do it. The soup was fine. "That chef's a peach," he said to Jimmie. The wine was good. Thinking of wine confused him. Names of old vintages, bottles appearing, glasses clinking, swell names, green Chartreuse — very rare, ladies and gentlemen, very rare, fifty bucks a bottle, forty years old — five cases of Chambertin, all to go on the table, ten cases of Château Yquem and that Italian wine the chef had called "Tears of Jesus," the kind of a name to interest and please Vera. She would say, "What a lovely sad name." It was a rotten time to think of Vera. He looked at Anna. She had a nice face. She was just finishing the soup. Her neck and shoulders were the best in the world.

The ballroom door opened and a line of waiters in single file appeared, each one carrying a platter and a young pig, skinned, roasted, a whole apple in the mouth, jelly in the eyes, lying in a sea of jelly. Twenty waiters served the young roast pig. For those who did not like pork there was planked steak, the meat on ice for three months to give it flavour.

"It's all so splendid," Anna said to him.

"It's nothing. Wait till next time," he said.

"You're wonderful, Harry."

"Boy, this is a feed," Jimmie said.

"What's O'Reilly thinking?" Harry said to Jimmie. They looked at O'Reilly. He was eating slowly without paying attention to the girl beside him. He was eating too attentively. "That guy bothers me," Harry said.

"Why did you ask him along?"

"You know what I was after, Jimmie. I wanted him to see everything was all right with me. It's a thing you get to do with a guy like O'Reilly."

"Well, don't let him crab the party for you."

"He hasn't got a chance to crab my party, only he's got something on his mind."

"Maybe he'll go home early."

"Go home or get drunk, I wish."

Everybody was happy. Everybody was drinking. O'Reilly smiled blandly at the eager girl. Harry forgot O'Reilly and ate hungrily until it wasn't safe to eat any more. He drank two glasses of wine, then asked the waiter for a highball. Mr. Johnston had a highball with him. Then Mr. Johnston had another highball, a good sort Mr. Johnston when he got really going. The Negro orchestra played a blues number and Harry had taken just enough liquor to make him feel sad. The woeful weary niggers sang a blues that got inside him and made him sad. The dinner was no longer important. Looking along tables, listening to girls squealing and men eating, he felt it had all become unimportant. He was missing something. He wanted suddenly to be alone, far away from music in an absolutely silent world, loafing in the shade and having idle thoughts, and looking at Vera sprawled on her belly. He took another drink. He became much more buoyant. He laughed out loud. He wiped his neck behind the collar with a silk handkerchief. "I'll be the biggest guy in town," he thought.

People, getting up from the tables, started to dance, at first gracefully but becoming careless of the rhythm they danced sloppily. O'Reilly came to the end of the table and asked Anna to dance. Harry watched them on the floor. O'Reilly was not a good dancer. He was pleased to think O'Reilly was such a poor dancer.

Harry danced with a slim, supple-bodied bleached blonde, her hair dark at the roots. They danced slowly, the blonde brushing lazy limbs against him, her head drooping back from the arched throat and her breast pressed forward. He tried to dance faster but gradually relaxed lazily into the slow time. Then he opened his eyes and watched O'Reilly bear-hugging Anna. He stopped dancing and walked off the floor to get a drink.

Jimmie and Eva were having a drink. Eva was quite drunk but in a contained, hilariously dignified way.

"I was talking to O'Reilly," Jimmie said.

"What's eating him?"

"Nothing's eating him only he wants to talk to you."

"Sure, I'd like to talk to him. What's eatin' him anyway?"

"Nothing I tellya, only he thinks it's important."

"Well?"

"That's all."

"Listen, Jimmie."

"What?"

"I'm a bigger guy than O'Reilly. I can knock hell out of him. If things go right I'll soon be able to knock hell out of everybody. Now if that guy's got anything to say and I don't like it, I'll tell him off, see?"

"Suit yourself, only there's no harm in listening."

"Forget him, Jimmie. Watch the waiters pile the stuff up."

Waiters were carrying cases of champagne to an impro-
vised bar in a corner near the door. People stopped dancing,
crowding near the corner, counting cases. Cases were opened
rapidly. Ten waiters kept coming in, carrying cases. Some
women laughed happily and men cheered. The cases were
piled up. Three waiters could not fill glasses rapidly enough.
Everybody linked arms, cheering when the cases counted up
to a hundred. They would never drink it all but went at the bottles placed on the long bar.

It was only half-past one but some girls were being
attended to by waiters who carried them to rooms where waitresses worked on them. Later on the girls came back and
couldn't smile easily and make-up stood out in blotches on
their faces. They kept going just the same.

The orchestra, nearly exhausted at three o'clock, was resting when O'Reilly came over to the bar. Harry was sitting
down in a corner. A slim girl had fallen asleep on his shoulder.
Harry, sitting there on the floor, didn't have any thoughts. He
asked O'Reilly to sit down beside him. O'Reilly shook his
head and said, "I'm going home now, Trotter."

"Have a good time?" Harry asked.

"He's not so bad, he's a good sort," Anna said, leaning on
O'Reilly's arm. "He wants me to go home with him. Think I
will, as a matter of fact."

Harry got up slowly. He was sore at Anna. Maybe she was
kidding, but it seemed he had really been sore at her for
months, and unable to understand it.

"I was talking to Nash," O'Reilly said, fumbling with his
limp collar.

"That's right."

"Did he tell you about tomorrow?"

"No." Harry was hanging on tightly to his thoughts, watching O'Reilly. He didn't like his soft fat face. He didn't like the way he shook his head sadly. "What's up?" he asked.

"We want you to meet us tomorrow in my hotel. Asche and Weinreb and myself'll be there. They think one of your boys got Cosantino."

"The hell they say so."

"Not me though. I don't know, but let's get together anyway, eh?"

"Sure Mike, it's all the same to me."

"Nice and friendly too, eh, no need to get excited either, I mean, just friendly and peaceable like. See what I mean?"

"It's all right with me, O'Reilly. Only I ain't taking anything. I know just how I stand."

"Sure, but we're friendly, ain't we? And it's too bad about Cosantino, isn't it?"

"It is. It really is."

"Tomorrow then, eh Trotter, two o'clock, eh?"

O'Reilly went home. Anna stood there, uncertain of herself, looking stupidly at Harry. He regarded her as if he had known her a long time, and there was no use saying anything. There was really no reason for feeling that way about her but he wouldn't talk. He wanted her to go so he could be alone.

A few people still danced slowly on the floor. Some of the orchestra were dozing. Women had fallen asleep on chairs, or stretched out awkwardly on sofas. Three waiters were clearing tables. At eight o'clock in the morning a good breakfast would be served. Harry walked over to a sofa and stood beside Jimmie who had fallen asleep with Eva in his arms. Eva was a peach of a girl, the same build as Vera.

His thoughts, he realized, were getting confused and he was thinking of Vera, Anna, Cosantino and O'Reilly, all at the same time. Their faces blurred into each other and he could not separate them. He wanted to go home. In the morning the edge would be worn off the good time. Girls at breakfast would look bad. Nobody really happy. Talk would not come easily. He decided to go home. He didn't awaken Jimmie. People in the morning could look after themselves.

He took Anna's arm and they went into the cloakroom and got their coats. The elevator went down rapidly and Anna's knees fell away, but she straightened up. In the cool air they walked a block to the parking space. They drove home. The streets were quiet in the gray morning light. The air was wonderful. He didn't speak to Anna on the way home.

3

He got into bed clumsily. He lay flat on his back, his body very tired. He lay on his back to get the maximum of feeling from sheets resting lightly on him. He had imagined he would go right to sleep and coming home in the car had thought of bed. "I would rather be in bed than any place on earth," he had thought. He was so tired, his body so heavy it ached and he couldn't get to sleep. Anna had gone to her own room. He turned over on his side, wide-awake. Anna was probably sound asleep, stretched out, sprawled, breathing heavily. Too many pictures in his head. He tried thinking of tomorrow and talking to O'Reilly and Asche, getting difficulties straightened out. Asche, O'Reilly, Weinreb, sitting there in front of him, talking, explaining, getting sore occasionally. He couldn't get beyond a point where he imagined himself sitting talking to them. Beyond that his thoughts drifted and he had to keep coming back. He stopped thinking about them. He had a clear picture of Anna in the next room sound asleep, untouched, probably wishing, before going to sleep, she had gone home with O'Reilly. Any new kind of adventure was good enough for her. Anybody's dame. Any big guy's meat. Still, they were getting along all right, he had nothing against her; only he couldn't get hold of her and exhaust her. He clenched his hands, detesting her so much he thought of going into her room and shaking her.

Then he was sorry for himself and thought of Vera. This time last year she had wanted him to buy a house, so they could have a garden and flowers. Vera, with her legs, wonderful Vera. He was alone in the bed, his body very heavy. "Anna ought to be thrown out on her ear," he muttered suddenly. His thoughts becoming disinterested hardly seemed to belong to him, then he was asleep.

In the morning he woke up at ten o'clock, tired but without any kind of a head. He took a bath and rubbed himself with the towel. Standing in the bathroom, the towel around one shoulder and under the other arm, he jerked and rubbed so vigorously that his shoulder and back glowed and he felt the hot sting. He rubbed his big chest, slapped his hips and stood looking at himself in the mirror.

He dressed slowly, and pulling on his socks, wondered if Anna were awake. He had been thinking of Anna the night before. His feeling for her had so changed he wondered why she was sleeping in the next room, and why they had been living together. He began to dress rapidly. "The trouble is I'm really thinking too much of Vera," he said, sitting on the bed.

He went into Anna's room. She was still sleeping, the covers thrown back from her right shoulder. Her face looked flabby. He sat down on the edge of the bed and shook her roughly. She tossed her head slightly, opening her eyes.

"Whasamatter?" she said.

"Get up."

"Won't get up."

"Get up, I tellya."

"Oh hell," she said, turning over on her side, trying to get comfortable again.

He shook her. Her eyes, wide open, stared at him angrily. "You go to hell," she said.

"Anna, get up."

She looked at him steadily, then grinned. She sat up in bed stretching slowly, her wide shoulders and full breasts moving easily, then at rest again, one hand patting her hair. She rubbed her eyes and yawned, ready to stretch again. She looked at him, pouting her lips, then laughed out loud, wide awake.

"Get into bed," she said.

"No, I'm dressed."

"What's the matter, what are you sore about? You look like a ton of bricks fell on you." She threw off the covers and attentively examined the length of her body, and the tips of her toes. She had nice feet for a big woman.

"I want to talk to you. That's why I wanted you up."

"What do you want to talk about, Harry?"

"Nothing much I guess, nothing in particular."

"Just feeling talky eh, atta boy."

"Go on, get dressed," he said, turning away, going over to the window. He heard Anna getting out of bed, heard her bare feet moving on the floor, slowly, lazily. Her bare foot lifted, then put down again, stockinged. There was a pause. He was thinking only of Anna's bare feet. "She gets on my nerves," he said to himself. He tried following her movements while she dressed. She still had the one bare foot, he thought, as she moved around slowly, standing up, silk rustling. A garter snapped. She was dressing more rapidly. Why the one bare foot? He turned quietly, feeling silly. She was standing in her stocking feet. She had fooled him by putting on the other stocking. He knew he was irritable and told himself not to be a fool and quarrel with her. "I'm sick and tired of her," he thought.

With his chin down he went out of the room. He looked at his watch, eleven o'clock. The maid came along the hall to go into Anna's room. He told her to go back and get some breakfast ready. He went into his own room, walking around slowly, gradually letting himself think about O'Reilly. He went down the hall to telephone Jimmie, mainly to hear him talking. He sat down and, lifting up the receiver, suddenly thought of phoning Vera. The operator said, "Number, number," and he sat there thinking of Vera. He had nothing to say. It would be stupid to phone her. He put down the receiver and got up to walk around the room.

Anna came along the hall, talking casually to the maid, and they went into the dining room to have breakfast. He didn't talk while eating. She was in a good mood, but knowing he was sullen, didn't pay attention to him. Watching her eating, and looking at her face and neck, he was interested because her face looked entirely different from the face he had seen in the bed. After all, she was a good sport and so they exchanged talk in good humour.

Anna, quite hungry, ate rapidly. They were both hungry. He drank black coffee and laughed very agreeably. They smoked a cigarette, and Anna, putting plump elbows on the table, blew smoke at Harry, making pretty faces behind the thin cloud. The food made him feel better, and sensing it, she became lively, instead of lazy; talkative, anxious to hold his attention. She was entertaining him, not merely sitting there having breakfast. The black coffee awakened her and she laughed voluptuously as though having breakfast after a night of love-making. At first he enjoyed it very much, smiling, reaching over the table to pat her shoulder.

They got up from the table.

"What are you going to do now?" she said.

"Guess I'll go downtown."

"I guess I'll lie down and read."

She lay down on the sofa in the front room, linking hands behind her head, eyeing him. He stood in the middle of the floor, frowning.

"For God's sake, stop flirting with me," he said.

"Hello, big boy."

"I don't feel like it I tellya."

"Kiss momma, big boy."

He did not move. She made it impossible for him to take her for granted and be sure of her, treating him as though he had come along the street and on a corner she had winked at him, feeling her way, deliberately voluptuous, anxious for an adventure. No peace nor rest with her, and at this particular time he wanted to enjoy a feeling of security and quiet possession. "God knows what'll happen this afternoon," he thought.

"Kiss me bye-bye. Right here behind the ear."

"Lay off, Anna, I don't feel like it. I'm fed up."

"Fed up with what?" she said, sitting up.

"Fed up with all this stuff. Why can't you go slow and easy, instead of monkeying around like a mink all the time. D'ya have to keep it up, can't ya get on without it? Can't you come down to earth and be normal? Do you think you're trying to pick me up and keep me on the merry-go-round? Stop workin' at it."

"Say big boy, what's got into you?"

He sat on the arm of the sofa. She stretched her leg, touching his thigh with the tip of her toe. She smiled, then was serious, smiled again, then sneered.

"Why so high and mighty all of a sudden?" He didn't answer her, staring at her moodily. "Jump off the high horse," she said, sitting up, her arms around her knees. "Harry old boy, don't you like Anna? You wouldn't really give me the run-around, would you, Harry?"

"You have a hell of a time, don't you?" he said.

"Hell of a time doing what?"

"Just living."

"Sure, just living, that's me all over. Should I be sad when you're sad, and grow bunions on my feet when you get corns, eh? Just living, sure, that's me. I figured that stuff out years ago when Jennie Wren was young. I'm not missing anything coming my way, see. I'm happy, I'm born happy. I'm not born sad like all the bums who sing hymns. I'm born happy and all I've got to do is to keep on being happy, see?"

"You haven't got the brains to be unhappy."

"What, brains?"

"Sure, brains. I said it."

"Yes, I heard you, but brains don't mean anything to me. I know what I want and I'm going to stay happy, and when I ain't got any pep left I want to die, that's all."

"Shut up, shut up."

"Well, take off the high hat."

"I'm fed up. There's no use talking, I'm just fed up."

"Fed up with what?"

"You. Who do ya think, the guy next door?"

"Fed up, eh?"

"Yeah, you heard me didn't ya? I don't need a megaphone. I said fed up."

She laughed out loud, her head down on the arm of the sofa. She sat up quickly and crawled along the sofa and put her forehead on his knee. He pushed her head away but she hung on to his leg and he looked down at the back of her neck. He stood up, feeling she was alien, someone he had never known. Her head bounced on the sofa. She got up, following him across the room, her big body trembling. "Don't do that," she said. "Listen, big boy, what'll I do if you don't want me? You know what I'll have to do? I'll have to go back to my husband. He's only a little runt, Harry. You're a big guy, see? He simply don't belong, see?"

Her soft arms slipping around his neck held him and he was staring at her eyes but couldn't go on thinking of her. He tried to shake her, loosen her arms, but she hung on tightly, rubbing against him, smiling drunkenly, her lips pale under the rouge.

"Lay off that, you little slut," he said, pushing her roughly. She sat down clumsily on the floor, legs spread out, a puzzled look on her face, her lips moving but unable to form words. "I'm through," he shouted, going out the door. He heard her dragging herself up from the floor. She yelled after him: "You're the biggest guy in town, you are, oh yes. You'll get it, do you hear?" she screamed. "You'll get it, right where the chicken got the axe."

4

He went downstairs to the street. He didn't take his car out of the garage because he felt like walking in the spring air. He took off his hat. At noontime not many cars were on the avenue. Apartment houses looked new, brick-fresh and clean, some lawns not sodded yet, a gardener working on a flowerbed parallel with a walk. Harry watched the bent back of the gardener. He would phone Vera from the store, he thought. The bent back straightened, the gardener, kneeling, put his hands on his hips.

He left the avenue and turned down the hill. At the top of the hill houses were big, further down they got smaller, dirtier, older, many rooming houses. Then the houses further down were bigger — tea rooms near Bloor Street. He walked down the hill and all the way downtown. On Bay Street some show-girls were walking a few paces ahead, three girls, poorly dressed. "That show isn't doing very well," he thought, passing the girls at the corner, the book-store sign in sight "The show will close at the end of the month."

In the store Eva Lawson was talking to a fat man with a new soft hat, her best customer. Smiling, Harry took off his hat and went into the office. He sat down and got up at once, the office seemed to have become uncomfortable. He looked out of the window to the lane leading to the stage door. The three girls he had passed at the corner were going up the lane, two of them arguing vehemently, the other one holding aloof, a few paces away. The two girls appealed to the third one excitedly, but she shrugged her shoulders. They went in the stage door. He sat down again. He lit a cigarette, his feet up on the desk. He closed his eyes, closing them tightly, having only vague improbable thoughts.

The main thing was he was rid of Anna, positively free of her. He knew he would never go back to the apartment while she was there. He wanted to be absolutely alone, and the thought of it seemed surprisingly fresh and exciting. Anything O'Reilly, Asche or Weinreb had to say was unimportant, of no interest at the moment, for he was enjoying a fine feeling of relief. For a long time he hadn't bothered about Anna. He took her for granted till he was unable to stand aside, and she was a part of his life and thoughts. For the first time in months he could look all around him.

He heard a car outside the store. He knew Jimmie and Sam and Eddie were coming in. They came through to the office.

"'Lo, Jimmie."

"'Lo, Harry."

"'Lo, Sam."

"Hello, Harry."

"'Lo, Eddie."

"How'do, Mr. Trotter."

Jimmie, smoking a cigar, puffing it slowly, blew out smoke carefully. They all sat down.

"What's the move?" Jimmie asked.

"We'll be taking Sam and Eddie along eh, Jimmie?"

"I'm for taking more than that."

"That'll be plenty. Go sit in the car, Sam. You too, Eddie."

Sam and Eddie got up. They walked out with quaint dignity. Sam sucking his cheeks, let them out with a whistling noise. He was practical. His clothes didn't fit him very well. Eddie hadn't been the same since Joe disappeared. He had cultivated a sad smile and whenever he went out he carried two guns. He used the guns when there was trouble and was much sadder. The two men left the office.

"Soon be time to go up to O'Reilly's," Harry said.

"Yeah."

"I been thinking. We got to watch our step," Jimmie said. "There's no knowing what's on their minds. They'll talk a lot about Cosantino but I don't think any one of them gives a damn for him. How you feeling after last night?"

"Fine, good party wasn't it?"

"A swell party."

"Say Jimmie, I was thinking of phoning Vera now."

"Why now? Still I don't know. We may both want to get out of this any time now, eh?"

"It's a hard thing to get out of. You simply can't get out of it once you're in deep, see what I mean?"

"Sure, only you've either got to keep going ahead or get walked on. One or the other. Why think of Vera? How's Anna?"

"Anna's a slut."

"Holy smoke, what's up? Why?"

"I don't know, she just is."

"Well, don't let her bother you, don't let her get on your nerves."

"She's got a fat chance, I'll tellya. What time is it?"

"Half-past one."

"Should we have a bite to eat or go right up there?"

"I'm not hungry. I got up late."

"Me too. Let's go then; only listen, we don't know a thing about Cosantino."

"Not a thing."

"Sometimes I kinda wish I hadn't got that guy," Harry said.

"Lord, Harry, you're not getting the woolies, are you?"

"That's crazy, Jimmie you know I'm not."

"Sure, old boy, I know you're not."

"Only it's just a feeling."

"I don't think about it."

"It's a feeling coming out of a lot of things. I didn't have anything against Cosantino, you know."

"I know, it was just tough luck for him. But they got Joe, didn't they?"

"That's right."

"And they didn't send flowers, did they?"

"That's right. Oh hell, I've just a rotten feeling. I guess it's got nothing to do with Cosantino. Let's go."

They went out of the store and got into the car. Sam drove. Harry sat between Eddie and Jimmie, and they did not talk for a few minutes. The car turned north and then east. O'Reilly's hotel was over the river. Jimmie explained to Sam and Eddie that they were to go into the hotel and sit around looking wise and Sam shook his head without talking, for there were many things he understood instinctively. Looking at the back of Sam's neck Harry counted the dark creases and wished he had phoned Vera before leaving the store. He leaned back in the car, restless, and not listening to Jimmie. At two o'clock she would likely be sewing in the front room, or talking to Mrs. Farrel. He should have phoned her before he left the store but there wasn't much to say. It would be hard to talk. The car, going more rapidly, left the business section, heading out east in light traffic.

They crossed the river, very muddy and sluggish. The willow trees on the banks were green and over beyond the trees across the park the hills were green. Dark clouds were over houses on the other side of the park. It would rain shortly.

They passed the jail and the corner at the Public Library and turned down to the hotel.

The hotel was on a corner, a brick building, respectable, woodwork well-painted, three stories high, and on the opposite corner a store for the sale of malt and home-brew, owned by O'Reilly, and formerly a house in which a nigger had killed a white woman five years ago. No one would rent the house and O'Reilly got it cheaply. The store was painted light brown, the window filled with brightly coloured signs.

They parked the car a hundred paces away from the hotel and walked back. The palms of Harry's hands got moist, then very hot and dry, and inside him was a nervous eagerness to be actually inside the hotel talking to men. The heavy feeling of depression left him. Walking along the street and thinking of talking about Cosantino he felt almost sure he had never known him.

"They're not going to bother me about Cosantino," he said.

"What's that?"

"They're not going to bother me about the wop, I tellya."

"That's the stuff."

"We're being good to these guys to even come here."

"Sure, here we are, anyway."

5

O'Reilly, Asche and Weinreb were sitting smoking in the small hotel rotunda. O'Reilly had on a derby hat. Asche, hatless, his high forehead shining, was lightly tapping the back of his hand with smooth fingers. Weinreb, well-dressed, sullen-looking, cleaned his nails with a small file. The three men did not get up. Harry and Jimmie walked over to them and Sam and Eddie sat down near the door. O'Reilly said: "Hello boys, glad to see you."

"Hello," Asche said. Weinreb went on cleaning his nails.

"Well, here we are," Jimmie said.

"We see you."

"How do we look?" Jimmie grinned.

O'Reilly got up, thrusting his hands into his pockets, glancing casually at Sam and Eddie. Eddie was scratching his head. Sam had his eyes closed.

"Let's go upstairs," O'Reilly said.

They went up one flight of stairs and into a bedroom. In the room there were only three chairs, so O'Reilly sat on the bed, facing the window. Harry sat opposite Asche and Weinreb. Jimmie stood near the window.

"Nice party you boys gave last night," O'Reilly said.

"Sure," Harry said. "Listen, O'Reilly, why the get-together? Let's get down to brass tacks, eh?"

"Who got Cosantino?" Weinreb said suddenly.

Harry looked at him. Weinreb was leaning forward, his low forehead wrinkled. They stared at each other and Weinreb, sucking his lips, kept on staring.

"It's funny, but a lot of people seem to think you fellows know something about Cosantino," O'Reilly said. "It's funny, I mean, people have that notion."

"It sure is funny."

"To hell with this," Asche said. "Listen, Trotter, you know all about Cosantino. Who did it, see? That's what I want to know."

"Search me," Harry shrugged his shoulders.

"Cut it out," Asche said.

"Lay off that stuff," Harry said, wanting to paste Asche. Such a nice Jewish boy. Such nice hair. Such a nice face.

"Keep your shirts on, boys," O'Reilly said. "All it means," he said, turning to Harry, "is we don't feel safe. Good lord, put yourself in my place. I got a wife and kids. I got a father too, and what would happen to them if I got bounced off like Cosantino was? See what I mean? I don't want to have a slab in the morgue. We all should be friends. I hate this sort of thing. I don't want to have anything to do with bloodshed. There's enough booze in the world for all of us, ain't there, and we should be peaceable. But the point is, someone got Cosantino, see what I mean, and we should know, take him for a car-ride maybe, 'cause it ain't safe for us to have a man like that floatin' around, see? I got a wife."

"Sure I see, but for Christ sakes, what's it to me?" Harry said. "I want to go on living as well as you guys do, don't I?"

"It don't mean anything to me," Jimmie said. "Only when I hear you talking that way I want to go to sleep."

"Don't be in a hurry," Weinreb said quickly.

"Lay down," Harry said. "Listen, O'Reilly, I'm getting tired of this. Who do these two kikes think they are? Are they looking for trouble? If they are they'll get it."

Asche jumped up, his hand swinging to his hip. Weinreb held on to him. "Take it easy, Sime," he said. "Keep your pants on. You don't need to take nothing from these birds. You know what's d'matter wid 'em."

"He called me a kike, the bastard."

"All right, didn't he call me a kike too, eh? Didn't he, huh?"

"We don't need to sit here and take it. Dese guys, dey need d'blocks put to 'em." Asche's words blurred into each other.

Talking quietly, he had no accent, but when excited, could not talk carefully.

O'Reilly, smiling, sat on the bed. "Let it pass. Let it pass. You boys have done rather well, Trotter. Got a good thing, I imagine."

Harry watched Asche but listened to O'Reilly, who was getting to the point. O'Reilly didn't give a damn for Cosantino.

"Come on, O'Reilly," he said. "What's on your mind? You don't give a hoot in hell for Cosantino. There's something else worrying you. Out with it. We're not going to sit around singing hymns for Cosantino. We'll move along if you've got nothing better to say, eh, Jimmie?"

"I'm fed up listening to these guys. That's all I got to say," Jimmie said.

O'Reilly stopped smiling. He tossed his cigar-butt at a spittoon. He tilted his derby back further on his head. "You're shipping too much stuff outside the city," he said.

"Who said so?"

"I'm telling ya. I'm peaceable enough, ain't I? I've got a wife and kids and I don't want trouble, but you're shipping too much stuff outside the city, and let it sink in."

"What do you want to do about it?" Jimmie said. "Now we're feeling practical, what do you want to do about it?"

"You boys have done well, why not lay off the out-of-town stuff? There's enough in it for all of us, just lay off the out-of-town stuff."

"We ought to be able to agree," Harry smiled.

"Sure."

"Now, what about Cosantino?" Asche said, linking hands around his knee and tilting back in the chair.

"I'm asking you for the last time to shut up, lay off that racket," Harry said.

Asche smiled at him. He turned to Weinreb and smiled, "Nice innocent boy, ain't he, hmmm?" Weinreb stared at Harry. He rubbed his hand across his mouth, looked at the palm, then glanced again at Harry. O'Reilly leaned forward. "I got this to say. You and me may fix up the out-of-town stuff, Trotter, but I'm with these guys about Cosantino."

"All right, ain't I with you, too?"

"Jesus, yeah," Jimmie said. "Wasn't it only the night before last I said to Harry — 'Now Cosantino's bumped off, any one of us is apt to go?'"

"Bunk," Asche said.

"Is that so, Mr. Asche? Maybe you know something about Cosantino, eh?"

Asche didn't get sore. He grinned. "All sorts of noise in dese guys, huh. Listen, wasn't Cosantino watching dese guys day and night? Wasn't I a pal of his? Don't I know what I am saying? Were dey razzing Cosantino from d'start? I was Cosantino's friend."

Weinreb said in a practical monotone, "Hand over d'guy that got Cosantino."

"That's right," O'Reilly said. "We've got to do it. Hand over the man that got Cosantino."

"I can't, I tellya."

"You got to."

"For the love of Mike, I tellya I can't."

"Hand d'guy over."

"Are you dumb, you saps. I tellya I can't. I don't know. Honest to God, I don't know. I hardly knew Cosantino. Didn't have a thing against him. Best guy in the world, for all I know."

"Just tell us who did it and we'll take him for a ride. He ought to get his, just to square things up."

"Come on, Trotter," Asche said.

"There's no use talking to these guys," Jimmie said wearily. "We might as well be at home reading the paper. We're not getting anywhere." He got up, walking the length of the room. Harry watched him. Jimmie was pale but absolutely indifferent. He walked over to the window and stood there looking out. They all looked at Jimmie's back.

"Well, what are you going to do about it?" O'Reilly was sullen.

"Listen, O'Reilly, what the hell can I do about it? Use your head."

"Don't tell me to use my head."

"I don't care what the hell you use but talk common sense."

"How do you like this then? Tell us the guy that got Cosantino or there'll be a hell of a lot of trouble and God knows where it'll end."

Harry listened, his eyes half-closed, waiting for him to go on talking about his wife and child, but O'Reilly stopped suddenly. Harry opened his eyes and O'Reilly was observing him, very pale eyes, his face fat and round. Asche and Weinreb were looking at O'Reilly. It was up to him. They sat back expectantly to let him do the talking. Asche put his thumbs in the armpits of his vest.

"What's it going to be?" O'Reilly said quietly.

Jimmie turned from the window. "You guys make me smile," he said. "You'd think you were all in Sunday school. The lesson for today is 'Who Killed Cosantino?'"

"Smart fellow, heh?" Asche said.

"Great help to his mother," Weinreb said.

"Cut the kidding." Harry got up. "I tellya again and again I don't know and I can't help you. That's final. How can I do it? How do I know? Do you think I have to sit here listening to those guys?" he said to O'Reilly. "They're back numbers, I tellya. They're just hanging on. They're scared if they don't hang on someone'll run away with their pants. They don't belong, see. What does a guy like you want with them?"

"That's got nothing to do with it," O'Reilly said.

"It's got everything to do with it."

"For once you're not lying, O'Reilly," Jimmie said. "All this bull's got nothing to do with it, as far as you're concerned."

"Back numbers, huh? Get that, Sime?"

"Back numbers, sure, and he's sittin' so pretty."

"I'm getting tired of it." O'Reilly took off his hat and wiped his forehead with a handkerchief.

"I was fed up fifteen minutes ago," Harry said.

"What's it going to be then?"

"Anything you like."

"I hate to think of you going ahead and looking at it in that way, Trotter. There are some things we got to do, you know."

"Sure, I know."

"Work with us then, hand over the egg that got Cosantino. Let's all stick together."

"Oh hell," Harry said. "There's no use talking, you guys don't understand English, and you're simply a sad pair," he said to Weinreb and Asche.

"Sad pair, huh?" Weinreb pounded the table. "Get that, eh. I guess I can go where you never could, you bum. I guess I got friends. I have. I have. I got clubs, too. I got everything you guys ain't got."

"Oh, dry up," Jimmie said.

"Then we're through, Trotter," O'Reilly said.

"All right, we're through. I'm sorry but we're through."

"Think it over."

"There's no use thinking it over."

"You know it means trouble, the end of the whole racket for you. I'd like to stop it if I could. I got nothing against you."

"Sorry, O'Reilly."

"You'll be Goddamned sorry," he shouted.

"Come on, Jimmie."

"Listen, Trotter, you ain't got a chance in a million, I tellya. We'll sew you up tighter than a drum. You're just a stubborn damn fool. You're crazy, you're off your nut, you're loco."

"Sure."

"Tell it to Asche," Jimmie said.

Asche and Weinreb stood up, not smiling, but quite satisfied. Then Asche grinned at Harry. His boyish face had a mean self-satisfied grin on it. Weinreb stood up, as if suddenly important. He looked stupidly serious.

O'Reilly left the room first. Jimmie followed, then Asche and Weinreb, then Harry. They went downstairs. Sam and Eddie were sitting together in the rotunda. Eddie, still looking sad, blinked his eyes at O'Reilly.

Harry turned. "Well," he said. O'Reilly started to say something, then hesitated, turning away his head. Asche was still grinning. Weinreb was looking sullen. "Don't mind us," Asche said. "We're just a pair of kikes, huh."

Harry walked out the door. Jimmie, talking to Sam and Eddie, followed. They walked down the street to the car.

"Let's go down to the store and talk this mess over," Harry said.

"I'm feeling kinda low."

"I know, but let's talk it over."

A few drops of rain were falling.

"It's going to rain hard," Jimmie said. "Get the top up on the car quick, Sam."

They got the top up and the rain came down hard, the biggest shower in months. Harry, driving the car, couldn't see twenty paces ahead. They passed streetcars that had stopped.

6

They went into the store, shaking raindrops from their hats, and when Eva Lawson looked steadily at Jimmie he shrugged his shoulders.

"Some rain." He smiled at her.

"Just like a cloudburst," she said.

"I jumped from the car and took about ten steps and look at me."

"Your collar's soaking wet."

They followed Harry into the office.

"How'd it go?" Eva asked.

"Rotten." Jimmie, sitting on the desk, tapped a pen.

"What's the word?" Sam asked.

"Nothing yet."

He turned round on the swivel chair, facing the window. The rain was stopping as suddenly as it had started. Eva went out of the office. Harry said: "I'm kinda hungry. Come on over to the corner and have some toast and coffee, Jimmie." Sam and Eddie didn't get up.

"Has it stopped yet?"

"Just a few drops falling."

They walked on the wet pavement over to the corner. Water was rushing along the gutters and up over curb, swinging past gurgling drains that couldn't take it in. People were coming out on the street after the rain, women walking timorously, doubtfully putting down umbrellas, coming from doorways and from under awnings, hurrying along the street.

In Bowles, men in white jackets stood idly behind the glass counter. The rain had kept out customers and given the boy a chance to clean white armchairs. The tiled floor was clean but there was a line of muddy boot marks to the counter. "Whole-wheat toast, well-browned, well-buttered," Harry said. "Toast the same," Jimmie yelled.

The bald-headed man with glasses had lots of time to sing, "Holeee-wheat toast have it well-browned and we-l-l-buttered twice." The man in the kitchen yelled, "Holeee-wheat toast on the fire twice." They waited, a hand shoved the toast along the slab from the kitchen. The man at the counter held up his forefinger. "Coffee," Harry said. "Coffee," Jimmie nodded.

They sat down in the armchairs. The coffee was very hot.

"Well, Harry."

"Well, it looks damn bad, don't it?"

"It looks damn bad but what can you do?"

"You can't do nothing, just see what turns up."

"We either got to go ahead, or get out quick. What's it going to be, that's the point."

"I got a rotten feeling it ain't going to be neither."

"Oh rot."

"I know, it's just a feeling."

"Hell Harry, we've made 'em say uncle before, haven't we? We've made 'em touch wood, haven't we?"

"I kinda wish I was home right now."

"You've been on the way home a long time."

"Yeah, but this is different. It's got to happen sometime. Trouble is in this racket, we all go the same way home. I'm worrying about Vera, I am."

"Listen Harry, let's go right ahead and give Asche and Weinreb the works. I don't like those guys. Then O'Reilly'll come down to earth. We can't lose anything by socking Asche and Weinreb, eh?"

"Maybe. I don't know. I had this bad feeling this morning."

"Lord man, shut up, stop thinking about it."

"All right, I'll stop."

"Now how about Asche and Weinreb?"

"The bastards," Harry said, feeling better. He swallowed the hot coffee, at the moment wanting to slug Asche. The old feeling was inside him.

"We're crazy to even bother about them," he said.

"Sure."

"Anyway, neither one of us is going for a car-ride. We're sure of that, so we got as good a chance as O'Reilly, eh?"

"Sure, but if they get you then I'll get out of the country quick with Eva and I'll be fixed, too."

"But they won't get me, the bastards. They won't get me."

"They won't get me with my boots off, that's settled."

"Listen, Jimmie, we'll get right to work on O'Reilly tomorrow. He's the guy we want to nail. Who in hell is that guy anyway? I don't like him. Those other guys simply don't count."

"Come on back to the office."

"Come on then."

They walked back to the office.

"I'm going to take Eva home," Jimmie said.

"I'll sit in the office. I don't want to go home."

Sam and Eddie went out to eat and Harry sat in the office. He heard Jimmie talking to Eva, then she came into the office to get her coat. "It won't do any harm to close the place a few minutes early," Jimmie suggested.

"I guess not, I don't care anyway."

"Listen, Harry, phone me before you go out tonight, eh?"

"All right."

"So long."

"Goodnight, Harry."

"Goodnight, Eva."

"Goodnight."

He was alone in the office and Eva was locking the door. No sounds in the lane, the store quiet. "Eva's a peach of a little girl," he thought, miles ahead of Anna whom he didn't want to see again, nor the apartment either while she was there. He wouldn't even think of her. That was over.

Something, getting him all mixed up, slipped away and leaning forward on the desk, his head on his arms, thoughts came easily along old channels, little thoughts of a few years ago. He was looking at Vera, but not talking to her. She had on a ball-dress with a red flower, and was walking toward him. Then she had on a light brown dress and tan shoes and stockings. He was depressed, his head heavy, and aware of being so practical, it was an effort to think of her, making pictures of her in his head when he merely wanted to talk to her. He had many words ready but no interesting thoughts. He began to feel lonely, wondering why he had left her. Tomorrow he would go and see her, but inside him was a feeling that he would not see her. He looked at the telephone, the number coming into his mind quickly, as it used to when working in the yard and calling her in the afternoon. Hesitating, he took up the receiver and called the number. He steadied himself, ready to talk quickly but the number was ringing a long time and no one answered the phone. The steady relentless ringing in his ear was irritating and his heart was beating too loudly, and he might not be able to talk to her. At the moment he wanted to talk to her more than he had ever wanted to talk to anyone. He had to get out of the room, he thought. At last it had become necessary to move rapidly, leave the store quickly, take a taxi. But the uneasy feeling returned. He couldn't go alone, not until Sam and Eddie came back, then he might go out and see her. The restive, uneasy feeling got between him and the notion for speed and all the eager thoughts, making it impossible to think clearly, waiting for someone to answer the phone. He looked out of the window to the lane. The window was streaked with rain and dust.

Someone answered the phone, Vera's voice.

"Hello," she said.

"Hello," he said carefully, so she would recognize his voice. He cleared his throat, repeating, "Hello."

"Who do you want?"

"Hello, Vera," he said eagerly.

"Harry."

"How are you, Vera?" he asked casually.

"Fine. How are you?" she repeated just as casually. He was steering the conversation the wrong way. He looked at the perforated mouthpiece, slightly puzzled, wanting to start over again but she was saying something mechanically, and he shouted in the phone: "Vera, Vera, I want to see you." She answered very practically: "Is that so?"

"Vera, dear, please, Vera, don't talk like that, what's the use of talking like that? Listen, Vera, let me go on talking to you, anyway. It's important, it really is important. For a long time I've wanted to talk to you."

He heard her say, "Well, you might have, you know."

She said it so practically, with so much finality, he became almost inarticulate. He shook the receiver. He glared at the mouthpiece. He said only: "Listen, listen, Vera."

"You could have phoned me before," she was saying.

"I know I could've, only I couldn't," he said emphatically.

"What do you mean?"

"Never mind that now, I simply got to see you sometime. I simply got to make things right with you. Do you hear, Vera? It's all right, isn't it, Vera. You want to meet me too, don't you, Vera. Listen, Vera. I've always thought of you and I've got to fix it now if you'll only let me. There wasn't a day I wasn't thinking of you." Eagerly he squeezed the receiver against his ear but she was silent. He thought she was getting ready to ask what he had been doing all winter.

"Why did you go away?" she asked softly.

"I don't know, Vera. Honest to God I don't."

He heard her crying. He heard her say something then choke over the words. She tried again to speak and he knew she was turning away from the mouthpiece. Once before, two years ago, he had heard her cry over the telephone. When she cried like that and he couldn't see her, he was bewildered, unable to find satisfying words. There was a clear picture of her in his head and because he could not see, his thoughts ran loose, distorting the image, and he was entirely miserable.

"Vera, for Christ sake, don't Vera."

"Don't what?"

"Don't go on crying. There's no use crying."

"All right."

"Let's talk now. You're feeling better, so let's talk."

"Go on."

He had nothing whatever to say. The main thing had been to get talking, to feel they were going along the same road in the old way and had become one again. Now he felt that he had got to that point, things were clearing away. He was happier but words he might use were of absolutely no importance. In the old days when they were happy they never used to bother to talk much or say anything really important, and now it was soothing to listen to her.

"Where are you?" she asked very agreeably.

"Downtown," he said, sure of himself again.

"Come up and see me."

"I want to see you, Vera, I'd rather be near you than any place on earth but I can't go right now. A little later maybe, but not right now. Tomorrow anyway."

"Harry?"

"What?"

Now that uncertainty had left her he knew she would become curious. He didn't want to give any explanations. He wasn't ready for explanations. Explanations had nothing whatever to do with his reason for phoning her. Satisfied in his own mind, he felt better. He was sad but not so lonely.

"I got to go right now," he said. "Tell you all about it later. I'll be up later," he added wildly, finding himself getting indignant at the thought of not being able to see her. "I'll be up later," he repeated. "Goodbye, dear."

"Goodbye," she said, her voice expressionless.

He hung up the receiver quickly and groped in his pocket for a handkerchief. He swallowed hard. He rubbed his fore-head with the handkerchief.

7

He got up and walked the length of the office. He rubbed the palms of his hands together. He sat down again, looking around the room, slowly becoming aware of every object in the room. He noticed the desk, its size, glass pen-container, four pens in it, big blotting-paper, mahogany chairs, carpet, the pattern. He was alone in the room and each one of these objects had assumed an identity of being for him. He became so conscious of them he felt he couldn't be really alone while they were in the room. Looking at the objects he was unable to think clearly. He got up and walked into the store and stood looking at the pictures on the wall. "I think I'll go out," he thought, but knew he wouldn't for any consideration go out before Sam and Eddie came back. If he did go out, where would he go? His thoughts hadn't got to the point of actually seeing Vera. At the moment, his world was the store, the office, books, pictures, carpets. Anything outside was beyond him. He walked over to a shelf and picked out a book. The small book had a leather back but that was all he noticed. He opened the book, saw the printed page, but was aware only that the small book had a leather binding. He picked up three or four books in succession and opened them but the binding alone interested him. "We must have some good books here," he thought. He walked the length of the store to look out on the street. No one walking along the street. A man washing the flower-store window across the street. He was glad to see the man on the street washing the window. He looked at his watch, half-past six. Sam and Eddie ought to be along any minute. He expected to get a good feeling thinking of Sam and Eddie coming back but remained depressed. He went back to the office and sat down, elbows on the table, chin in his hands.

There was a thought in his head he could touch only gropingly. "The whole thing would come to an end." Sooner or later they would get him. O'Reilly would try and get him anyway. He was sitting in the office because it was safe. He explained to himself why he was sitting there. He jumped up suddenly. "Not by a damn sight," he said aloud. "Not by a damn sight." He stood still, looking out of the window to the lane and down the lane and over the top of a small building to the sky which had cleared up. A patch of blue sky. He turned eagerly toward the mirror hanging on the wall near the door and regarded himself, sucking in his lips, his hands on his hips. He felt strong, he looked strong and wanted to get his hands working, smashing, swinging. He shook his head a little, longing to feel the impact of his fist against flesh. A dandy feeling. He held it, but moments passed and he lost it. Again he looked into the mirror, with a new feeling of exhaustion and laziness. He sat down and slumped aback on the chair. "I won't go out for a while," he thought, and the finality of the decision pleased him.

He heard someone at the store door. He hurried out and through the window saw Eddie and Sam. He opened the door. He grinned at Sam who came in first. "How goes it?" he asked.

"Eddie's got a bad headache."

"What's the matter, Eddie?"

"I don't know, I got a hell of a head."

"Go on over to the drugstore and get a powder or something."

"I guess I'd better, maybe."

"Go on, Eddie."

Harry and Sam went back to the office. Sam had his hat on. He needed a shave. He seemed quite happy.

"Anything bothering you, Sam?"

"Not a thing."

"I'll bet a dollar you were never bothered about anything, eh?"

"I been bothered in my time as well as anybody else. I was bothered when the missus had bronchitis in the winter and was on her back for a few months afterward. Sure I been bothered."

"Eddie's the guy to get bothered, eh?"

"Like hell he is."

"Didn't Cosantino bother him?"

"The wop, huh?"

"Yeah."

"Not Eddie. Look at the funeral Cosantino had, a duke wouldn't get such a funeral. Not many guys can ever hope for a funeral like that."

Eddie rapped on the front door and Sam let him in. Harry wondered why he had asked the men to come back to the store when he had no place to go. "I'm going to see Vera," he thought mechanically. The thought didn't impress him. He didn't expect to see Vera tonight.

He took his hat from the peg. He tapped his hip pocket and an inside pocket. Eddie looked at him curiously. He hesitated, thinking of phoning Jimmie. "What's the use," he thought. He turned out the office light and they went into the store and he turned off the store lights. He unlocked the door and they went out. He turned around and locked the door. The air on the street felt cool after the rain. He buttoned up his spring coat. He walked west, between Sam and Eddie. The sidewalks were dry but water ran along the gutters to the sewers. They walked as far as the newsstand on the corner. They were alone on the street, except for an automobile coming along behind them. Harry heard the car coming. He turned, hardly able to get his breath, and ducked, his hand swinging to his hip. Six men were in the automobile and they fired rapidly, using sawed-off shotguns. A bullet hit Harry in the shoulder. He sat down slowly, one leg buckling under him, and he tried to crawl into an entrance, but could feel only a cement wall. The newsstand dealer ran out, turned, ducked back into the stand. Eddie and Sam were on the pavement. Sam had his gun and was firing but the car had gone by. A policeman's whistle sounded. The car turned at the corner and came back. Harry saw the car coming back and got out his gun, a pulse pounding on the side of his head. He looked at Eddie lying stiff on the pavement and wanted to stand up and scream wildly, but the car was passing and he fired and Sam fired and one of the man in the car yelled and jumped up, throwing his gun out on the road. The men in the car fired. Sam grunted. Harry dropped his gun, hit in the neck, his head dropping down slowly till his forehead rubbed against the pavement. He saw the wheels of the car going round and round, and the car got bigger. The wheels went round slowly and he was dead.

ENDNOTE

A Letter from William Carlos Williams
to Maxwell Perkins: 1928

There's much of the starkness of the tragic drama in Callaghan's book. It might be Greek, it may be Racine, it might be Ibsen. It is not Shakespeare, for in Shakespeare there is less hewing to a line; as much corollary as principle, the body is less clearly defined, the mind less pared, more provincial, gayer — even at the death. "Good night, ladies, good night, good night!" There's nothing of that in Callaghan. In Hemingway, whom Callaghan superficially but slightly resembles, there's no tragedy and little of the humor that it sometimes inspires.

At the head stands Vera, the truth at the core for Harry, a strange fugitive. Between them unfolds the unfailing story . . . And the success of it is that toward the end there is tragedy and not just a logical conclusion.

Realism? What of it? Experiments with language in order to reach through the obscurations brought on by the mold, even the fungi of accidental connotations, that is the work of Joyce, even of Stein. These are things Callaghan does not find himself concerned with. But writing —

There is a truth or a principle which governs this book. I have intimated that it is the tragic principle of classic drama. The book is a play of studied moves. It does not grow, it is made by terrifying rules from which the characters do not escape, but they do live. Thus the truth of the writing outside the story.

I don't want to write this way.

I like to speak of a modern writer as an experimentalist, someone working with the language, trying for effects, colors, new lines and arrangements, someone trying to embody his day with tentative insights, perhaps gaiety. But Callaghan won't have that.

I don't know; the thing frightens me. There's some mystery outside the book I cannot see, something working at the moment that may be working at other things later and out of the mystery, stark as letters, these characters come to us, with a bare — one might almost say theological — force. It governs Callaghan's technique, his selections of character. It holds him in one social plane, more from desire for simplicity of the requirements than anything else. In other words the problem would be the same no matter what the factors involved, high or low. He seems to prove by laying his tale among bootleggers and whores that the tragic principle holds as good with ignoble metal as with noble, as good here as with the mythological kings of Attica.

My own interest is in asking, What is this thing? It is the Vera of the story. Harry wavers around it like a moth. Its failure in Harry is his death, his inherent inability to realize it and to hold it under any circumstances is his tragedy. Harry is, in a way, an appealing figure — because of his bewildered circling around the flame of his love for Vera. Or so it seems to me.

There is a dryness in the story which goes with this logic, something which at times makes the characters a little less than human beings — which Shakespeare's characters, we'll say, are always. But the types are accurate and they move convincingly even when they seem a trifle still, even automatic.

As for the story, it's as good as may be found. Like the newspapers, it gives the sense of something quite improbable actually having happened, something grotesque, of no particular consequence — a relative or someone we've never seen having shot his wife or somebody or other; it doesn't matter . . . The thing is that under the story is a design, bare, harsh, terrifying. I confess I wouldn't quite like to say what it is, if I could . . .

W.C. Williams

P.S. This is most haphazard, sadly. incomplete . . . use it as you may.

Bill

James Dubro has been a well-known crime writer, documentarian and author for the past three decades. He has published five best-selling books, including *Mob Rule, King of the Mob: Rocco Perri and the Women Who Ran His Rackets,* and *Dragons of Crime,* and he helped to produce many major television documentaries, including the award-winning CBC television *Connections* series on organized crime. He co-authored the definition of organized crime for the *Canadian Encyclopedia.* He is the past President of the Crime Writers of Canada, recipient of the CWC's Arthur Ellis Award in 2002, and a contributor to magazines as diverse as *Canadian Business, Hamilton Magazine, Xtra, Toronto Life,* and *Eighteenth-Century Life.* He has a BA from Boston University, an MA from Columbia University, and has taught biography and eighteenth-century literature at Victoria College at the University of Toronto.

Questions for Discussion and Essays

1. It is often said that Callaghan, a political liberal with anarchist inclinations, believed in the nobility of individual independence. It has also been said that he consistently refused to pass any kind of moral judgment on his characters. Does Harry Trotter possess a nobility of independence?

2. "A great writer is always a contemporary." In what way is *Strange Fugitive* still a contemporary story?

3. "Being a homespun existentialist, Callaghan believed in the contemplation of the object, the thing in and of itself." Because he allowed nothing – no ideology or conventional wisdom or prejudice – to intervene between himself and the object, he achieved a style of wonderful clarity and directness, a style that was praised for being "fresh and vivid" in his time. Is this still an accurate description of his style? Cite examples of his style from *Strange Fugitive* to argue your case.

4. It has been said that all his characters are "insulted and injured" and, therefore, "shame and humiliation" are the driving concerns of his stories. Do you find this to be true?

5. Some readers feel that, because Harry Trotter has no articulated inner moral life, that there is nothing heroic about him, that he is something of an emotional robot. Yet William Carlos Williams, the great American poet, said that the truth in principle that governs the book is the tragic principle that governs classic drama, a principle that is usually centred in a figure who is heroic because he has a moment of catharsis, a moment of blinding moral awareness in which all is illumi-

nated and given meaning. Can you resolve these conflicting arguments in the figure of Harry Trotter?

6. Considering all the gangster films and gangster stories available – Cronenberg's *History of Violence*, for example, or *The Godfather* in all its parts – and bearing in mind that "honour" in such stories usually has nothing at all to do with what we would call "morality" – do the gangster figures of our time represent any kind of enlargement, in terms of character, on Harry Trotter?

7. Discuss the relationship between sexuality and violence as it plays out in *Strange Fugitive*.

8. Most would agree that at the heart of a Morley Callaghan story is the figure of a man or woman who is going through the process of a moral disintegration; is it possible to talk about Harry Trotter in these terms, and if so, do so.

Related Reading

Aaron, Daniel. *Morley Callaghan and the Great Depression.* The Callaghan Symposium. University of Ottawa Press, 1981.

Callaghan, Barry. *Barrelhouse Kings.* Toronto: McArthur & Company, 1998.

Callaghan, Morley. *A Literary Life. Reflection and Reminiscences 1928-1990.* Holstein: Exile Editions, 2008.

Cameron, Barry. "Rhetorical Tradition and the Ambiguity of Callaghan's Narrative Rhetoric." The Callaghan Symposium. University of Ottawa Press, 1981.

Clark, O.S. *Of Toronto the Good: A Social Study.* 1898. Toronto: Coles Canadiana Collection, 1970.

Conron, Brandon. *Morley Callaghan: Critical Views on Canadian Writers, No. 10.* Toronto: McGraw-Hill Ryerson, 1975.

Edwards, Justin D. *"Strange Fugitive,* Strange City: Reading Urban Space in Morley Callaghan's Toronto." *Studies in Canadian Literature,*Volume 23.1. 1998.

Ellenwood, Ray. "Morley Callaghan, Jacques Ferron, and the Dialectic of Good and Evil." The Callaghan Symposium. University of Ottawa Press, 1981.

Marcus, Steven. "Reading the Illegible: Some Modern Representations of Urban Experience." *Visions of the*

Modern City: Essays in History, Art, and Literature. Ed. William Sharpe and Leonard Wallock. Baltimore: Johns Hopkins UP, 1987. 232-56.

Mathews, Robin. "Morley Callaghan and the New Colonialism: The Supreme Individual in Traditionless Society." *Studies in Canadian Literature* 3.1 (1978): 78-92.

McDonald, Larry. "The Civilized Ego and Its Discontents: A New Approach to Callaghan." The Callaghan Symposium. University of Ottawa Press, 1981.

McPherson, Hugo. "The Two Worlds of Morley Callaghan: Man's Earthly Quest." *Queens Quarterly*, LXIV, 3 (Autumn 1957). 350-365.

Snider, Norman. "Why Morley Callaghan Still Matters," *Globe and Mail*, 25 October, 2008.

Walsh, William. *A Manifold Voice: Studies in Commonwealth Literature*. London: Chatto & Windus, 1971.

White, Randall. *Too Good to Be True: Toronto in the 1920s*. Toronto: Dundurn, 1993.

Wilson, Edmund. *O Canada: An American's Notes on Canadian Culture*. New York: Farrar, Straus & Giroux, 1964.

Woodcock, George. "Callaghan's Toronto: The Persona of a City." *Journal of Canadian Studies* 7-2 (1972) 21-24.

Zucchi, John E. *Italians in Toronto: Development of a National Identity, 1875-1935*. Montreal: McGill-Queen's UP, 1988.

Of Interest on the Web

www.MorleyCallaghan.ca
– The official site of the Morley Callaghan Estate

www2.athabascau.ca/cll/writers/english/writers/mcallaghan.php
– Athabasca University site

www.editoreric.com/greatlit/authors/Callaghan.html
– The Greatest Authors of All Time site

www.cbc.ca/lifeandtimes/callaghan.htm
– Canadian Broadcasting Corporation (CBC) site

Exile Online Resource

www.ExileEditions.com has a section for the Exile Classics Series,
with further resources for all the books in the series.

THE EXILE CLASSICS SERIES

THAT SUMMER IN PARIS (No. 1) ~ MORLEY CALLAGHAN
Memoir 6x9 247 pages 978-1-55096-688-6 (tpb) $19.95
It was the fabulous summer of 1929 when the literary capital of North America had
moved to the Left Bank of Paris. Ernest Hemingway, F. Scott Fitzgerald, James Joyce,
Ford Madox Ford, Robert McAlmon and Morley Callaghan... amid these tangled
relationships, friendships were forged, and lost... A tragic and sad and unforgettable
story told in Callaghan's lucid, compassionate prose.

NIGHTS IN THE UNDERGROUND (No. 2) ~ MARIE-CLAIRE BLAIS
Fiction/Novel 6x9 190 pages 978-1-55096-015-0 (tpb) $19.95
With this novel, Marie-Claire Blais came to the forefront of feminism in Canada. This
is a classic of lesbian literature that weaves a profound matrix of human isolation,
with transcendence found in the healing power of love.

DEAF TO THE CITY (No. 3) ~ MARIE-CLAIRE BLAIS
Fiction/Novel 6x9 218 pages 978-1-55096-013-6 (tpb) $19.95
City life, where innocence, death, sexuality, and despair fight for survival. It is a book
of passion and anguish, characteristic of our times, written in a prose of controlled
self-assurance. A true urban classic.

THE GERMAN PRISONER (No. 4) ~ JAMES HANLEY
Fiction/Novella 6x9 55 pages 978-1-55096-075-4 (tpb) $13.95
In the weariness and exhaustion of WWI trench warfare, men are driven to extremes
of behaviour.

THERE ARE NO ELDERS (No. 5) ~ AUSTIN CLARKE
Fiction/Stories 6x9 159 pages 978-1-55096-092-1 (tpb) $17.95
Austin Clarke is one of the significant writers of our times. These are compelling stories of life as it is lived among the displaced in big cities, marked by a singular rich-
ness of language true to the streets.

100 LOVE SONNETS (No. 6) ~ PABLO NERUDA
Poetry 6x9 225 pages 978-1-55096-108-9 (tpb) $24.95
As Gabriel García Márquez stated: "Pablo Neruda is the greatest poet of the twen-
tieth century – in any language." And, this is the finest translation available, anywhere!

THE SELECTED GWENDOLYN MACEWEN (No. 7)
GWENDOLYN MACEWEN
Poetry/Fiction/Drama/Art/Archival 6x9 352 pages
978-1-55096-111-9 (tpb) $32.95
"This book represents a signal event in Canadian culture." –*Globe and Mail*
The only edition to chronologically follow the astonishing trajectory of MacEwen's career as a poet, storyteller, translator and dramatist, in a substantial selection from each genre.

THE WOLF (No. 8) ~ MARIE-CLAIRE BLAIS
Fiction/Novel 6x9 158 pages 978-1-55096-105-8 (tpb) $19.95
A human wolf moves outside the bounds of love and conventional morality as he stalks willing prey in this spellbinding masterpiece and classic of gay literature.

A SEASON IN THE LIFE OF EMMANUEL (No. 9) ~ MARIE-CLAIRE BLAIS
Fiction/Novel 6x9 175 pages 978-1-55096-118-8 (tpb) $19.95
Widely considered by critics and readers alike to be her masterpiece, this is truly a work of genius comparable to Faulkner, Kafka, or Dostoyevsky. Includes 16 Ink Drawings by Mary Meigs.

IN THIS CITY (No. 10) ~ AUSTIN CLARKE
Fiction/Stories 6x9 221 pages 978-1-55096-106-5 (tpb) $21.95
Clarke has caught the sorrowful and sometimes sweet longing for a home in the heart that torments the dislocated in any city. Eight masterful stories showcase the elegance of Clarke's prose and the innate sympathy of his eye.

THE NEW YORKER STORIES (No. 11) ~ MORLEY CALLAGHAN
Fiction/Stories 6x9 158 pages 978-1-55096-110-2 (tpb) $19.95
Callaghan's great achievement as a young writer is marked by his breaking out with stories such as these in this collection... "If there is a better storyteller in the world, we don't know where he is." –*New York Times*

REFUS GLOBAL (No. 12) ~ THE MONTRÉAL AUTOMATISTS
Manifesto 6x9 142 pages 978-1-55096-107-2 (tpb) $21.95
The single most important social document in Quebec history, and the most important aesthetic statement a group of Canadian artists has ever made. This is basic reading for anyone interested in Canadian history or the arts in Canada.

TROJAN WOMEN (No. 13) ~ GWENDOLYN MACEWEN
Drama 6x9 142 pages 978-1-55096-123-2 (tpb) $19.95

A trio of timeless works featuring the great ancient theatre piece by Euripedes in a new version by MacEwen, and the translations of two long poems by the contemporary Greek poet Yannis Ritsos.

ANNA'S WORLD (No. 14) ~ MARIE-CLAIRE BLAIS
Fiction 5.5x8.5 166 pages ISBN: 978-1-55096-130-0 $19.95

An exploration of contemporary life, and the penetrating energy of youth, as Blais looks at teenagers by creating Anna, an introspective, alienated teenager without hope. Anna has experienced what life today has to offer and rejected its premise. There is really no point in going on. We are all going to die, if we are not already dead, is Anna's philosophy.

THE MANUSCRIPTS OF PAULINE ARCHANGE (No. 15)
MARIE-CLAIRE BLAIS
Fiction 5.5x8.5 324 pages ISBN: 978-1-55096-131-7 $23.95

For the first time, the three novelettes that constitute the complete text are brought together: the story of Pauline and her world, a world in which people turn to violence or sink into quiet despair, a world as damned as that of Baudelaire or Jean Genet.

A DREAM LIKE MINE (No. 16) ~ M.T. KELLY
Fiction 5.5x8.5 174 pages ISBN: 978-1-55096-132-4 $19.95

A Dream Like Mine is a journey into the contemporary issue of radical and violent solutions to stop the destruction of the environment. It is also a journey into the unconscious, and into the nightmare of history, beauty and terror that are the awesome landscape of the Native American spirit world.

THE LOVED AND THE LOST (No. 17) ~ MORLEY CALLAGHAN
Fiction 5.5x8.5 302 pages ISBN: 978-1-55096-151-5 (tpb) $21.95

With the story set in Montreal, young Peggy Sanderson has become socially unacceptable because of her association with black musicians in nightclubs. The black men think she must be involved sexually, the black women fear or loathe her, yet her direct, almost spiritual manner is at variance with her reputation.

NOT FOR EVERY EYE (No. 18) ~ GÉRARD BESSETTE
Fiction 5.5x8.5 126 pages ISBN: 978-1-55096-149-2 (tpb) $17.95

A novel of great tact and sly humour that deals with ennui in Quebec and the intellectual alienation of a disenchanted hero, and one of the absolute classics of modern revolutionary and comic Quebec literature. Chosen by the Grand Jury des Lettres of Montreal as one of the ten best novels of post-war contemporary Quebec.

STRANGE FUGITIVE (No. 19) ~ MORLEY CALLAGHAN
Fiction 5.5x8.5 242 pages ISBN: 978-1-55096-155-3 (tpb) $19.95

Callaghan's first novel – originally published in New York in 1928 – announced the coming of the urban novel in Canada, and we can now see it as a prototype for the "gangster" novel in America. The story is set in Toronto in the era of the speakeasy and underworld vendettas.

IT'S NEVER OVER (No. 20) ~ MORLEY CALLAGHAN
Fiction 5.5x8.5 190 pages ISBN: 978-1-55096-157-7 (tpb) $19.95

1930 was an electrifying time for writing. Callaghan's second novel, completed while he was living in Paris – imbibing and boxing with Joyce and Hemingway (see his memoir, Classics No. 1, *That Summer in Paris*) – has violence at its core; but first and foremost it is a story of love, a love haunted by a hanging. Dostoyevskian in its depiction of the morbid progress of possession moving like a virus, the novel is sustained insight of a very high order.

AFTER EXILE (No. 21) ~ RAYMOND KNISTER
Fiction 5.5x8.5 240 pages ISBN: 978-1-55096-159-1 (tpb) $19.95

This book collects for the first time Knister's poetry. The title *After Exile* is plucked from Knister's long poem written after he returned from Chicago and decided to become the unthinkable: a modernist Canadian writer. Knister, writing in the 20s and 30s, could barely get his poems published in Canada, but magazines like *This Quarter* (Paris), *Poetry* (Chicago), *Voices* (Boston), and *The Dial* (New York City), eagerly printed what he sent, and always asked for more – and all of it is in this book.